Hastening west with the information that will clear his brother's wife of murder, the last thing Deputy U.S. Marshal Kendrick Parker expects when he arrives in St. Louis is to come face to face with the notorious Black Bette Barclay. Knowing the San Francisco Marshal's office has a warrant for her arrest, Kendrick arranges to bring the dastardly woman as far as his brother's home in Adler Creek, Wyoming where he will turn Bette over to fellow lawmen. To avoid bringing undue concern to his fellow wagon train travelers, Kendrick concocts the story that Bette is his wife, Mandy.

Mistaken Bride
Copyright © 2019 Regan Taylor
ISBN: 978-1-4874-2671-2
Cover art by Martine Jardin

Published by eXtasy Books Inc or
Devine Destinies, an imprint of eXtasy Books Inc

Look for us online at:
www.eXtasybooks.com or www.devinedestinies.com

Mistaken Bride
The Bride Book 2

By

Regan Taylor

DEDICATION

Karin and Jan – thank you for being there with me on my journey.

CHAPTER ONE

New York City — 1860

BRETT, INFORMATION REQUESTED — STOP
CARLMAN EXTREMELY DANGEROUS — STOP
CARLMAN POSSIBLY MURDERED DOROTHY MATTHEWS — STOP
CARLMAN MURDERED WILLIAM MATTHEWS — STOP
CARLMAN INVOLVED IN SHADY DEALS — MANY — STOP
DEALS INCLUDE FORGERY, HUMAN TRAFFICING, SMUGGLING — STOP
MAY HAVE KILLED OR SOLD NIECE JENNIFER MATTHEWS — STOP
IF STILL IN YOUR TOWN, ARREST, HOLD FOR FEDERAL OFFICER — STOP
HARD COPY REPORT FOLLOWS FASTEST ROUTE — STOP
U.S. MARSHAL KENDRICK PARKER, NEW YORK, NEW YORK — STOP

Deputy United States Marshal Kendrick Parker read the telegram one more time before giving it to the clerk to send. He and his younger brother, Brett, didn't contact each other often, but when they did it was for something important.

Brett hadn't told him anything when he married his wife, Jenna.

However, he didn't waste any time contacting Kendrick when his bride was in trouble. Not that Kendrick knew

1

exactly what the trouble was. In fact, all Brett had told him in a short telegram was *Wife Jenna in trouble, possible murder charge. Check on background of Julian Carlman and possible link to death of William and Dorothy Matthews of New York.*

What was interesting was Carlman had come up in a number of discussions in the D.C Marshal's office over the past couple of years and not in a very favorable way.

With time on his hands between cases in the Washington, D.C. office, Kendrick was on the first train to New York and, within hours of his arrival, began looking into the deaths of the Matthews. Just the surface findings were enough to make the hair on the back of his neck stand up. Simply the possibility that Carlman had killed his sister, Dorothy, was chilling. The other things the man was into were beyond the pale. For years the Marshal's service had been after Carlman. Now it looked like they finally, with Brett's intervention, had him in custody and Kendrick would be the man to bring him in.

"I'm ready," he told the clerk. Despite the words spoken in a soft tone, the timber of his voice was enough to make anyone standing nearby take notice of the tall, blond haired man dressed in the height of fashion. The crisp white cotton shirt was a stark contrast to the jet-black wool suit and the silver buttons that held his suspenders. The only other splash of color was the silver pocket watch chain settled across his waist. His vest was a patterned black satin with thin silver pinstripes all which served to give him the appearance of a prosperous lawyer rather than the lethal Deputy United States Marshal he was.

The clerk glanced at the telegram. One of his gray eyebrows, thick from age, lifted at the contents of the message, but he said nothing.

Sitting at his table, the clerk tapped out the message with precise movements, not at all concerned about the man with the cold blue eyes watching each tap of the key. The clerk sat a moment after completing the message before asking, "You expecting an answer?"

"I would hope something." Kendrick stood a few minutes, waiting to see if an answer would be forthcoming and was rewarded in a short time with the machine's steady tap, indicating an incoming message. If he was impatient at the clerk's deliberate, painstaking writing, he didn't let it show. If there was one thing his fellow Marshals would say about Kendrick Parker, it was that the man had ice in his veins. He was the last to show temper, methodical in a boxing match to the point his opponents seldom touched him. None were faster on the draw with their guns, which seemed almost incongruent to the Washington raised and bred man. Dirt wouldn't dare mar his signature pristine white shirts.

The clerk finished writing the short note that said only *Received, thanks. Brett*, stood and handed it to Kendrick. He gave it a quick glance and nodded to the clerk as he put his coins on the counter. "Thanks."

He turned and strode to the door. With most of the investigation done in New York, he only needed to tie up a few loose ends before leaving for Washington where he'd have his boss assign another deputy to finish the work there so he could bring the information he'd found out to Adler Creek, Wyoming where Brett waited with his bride. Exiting the Western Union office, he lifted his black bowler and placed it on his head. A few of the proper ladies strolling along the lower Manhattan street gave him the once over, only to be disappointed when he moved on without even a glance. He liked women well enough, but the simpering misses of polite society just weren't on his agenda today.

A short while later, having picked up his bags from his hotel, he was on his way back to Washington. Sitting back in the seat of the southbound railcar, he drew a long pull off his cheroot. It was a rare ritual, one reserved for the conclusion of a case, and, despite the fact there were a few loose ends to tie up in Washington before he left for Wyoming, the telegram to Brett was a major milestone. Whatever was going on with his little brother's wife was something he intended to learn in person.

CHAPTER TWO

"So let me get this straight, Parker. You are heading out to some Podunk town in Wisconsin because your brother got married?"

"Not quite, Sir. I believe that the man that's behind these murders is a southern sympathizer as well as being responsible for some of the disappearances here in town. He may be the same man who is now out in Adler Creek, Wyoming, causing troubles for my brother and his wife."

"That so?" United States Marshal William Richardson leaned forward in interest. Being a man of few words, when Kendrick Parker spoke, it was worth Richardson's time to listen.

"Seems so. Apparently my little brother married a woman named Jenna who is somehow related to a Jennifer Matthews of New York City whose parents both died under mysterious circumstances. What I've been able to piece together is that her mother was killed in a carriage accident that the stableman is sure was rigged. Her father committed suicide under strange circumstances. Within days of her father's death, she was taken to Maryland, apparently against her personal wishes, to her uncle's home. Her uncle's a man by the name of Julian Carlman."

"Carlman? Well what do you know? We spend the past few years looking for something to tie to him and your brother drops him right in our lap, so to speak."

"That's the way it sounds. From the little I got from Brett, Carlman showed up there demanding Brett turn over this

Jennifer. That's why I was up in New York, following the lead up there. I sent word to Brett to keep Carlman in custody until I got out there."

"I'm not sure . . ."

"Sir, besides the fact that it's family, I want this man. He's cut a swath through the eastern states engaging in all manner of illicit activities. It's time he was brought in and made to pay for his crimes. I haven't seen my brothers in, gees, five years. And now that one of them's married, I think it's time I paid them a visit."

"Who do you want to go with you?"

"Don't need anyone. I'll travel faster going alone and, if it's the man we're looking for, I'll have a deputy from out in Wyoming travel back with me."

"Fine. If you're sure."

"Definitely."

"Then good luck. Keep in touch and let me know when you'll be back."

"Will do."

Strolling out of the well-appointed office a few minutes later, Kendrick stopped to look over the wanted posters covering the wall of the main office. Most of the wanted men were out west, but you never knew when you'd run into one of the low life miscreants that made his job worth doing. He almost missed the poster of a woman.

Despite the fact that the poster was black and white, it was obvious the woman had dark blonde hair, a few shades darker than his own, pinned back up in a severe bun. The caption below read:

$2,000 Reward
Will be paid for the capture or arrest of
Elizabeth "Black Bette" Barkley
For the murder of Sheriff Harvey Nichelman
DEAD OR ALIVE

The picture showed a woman in her early twenties, with softly rounded cheeks, a slightly upturned nose, and full lips. If he put aside the fact she was a killer, Kendrick would have thought her attractive even with that ghastly bun. Shaking his head, he pulled the poster off the wall and moved on. Capturing someone like that Black Bette wasn't about the money. It was about bringing them to justice. Maybe one day he'd make it out to California and see what all the talk about that part of the county was about. An untamed society, gold, and adventure. It certainly would be a change from the staid life he led here in Washington, especially with the threat of war on the horizon. Not that being a Marshal was boring; at times it could be outright interesting. But not with the adventure his gut told him he'd find out west. With his grandparents gone, he could pursue his own dreams instead of theirs. Law enforcement wasn't their idea of a career for him. In fact, they'd insisted he study law and pushed him to join his grandfather's legal practice. To this day, his grandfather dead and gone almost five years, he could still hear the old man harangue him . . .

"The law, Kendrick, the practice of law. That's what a gentleman engages in. You finish your education and come join my practice. A few years of hard work and I'll make you a partner."

"I appreciate your thoughts, Grandfather, but I'm not certain . . ."

"Not certain? Not certain!" He all but roared, "You listen to me young man. I know what is best for you and it's finishing your law studies and becoming a member of my firm."

They'd argued, *no, not argued*, Kendrick told himself. An argument takes two or more people. With his grandfather, there were pronouncements and he was expected to go along. If he didn't, even as a grown man, his grandfather'd taken his cane to him. The last time was when Kendrick had just turned twenty-three. Granted, the old man didn't have the strength he did when Kendrick was younger, not that it meant striking him was right in either case. It was just that with his grandfather's strength waning it was more symbolic than anything else.

He'd tried for a few years, but his heart wasn't in it. When he heard childhood friend, Rick Hansen had become Sheriff of Adler Creek, Kendrick thought it might be just the thing for him. The day after his grandfather's funeral, he walked into the United States Marshal's office, signed up and never looked back.

After checking in with the other deputies before returning to his home to prepare for his trip west, he surprised himself when Black Bette entered his mind. From what he'd read on the poster and heard in the office, the woman was despicable. She belonged behind bars or strung up from the hanging tree. She wasn't someone he even wanted to meet. So why had he taken her poster and why would he think of her?

A visit to the train station to check on trains heading west, at least to St. Louis, was a quick diversion before heading home to pack. Thinking about the journey ahead, he walked up the steps to his house . . . house, his grandparents had left him a mansion. With two well-appointed parlors filled with original artwork—one for family and one for visitors, an ostentatiously large ballroom, two kitchens, library, den, and fourteen bedrooms on the second floor, Kendrick wondered again why he didn't sell the place. It certainly wasn't because of happy memories.

Following his mother's death in Adler Creek, his father, Whitney Parker, reluctantly sent him back east to live with the Whitcombs, his grandparents. The Whitcombs hated the west with a passion, blaming their only child's death on it, causing them to put considerable effort into dissuading Kendrick from ever returning there.

"That Whitney Parker killed my little girl. You listen to me and you listen good, Kendrick. That man, that Whitney Parker is a no

good killer. He may not have held a gun to your mother, but he killed her just the same. Dragging my baby girl halfway across the country to that Godforsaken wilderness. Forcing her to endure those brutally cold winters, giving birth to you in the dead of the worst storm they had in years."

"My pa loves me."

"No he does not. Kendrick Parker, if your father felt even a modicum of warmth for you he would never have brought your mother, God rest her soul, to Wyoming and even then, as soon as he knew she was in the family way, if he cared, one iota, he would have brought you all back here. The man is evil. Pure evil. The only person he cares for is himself. You go out there I can guarantee you will not live long enough to return home here to the people who truly love you."

"But I want to go. I want to see my brother."

"Brother. Bah. Spawn of an injun. Those redskins are less than human. You turn your back on that frogspawn and he'll scalp you alive. That's what those animals do."

"He's my little brother. If my pa's his pa . . ."

"You don't want to go there, Kendrick. Not if you want to live to see your next birthday."

But when Whitney said he'd come east to get Kendrick, it was his grandmother who relented and said he could go for a visit. After the first one, every few years he was allowed to visit his father and younger brother.

Unfortunately for his grandparents, Kendrick had happy memories of the small town in the middle of Wyoming and his friends there. Every few years he'd manage to badger them into letting him visit. On those all too short visits he rode with Brett and Rick and later his younger brother, Wolf. The four boys learned to shoot, fish, and hunt. When Whitney died, despite the fact he didn't know his father well at all, he grieved. Adler Creek held happy memories that the mansion on the outskirts of Washington would never have.

Two days later, his bags packed, arrangements made for

his staff to be paid while he was away, his horse readied, there was little left for him to do before heading west.

"Yo sho now, Mista Kenrick?" Old Samuel, the butler who had worked for his grandparents and stayed on for Kendrick asked. "Yo sho you goins to Adler Crick is bes?"

"I am, Samuel, I am. I've left instructions with Mr. Deekins at the bank to release any funds to you you need to keep the house running."

"I dunno, Mr. Kenrick. Meebee I should go wit ya'll."

Kendrick chuckled and smiled. Samuel'd always had a hankering to travel but never managed to do so. At his advanced age this could be his last chance, but with the pace Kendrick would be traveling, it would be too rough on the elderly man. "No, Samuel, I'll be fine. I've decided to take the train to St. Louis and ride my horse the rest of the way to Adler Creek. With luck, there'll be a wagon train leaving about the time I arrive, so at least I'll have some company on the trip." Not that he craved company. Actually, the thought of riding the range with nothing but his thoughts was appealing. But traveling in the later winter months, companionship could have its benefits. Then again, traveling with a wagon train could slow him down and right now, getting the information he had to Brett, even with his telegram alerting the Wyoming authorities of Carlman's activities, was of paramount concern.

"Tell you what though, when I get back, let's you and me think about a trip up to New York to visit and see the sites."

"I dunno, Mr. Kenrick. With all the talk of war comin, wall you jes don't know."

"Well let's hope war doesn't come and you and I can have that adventure."

"Okay. Okay. If'n you change yo mine . . ."

Just before he fell asleep that night, the image of a blonde-haired woman, her hair tumbling out of her bun in wispy strands, like spun gold, flashed across his mind.

A few days later, his horse settled in a cattle car, Kendrick strode through the train to the private car he'd engaged. While he may not have adopted his grandparents' beliefs, it didn't mean he couldn't enjoy the trappings of their society. The private car with its comfy seats and sleeper gave him plenty of room to stretch out to his full length. He relaxed against the soft burgundy colored leather and watched the scenery passing by, his mind drifting, yet at the same time alert for danger. His ability to seem to sleep with one eye open was one of the reasons he was considered a top man in the Marshal's service. Gazing out the window, it wasn't Julian Carlman and bringing him to justice that occupied his mind. Rather, it was the woman from the poster, Black Bette. For the life of him he couldn't figure out why she kept meandering into his mind. His thoughts had never been so taken over a woman before, and certainly not one of her ilk.

Arriving in St. Louis a few days later, Kendrick gave a quick look around the city, taking note of the changes that had taken place in the few years gone by. Elevated wooden planks covered what had been muddy sidewalks. Each shop had a window with an enticing display drawing visitors to come in. Ladies of quality strolled the street while gentlemen tipped their hats. The city was quickly becoming a metropolis to rival any east coast city. He quickly saw as well that despite talk he'd heard a year or so earlier, there was still no bridge across the Mississippi River at St. Louis, passengers and freight were being hauled across by ferries to the City. While the Pacific Railroad could have taken him to Kansas City faster than on horseback, he quickly decided to continue with his plan to ride the rest of the way to Adler Creek. There was something about the freedom of being on the trail that somehow seemed more important than rushing in the confines of the train. Of immediate concern was a room for the night and then looking into just where any wagon trains or fellow travelers might be assembling to head out in the next few days. Not given to flights of fancy, Kendrick shook his head at himself when the thought crossed his mind that his life was about to change in a way he'd never imagined.

CHAPTER THREE

Stepping into his hotel room Kendrick Parker removed his black bowler, placed it on the wooden, four drawer dresser and made short work of checking the room's security. Even though no one knew he was in town . . . heck, he was certain hardly anyone in St. Louis even knew who he was, caution was his mainstay. Just the same, checking the room for easy egress if needed, as well as a defensible position should someone try to enter, was routine for him. One of his former partners, Dave McClusky, had just laughed at him about his caution hours before being shot in his hotel room not quite two years past.

Ensuring the room was as secure as possible, Kendrick peeled off his heavy wool winter coat and stepped to the small closet to hang it up. Following that, he removed his suit jacket before he turned and began to unpack his traveling bag. For all his appearance as a dapper, well- to-do man about town, Kendrick looked forward to the more relaxed fit of what he considered to be his western clothing. While the tailored suit pants may fit him like a second skin, the buckskin was far more comfortable to say nothing of shirts that were washed sans starch and ironing. The heavily starched white shirts he wore in the east were merely part of the persona he affected, not a part of the real Kendrick Parker. Even his Stetson was far more appealing than the black bowler.

He debated ordering his supper in the room when a knock on the door alerted him to the arrival of the hot bath he'd ordered. In that moment he decided to dine below. Despite it being late winter, he knew some brave souls would be heading west and if he could link up with them, so much the better. With the talk of war in the east, especially in Washington, he was curious what news had spread to the gateway metropolis. While he preferred traveling alone, this time of year it was better to have at least one companion. So he opted to take his evening meal below and see what news he could hear.

A short while later, his bath completed, he pulled on his boots, ran a comb through his hair and considered a trip to the barber before beginning his journey. Not that he minded wearing his hair longer . . . it would just be a couple of months at best before he could engage in any luxuries. Memories of the trail to Wyoming slowly seeped back into his mind. There would be long days on the trail with no conversation. It wasn't a hardship, at least not for a loner like Kendrick.

The dining room had a few patrons when he entered; no one of interest as he settled into a seat near the far wall where he could watch the comings and goings of the room.

He'd barely sat when the plump, dark-headed proprietor waddled over, her lips wreathed in a smile that seemed to go from ear to ear. "Evening, Mr. Parker, isn't it?"

"Yes, ma'am, indeed it is. And you are?"

"Mavis. Mavis Crowe. Pleased to meet you."

"And you as well. So, what do you recommend for supper?"

"Well, I had a smidge of the fried chicken a bit ago. That with the mashed potatoes, corn and gravy looked mighty good. Then again, the cook was roasting some beef that looked just delicious."

"Hmmm, well." He considered the choices a moment, "I'll take the chicken with a large glass of butter milk."

"Excellent!" She walked off, Kendrick noticed with a smile, a bit of a sashay to her hips.

He savored the meal. Mavis was right. The chicken was

mighty good with just the right blend of spices giving it a mouthwatering flavor. He ordered a helping of the fresh baked apple pie Mavis suggested after assuring him she'd sampled it herself, with coffee to top off the meal. When Mavis brought him the pie he ventured to ask, "Any chance you've heard about any wagon trains heading west in the next week or so?"

She considered his question a beat before answering, "Actually, yes, Dusty Hendricks got into town a few days ago and said something about resting up just a bit before heading out again."

"Hendricks?"

"Yes. He's been leading trains out to the gold country in California for a few years now. Nice man, but he could sure use a wife."

"A wife, huh? Why's that?"

"May I?" She gestured to the other wooden chair at Kendrick's table and at his nod she sat down, clearly pleased to be taking a moment with him.

"So why do you think Mr. Hendricks needs a wife?" he asked.

"Oh, well, I'm of a mind to think all you men need a good woman looking after you." She gave him a warm smile. One he was sure she thought was beguiling and come hither. "Him especially. Nice man. Good man, but he's on the trail most of the year. I'm sure he'd settle down if given the chance. About a year ago he led what they were calling a 'bride train' out west. I was sure he had his eye on one or two of those gals. Then again," she paused as if considering her next words, "that may be why he's all fired up to be heading back out. Maybe he did find a gal for himself and is heading back out to be with her."

It was clear to Kendrick the woman certainly liked the idea of match making.

"That sounds like a good enough reason to me. So this Mr. Hendricks, he kinda tall, red hair?"

"Yes! That's him!" She was clearly pleased that Kendrick appeared to know him although why, he didn't know or really care.

"Think I know him. You know where he's staying?"

"Why right here, at the hotel. In fact, he headed out just a bit before you came in to eat."

"He go up to his room?"

"No. He usually heads over to Delia's place."

"Delia?"

"The saloon." She leaned in conspiratorially, "he's been . . . friendly with a woman named Annmarie there when he comes to town, if you get my drift."

Kendrick smiled, "I do. Well, if you see him in the morning, could you let him know Kendrick Parker is in town and was wondering about his next trip west?"

"I surely will."

He stood and put out a hand to help her up. "Wonderful. I appreciate it."

He paid his bill and decided to venture out towards Delia's and try to meet up with Dusty that night.

Like most of St. Louis, Delia's had been upgraded. In lieu of the tarp like material that had covered the windows a few years ago there was now glass. The tinkle of the piano spilling lightly into the street caught Kendrick's attention. He'd barely entered the saloon when a petite woman, her hair so red it seemed almost burgundy, approached him. He was surprised to note that her seductive smile reached her dark brown eyes.

"Good evening." She purred, running a hand up his lapel.

"Evening." He tipped his hat and made to move past her towards the bar. While he had no problem enjoying a lady's company for an evening, this evening was not one he planned to share. It struck him as odd that the image of the woman known as Black Bette would jump into his mind again. Maybe it was a sign that he should head out to California to look into hunting her when he delivered the information to Brett. Then again, the poster had made reference to her having family somewhere up north.

She slid up behind him at the bar, the practically sheer top she wore slipping off her shoulder just low enough to show him the dusky pink areolas of her breasts. Kendrick smiled to himself before asking her, "How about I buy you a drink and after I conduct some business maybe I look you up if you're available?"

"Sure, Mister. That sounds real good."

He signaled to the barkeep, ordered them both a whiskey and turned to look around the room, sighting the man he thought was Dusty a few minutes later. Taking the bottle with him he headed towards the trail master.

"Dusty Hendricks?"

The red headed man glanced up, "That would be me. Who's asking?"

Kendrick placed the bottle on the table and waited for Dusty to lift his brow in question. "Kendrick Parker."

With that Dusty smiled and stood. "Why you old bastard! Sit down, sit down! What brings you to St. Louis? You headin out to congratulate your brother on his nup-tals?"

"I am at that." He poured them both a shot from the bottle. They clinked glasses and drank them down.

"Well good for you. Ah, you know he already tied the knot? Day after the brides got to Adler Creek, he waltzed his gal down the aisle, and she made him one happy man."

"That so? So it's clear Brett's a happily married man? Good. And what do you hear about our littlest brother, Wolf?"

Kendrick noted a look of sadness cross Dusty's features a brief second before the man again smiled, "Wolf is good. Brett, well now he is too. At first, well at first, Miss Jenna was a might shy. In fact, when we first got to St. Louis, she up and . . ."

Kendrick put his hand up. "You and she came to St. Louis together? Was she your gal?"

Dusty laughed and shook his head. "Nothing like that. The good Lord hasn't made the woman yet who is gonna claim my heart. No. This fella, Henry Bascom, from Adler Creek came up with this idea a year ago to bring these mail order brides there so's the men could find themselves some wives. I signed on to escort them west. They all got together in Virginia and Miss Jenna showed up right before we left. Two other women took her under wing. There was, oh, let's see. Twenty-three brides in all."

"So Brett got himself a mail order bride. Imagine that." Kendrick couldn't hold back a chuckle thinking about his younger brother having to send for a bride although that would explain some of the vagueness about his marriage. That was, until, it occurred him that he hadn't wanted to marry himself. What man didn't want a wife to warm his bed and cook his meals? Apparently Kendrick Parker and . . . Dusty Hendricks.

"He sure did! But she was a package all right. She tried to leave the bride train here in St. Louis and again on the trail. I'll admit she irked me some. After all your brother paid the way for a bride to come marry him and she got all testy about it. Guess maybe the idea of moving so far from her home was more scary than she originally thought. But she walked down that aisle with him and made him a happy man. When I left to head back here, they seemed more'n suited to each other."

"He'd written me he was married. Just a short telegram. No details. Thanks for filling me in. So is she pretty?"

"Real pretty. Brett did real well for hisself."

"They love each other?"

"I think so. Once she got used to the idear of bein married

I think she fell in love with him. And your brother, you know, it was about time he found hisself a good woman."

"True. True. Good. Good. So what about you? You gonna get yourself a bride?"

"Me? Naw. Not yet leastways. What about you?"

"No. No wife yet." For some reason that thought was starting to bother him. Maybe it was because his brother married before him and that just didn't seem natural.

"So what are you plannin then? Heading out to Adler Creek and gettin yerself a mail order bride like Brett?"

Kendrick laughed, "No. Not likely."

"Then . . ." Dusty glanced down at Kendrick's belt. Spotting his badge he asked, "you're on a case?"

"Something like that. It seems Brett's bride got herself in a bit of a fix."

"Beg pardon?"

"Seems like she . . ."

"I got that." Dusty rubbed his hand over his jaw. "Open case?"

"Yup." Kendrick reached for the bottle and poured them each another drink.

"Well," he lowered his voice to a whisper, giving the hint of conspiring with the deputy marshal, "I know how you lawmen can't talk about your cases when you are on them." He looked around the room before lowering his voice a tad more, "Kin I help ya in any way?"

"As a matter of fact, yes you can."

CHAPTER FOUR

The light-haired woman returned to the room she'd taken in the boarding house and began to pull off her boots. Working the laces undone she released a long sigh of relief from wearing the worn, yet still decent looking boots almost constantly the past few days. On the train to St. Louis, she could only afford the common, wooden seat and had slept sitting up, as had many of the less affluent travelers riding west with her. Spending one of her precious coins to have the young man carry her trunks to the room, she considered whether or not she could afford a bath before meeting with Mr. Pedersen about the teaching position. For now, despite the excitement of finally being in St. Louis, she felt a bit drained. Her backside was a tad sore, her legs stiff and a good night's sleep was in order. She wriggled her toes, enjoying the freedom from the boots. Tomorrow she'd be more than ready to meet her new employer.

Sitting at the plain vanity with its small mirror she pulled the pins out of her long dark blond hair, letting the thick locks tumble down her back. *Until you get settled in and learn the lay of the land, young lady, you need to watch how you spend your money. That said, I sure wouldn't mind a bath. Not tonight though, maybe tomorrow after you meet your new employer you can request a bath.* A long soak in hot water was certainly an appealing thought.

She checked the window to be sure it was locked, drew the dark blue cotton curtains closed more tightly and began to pull off her traveling dress. Hopefully the position she had answered for would still be open. She never thought she'd end up in St. Louis, but it was as good a place as any to begin a new life.

Slipping between the sheets she was surprised to find the bed so comfortable. Then again, after the hard-wooden seats of the train, anything would feel more pleasant. Tomorrow, yes indeed, tomorrow, she'd head out and check on that teaching job and hope it was still open. Only now, with a moment to think, did she wonder if it may not have been the most prudent thing to just up and head to St. Louis without that job firmly in hand. Oh the offer'd been real enough. She just hadn't waited for the letter confirming she had it.

Over a breakfast of eggs, home fried potatoes, thick strips of bacon, grits and a pot of hot coffee, Kendrick and Dusty went over the details for the trip. Noreen's Café with its green and white checkered tablecloths, wooden chairs with comfy cushions that matched the tablecloths and curtains providing a comfortable seat and room to sit back and relax after one of the well-made meals was touted as one of the best in the city. At Noreen's there was always plenty of food, served hot and fresh which generally made for a line of eager diners waiting. Arriving early, the smell of fresh brewed coffee tickling their nostrils, Kendrick and Dusty were quickly escorted to their table and had the time to savor their meals.

"I gotta tell ya," Dusty started before taking a mouthful of his grits, "I am glad to have another gun on board with us."

Kendrick finished his mouthful of food and dabbed at his lips before asking, "Any reason why except for the usual?"

"No, not really. Well, actually, there was a rumor abouts a few weeks ago that a bank robber from Frisco was headin out this way. Mean S.O.B. from what the fella I met on the trail said. I asked the fort to send some troops with us, but with the rumors of trouble in the Carolinas over Mr. Lincoln's speeches and all, they couldn't spare anyone."

"So you're thinking this bank robber may try to steal from the folks on the wagon train?"

"That, or worse. Never know."

"This robber . . . you got a name?"

"Yeah, Black something or other."

"Black Bette?"

Dusty considered that while he chewed on a piece of bacon. "Matter of fact, yeah. Black Bette. Sounds like a woman, don't it?"

"Matter of fact, it is." Kendrick reached into the pocket of his buckskin vest and pulled out the poster he'd been carrying with him. Not one for flights of fancy, there was something about the woman in the poster that stuck with him. When he left Washington, he couldn't shake the feeling he'd be meeting up with her one way or the other. He told himself that repeatedly looking at the poster only made sense so he could ensure himself that if he ever met her, he'd have the right woman. "Looks innocent enough, doesn't she?" He held the poster up to Dusty.

"She sure does. Then again, you ever met a woman who couldn't look as innocent as a lamb?"

"That's true. So this fella say she was in fact heading this way?"

"Nope, just speculation. Never know though."

Finishing up their meals Kendrick asked, "So when do we head out?"

"I got two more families due in today and some more supplies to load so I'm thinking day after tomorrow."

"I'll see you then, if not before."

As they passed out of the restaurant, a number of the young ladies, out for a morning meal with their families, eyed the blond deputy marshal, their appreciation of his form apparent. Much to their chagrin, he didn't notice a one.

Striding along the street he fingered his chin, or rather the beard and muttonchop whiskers covering his face. Never one for fashion, indeed, he only grew the whiskers to blend in while on an assignment, he searched out a barber to rid himself of the uncomfortable beard. A short time later, his face devoid of whiskers and his locks trimmed he felt a bit more at home in his own skin. One thing about life in Wyoming, they may have some of society's constraints, but not the burdensome ones of life in Washington, D.C. or New York. Yes, time in Adler Creek would be good in more ways than one.

Kendrick's next stop was the Sheriff's office to see if his old friend Jim Gromley was still the man in charge. He was pleased to see Jim behind his desk. Rising in recognition of his friend, the older man grinned, "Kendrick Parker! Long time no see. How are you? Come on in, have a seat."

"Jim. Good to see you."

"What brings you out this way? Not the war talk now, is it?"

"No. Not from me anyway. What do you hear?"

"Fortunately everything in these parts has been pretty peaceable. We hear the rumblings about South Carolina and them wanting to leave the Union, but that business won't be reaching us here in St Louie. I'm sure it will pass over before we even know it. That Mr. Lincoln though. I know there's some not very pleased with him winnin the election."

"Well, he is our President and it's up to us to do our part to enforce his laws."

"Amen to that. And with any luck he'll avert this talk of war."

"We can only hope so."

The men sat in silence a moment, each in their own thoughts, until Kendrick asked, "That robber from Frisco, Black Bette. You hear anything about her?"

"Black Bette? Cain't say as I have. From Frisco you say?"

"Indeed. She's killed a few lawmen out that way and there's been a rumor she may be heading this way."

The sheriff rapped on his desk, "Here's hoping she doesn't show her face in this town."

Kendrick stood. "Well thanks for your time. I'll be pulling out with Dusty Hendricks in a couple of days. If something comes up or you want to send some information as far as Wyoming, I'm staying at Hegleman's Inn."

"Hope to see you before you take off. Stop by before you go."

With the rest of the day at his disposal Kendrick ventured into a few of the shops, looking for a wedding gift for Brett and his bride and some sort of gift for Wolf. While not related to Wolf by blood, there still was an unspoken tie of brotherhood between them.

Toying with a hunting knife he thought back on his parents' story . . . Kendrick's father and mother, Whitney and Clarissa Parker traveled west, on their way to California. When they arrived in Wyoming though, Whitney fell in love with the land and decided they would settle in Alder Creek. Despite his grandfather's statements to the contrary, everyone else said his mother, Clarissa, loved Whitney, but hated the vast open spaces, desperately missing the society of Washington, D.C. Shortly after she gave birth to Kendrick, Clarissa died. While she was ill, an Indian woman by the name of Falling Leaf cared for Clarissa. When Clarissa died, Whitney married Falling Leaf who in turn gave birth to Brett. While Brett's hair was as black as coal, a striking contrast to Kendrick's light blond, both men shared the same vivid shade of blue for their eyes.

When Whitney died, Falling Leaf married a man from her tribe. The couple, in turn, gave birth to Wolf. Despite hearing about him in a few letters back and forth, Kendrick only met

Wolf for the first time when he was almost fifteen. At the time he not only spent time with his brothers, but renewed his friendship with Rick Hansen, who was now the Sheriff of Adler Creek.

Wandering through the shops, he searched for just the right items for his brothers, totally unprepared to run head long into a petite blonde-haired woman. His first instinct as he looked into her wide hazel eyes was to take her in his arms and hold her. When his gaze traveled to her lips his mind emptied of all thought except for the desire to kiss her.

"I beg your pardon, Sir." The cultured tones of an Eastern woman seemed to flow like a song from her lips. "I need to concentrate more on where I am stepping than on these lovely china cups."

Despite the tightening in his groin, a reaction Kendrick normally controlled with little effort, he found himself staring at the woman. She was, in a word, lovely. There was something so sweet, so appealing to her he wanted only to take her hand and ask her to tea. Even in the threadworn, faded pale pink walking dress she moved with the elegance and grace of the society ladies he knew back east. Without volition, he took her arm, imperceptivity drawing her to him. It was only when she tried to withdraw from his touch that he came to himself and realized he was looking into the eyes of Black Bette Barkley . . . right there in St. Louis. The rumors were true. There she was and he was going to take her into custody and return her miserable soul back to California to stand trial.

In one motion he spun her around and clasped a newfangled device he'd been given by a man by the name of W.V. Adams on her wrists. While manacles and other restraints had been around for centuries, they were generally of a fixed size. Too tight for a large man; too large for most women. Kendrick met Mr. Adams several months before, in of all places, attending a theatrical event in Washington, during an intermission. While obtaining refreshments for the party Kendrick was with, his suit jacket happened to be pulled backwards, revealing his badge. Adams approached him and asked for a moment of his time to discuss his new invention. While waiting for his patent he had been looking for a lawman to try them out. Kendrick readily agreed. He was intrigued by Adams' radical ratchet design in a cuff consisting of a square bow with notches on the outside producing a simple handcuff that could be adjusted to fit a wrist of any size.

Now, with the handcuffs, as Adams called them, on the woman he knew was Black Bette's wrists, Kendrick saw firsthand just how well the devices functioned. In a flash, her arms secured behind her, he led her off towards the jail, little knowing just how the petite woman was going to complicate his orderly life.

CHAPTER FIVE

"You, sir have made a mistake."

"Don't think so." Kendrick told Bette as he hurried her along the sidewalk her arm held firm in his grip.

"I know so. Now remove these devices from me immediately or I will have charges brought against you for false arrest and kidnapping."

Kendrick looked down at the woman he'd just taken into custody. Despite her appearance as sweet and innocent, he knew otherwise. He was sure of it — something told him he'd be meeting up with Black Bette and here she was. Marching her into the jail he informed a startled Sheriff, "Jim, if you don't mind, could you open a cell, I have a guest for you."

"Guest . . . ." The other man sputtered. "What the . . . Kendrick, what do you think you are doing?"

Kendrick continued to move the woman he was sure was Bette Barkley along towards the holding cells, calling over his shoulder, "This is Black Bette, the same woman who has robbed banks from Yuma to San Francisco and killed at least two men in the process." He glanced down at her, conceding for a breath that the wanted posters didn't do her fragile features justice. With her golden brown, almost blond, hair, big hazel eyes and a pair of lips that begged to be kissed he wished it would be a jury of women to try her case because any man looking at her would fall for her innocent look.

"Black Bette? What kind of name is that?" the blond woman demanded. "My name is Amanda Davis. Now release me this instant!"

Kendrick had to give her credit . . . her voice certainly brooked no defiance. The woman sounded almost like a schoolteacher for a group of rowdy boys instead of a cold blooded killer.

"Kinda thought you might enjoy being named something so evil."

"Evil? You, sir, are insane. Release me this minute or I promise you, I will bring charges against you."

"You can certainly try that Miss Barkley, but it won't be till after you're tried for robbery and murder, let's go." He urged her into the cell that the Sheriff had pulled open and hurried her inside.

"I never robbed or killed anyone although you are in the process of making me consider such action," the blond woman told him as she turned and stomped on his foot. She looked up in time to see his sapphire blue eyes register a moment's pain before he abruptly pushed her further into the cell and slammed the door shut. Turning to the Sheriff, Kendrick reiterated, "Jim, this is Black Bette Barkley and not the nicest lady you'll ever meet."

"Sheriff, you need to listen to me," Bette pleaded, "this man is crazy. I haven't killed or robbed anyone. This . . . this miscreant accosted me in Miller's Dry Goods and manhandled me here. I only just arrived here in St. Louis to begin a teaching job. I'm a teacher! Not a robber!"

"Here's the poster Jim . . . you tell me this isn't Elizabeth Barkley, otherwise known as the killer Black Bette."

"My name is *not* Elizabeth Barkley. As I said, it is Amanda Davis. I'm a teacher and I just arrived here from Massachusetts to teach."

Shaking his head Kendrick looked the woman over before telling her, "Step over here so I can take the cuffs off you and get on with my business." Moving to the sheriff's desk to fill in the custody paperwork he commented, "Piece of work, isn't she?"

Jim glanced up from the wanted poster Kendrick had handed him, studying it closely. "So it seems. Gotta wonder how she ended up here. You sure it's that Bette woman? I mean, maybe she really is a schoolteacher or has a husband here abouts."

"I have no doubt it's her. Little thief hightailed it out of California and probably thought she could lie low here and plan her next crime spree. Dusty told me this morning he heard rumors she was headed this way. Cold blooded killer to boot."

"That little thing?"

"Jim, you know as well as I do size doesn't matter nor does an innocent look when it comes to committing a crime and she's one of the worst."

"You sure this is the same woman from your poster? I mean, those pictures don't always . . ."

"Without a doubt. And she'll be on the wagon train with me headed back to California to stand trial. I appreciate you holding her the next two days till we head out."

As Kendrick finished the last of the paperwork, he let out a long, slow sigh. "My gut's never steered me wrong and it's served me now. I knew I'd be running into her." He gave the papers one last look before passing them over to the Sheriff. "I need to send a telegram to Frisco and let them know I have her in custody. Care to join me for supper after?"

Jim took a quick look and commented, "Sure enough on supper. My deputy will be in about a half hour. Meet you at Noreen's then?"

"Right enough."

"Say, Kendrick, there are serious charges there and if what she said is right, that her name is Amanda something or other and she's a teacher just arrived to teach, you'll be takin her a long ways away for nothing. You sure you got the right woman?"

"Oh yeah, she's the one all right. She's definitely the one I want."

CHAPTER SIX

After placing their dinner orders at Noreen's, Gromley handed over some papers to Kendrick. "Thought you'd like to see what came in on your Miz Barkley there. 'Parently it's more than what was on that poster."

Kendrick scanned the sheets the other man handed to him and let out a low whistle. "Like I said, she's some piece of work."

"You sure you'll be all right takin' her back out that way by yerself?"

"Shouldn't be a problem. I'll be traveling with Dusty and the wagon train. I'll just load her onto Dusty or the cook's wagon. Properly secured she won't be going anywhere. I telegraphed on ahead that I'll be getting her to Adler Creek and someone from Frisco will meet me there and take custody of her. If need be I'll travel west with whoever meets me."

"West, huh? You have a hankering to see California?"

"Maybe. My grandparents are gone. Except for my job, there's little for me in Washington. Sooner or later I need to find a wife and settle down. Might as well see some of the country before then."

"No one in your sights now?"

"No, not now. Although I'm sure I'm in some women's sights." Both men chuckled, "But no one I'd like to wake up beside every morning. Most of the eastern women I meet are very much like what I hear my mother was like. I loved her, or at least I love the memory of her. She died not long after I was born, but from what her friends in Washington told me when I was growing up, she was a fine, genteel lady. She had no sense of adventure and just wanted to have their lady's teas and things like that. From what little I heard from Dusty, my brother married a mail order bride. Who knows, maybe that's what I'll do too. But that's way ahead in the future. I figure for now, why not see the country?"

"And if war comes?"

"If it comes to that . . . well I'm gonna hold my cards close on that one. We're all going to have to choose at some point unless Mr. Lincoln can find a way to hold the peace."

Jim nodded his understanding. "Well I'm glad you recognized her in the dry good's store. Guess she thought she'd hit up a St. Louis bank before heading to wherever she was planning on going."

"Seems so. Schoolteacher my ba-hind. It will be a pleasure to see this one strung up, that's for sure."

"Well, it's only a six or seven week or so ride to Adler Creek, you keep her cuffed and an eye on your gun you'll be fine. I really wish I had someone to spare to keep an eye on her but right now . . ."

"Not to worry. Before we head out, I'm gonna wire Brett and see if he can head out and meet me half way. If not him, I'm sure Rick will come."

"Rick? Rick Hansen?"

"Yeah."

"Now that's a name I haven't heard a while either. How's he doing?"

"From what Dusty said he's still single. Unless he married one of those brides from that bride train Brett got his wife from."

Both men laughed a minute before Jim continued, "Smart man."

"I'd have to agree. I haven't met the woman yet that would make me want to put down roots."

"Well, I'll admit I wasn't too sure if it was right to marry Penelope, but she's a good woman and to be honest, I do love her."

"Glad to hear it. I'm happy for you and Brett, but I still think Dusty and I have the right way of it. Single."

The woman Kendrick called Bette watched the two men leave, mentally stomping her foot and wishing all kinds of nasty things to happen to the tall, blond haired Marshal. "I've seen frozen lakes warmer than those blue eyes of his," she told the wooden planked walls.

"Who in all that is righteousness does he think he is? Comes up to me in a store and says he's arresting me for murder and robbery? Based on a stupid wanted poster? How can anyone say there's a likeness to any living being based on those papers?"

Clenching her fist she pounded the air, wishing it was Marshal Parker instead. The man was frightening in his steadfast determination to bring her to California to stand trial based only on the similarity to a photograph on a wanted poster. Well, there was that and apparently a word of mouth description of her.

She stomped back and forth in the small cell, alternately inventing nasty ways of doing the arrogant deputy in and plotting her own escape. There had to be some way to get away from the man and somehow get back to Massachusetts where no one would know what had befallen her here. He'd never think to look for her there, would he?

No, of course he wouldn't. He was way too stupid and impressed with his arrogant self to consider she'd go east.

She hadn't wanted to leave Massachusetts. Despite the brave front she'd put up, it wasn't what she wanted at all. But with no family of her own and no job prospects there, she accepted a position in St. Louis or at least intended to. "What a liar you are Marshal, if in fact that's what you are."

Now here she was, alone with nothing to keep her company except her thoughts on just what she was going to do to Deputy Marshal Kendrick Parker when he realized he had the wrong woman. "Castration would be too kind."

Though spoke to an empty room she was still mortified at what she had said, covering her mouth with her hand. Ladies from polite company did not speak in such a manner. They did not even acknowledge that men's bodies bore such appendages.

Well, it was all his fault. Plain and simple, it was his fault she was now resorting to unladylike thoughts, words, and images.

The next morning Amanda found herself rudely awoken to the sounds of people yelling about wanting to string up some murderer or that they wanted guards posted around the clock so their bank wasn't robbed. It took her a few minutes to realize they were talking about her!

When she peered out the window to tell them they were mistaken and that the deputy marshal had the wrong woman someone threw a rock at her. Three more followed before the sheriff stepped up and told the crowd to disburse. When they were slow to leave, he pulled out his gun and fired a round into the air. Having ducked down she cringed when heard Marshal Parker's voice outside the jail. "Didn't think she'd be that much trouble. How'd word get out she was in town?"

"Wellll, I guess that would be my mistake," a young man softly admitted.

"Billy McCaffrey, what did you do?" She recognized the sheriff's voice as he asked the apparent newcomer.

"Aw, Sheriff, you know how it is . . ."

"No, Billy, I don't know how it is, but I'm going to in a few minutes. Inside. Now."

Marshal Parker, the sheriff and who Amanda could only guess was the troublemaking Billy McCaffrey entered the jail. She recognized the marshal and sheriff and concluded the other man was Billy. With his black hair, heavily slicked with pomade that one looked as if he'd just left a fancy house rather than being a lawman. The way he kept his hand on his gun, rubbing the butt as he looked past the Sheriff's shoulder at her made her realize that no matter how young he looked, he wouldn't hesitate to shoot now and ask questions later.

"Tell me this isn't your deputy, Jim." Parker stated the very question that Amanda would have if anyone had given her the time of day.

"Sorry to say he is. Billy's newly sworn and hasn't quite learned the job yet."

"Well . . . Billy." Parker moved to stand in front of the younger man. To Amanda's eyes the Marshal seemed to grow even bigger than he already was. "One of the first rules of law enforcement is you keep your mouth shut. What if she has accomplices she's meeting here in town? What if they waited till no one was around, or worse yet, broke in when you were here and killed you to get her out?"

"I'd kill anyone who tried to break a prisoner out." Billy blustered, his chest puffing out to match the arrogance of his words.

"I don't doubt you'd try. Just like I don't doubt you'd end up killing an innocent bystander." Amanda watched as Parker reached for Billy's gun. "Look at this, not only is it not secured in your holster, you have the safety off. It's any wonder you haven't shot yourself. Jim, I don't want this . . . boy . . ." Amanda could tell from the way Parker called Billy "boy" he meant it to be an insult. " . . . near my prisoner. Just because she's going to swing for murder doesn't mean she doesn't get a fair trial first."

"I don't see why that's necessary. I heared she kilt that

man, a lawman, she deserves to die."

"After a trial, Billy." The sheriff's exasperation was clear. "Listen, why don't you go on down to the post office and see if any mail's come in, huh?"

"Don't you need me to guard the prisoner?"

"Not today, Billy. Not today. I think you've done enough."

As the ornery young man headed to the door Parker called after him, "I think it best if you don't return here until we leave town. I'm sure you understand we don't need any more attention drawn to Miss Barkley."

Before Billy could answer, the sheriff gave him an order to bring the mail and then take a few days off.

Just before the door closed Amanda heard Parker ask the sheriff, "Where did you find him?"

"He's the mayor's nephew. I knew him when he was growing up. Too big for his britches, even then. Always causing scrapes. I tried to tell the mayor it wasn't a good idea to make him a deputy, but he insisted, and you know how it is with politics."

"Not really. I won't deny we have our problems in Washington and the Marshal's service, Jim, but nothing like that. You never talk about a prisoner to folks. Could get you and anyone else around killed by his . . . or her . . . accomplices. And just because I know we have the right person, it doesn't mean she isn't entitled to a trial. Who knows, maybe she'll give up her accomplices in exchange for a life sentence instead of the hanging she deserves."

"Right person my backside," Amanda muttered under her breath before calling out. "Excuse me! Sheriff, I need to . . . well I need . . . I have some personal . . ."

"Use the bucket Bette." Kendrick ordered her.

"You'd like that, wouldn't you, you pigheaded . . ." she stopped suddenly realizing that she was telling these strangers more than any lady should. Not that that stupid

Marshal Parker would know a lady if one announced it in big red letters across her chest. Well, make that big letters. The Sheriff, however, he might be much more understanding. If only she could speak with him away from the Marshal.

"Sheriff, please, if you could just come over here a minute."

"Bette, you are *my* prisoner, not the Sheriff's. You are only a *guest* in his jail. I decide what happens to you and when."

"Guest. Some guest. And my name is *Amanda*! Not Bette!"

"Put a lid on it, Bette."

"Amanda!"

"Call yourself anything you like, but you shut your mouth, or I'll cuff and gag you. Nature's calling you, use the damn bucket!"

"Sir, I am offended by your crude language." She huffed, folded her arms over her chest and glared at the two men.

She stepped back as Kendrick advanced on her, hands fisted at his side. She didn't know which frightened her more, the look on his face or the way he'd fisted his hands, as if he wanted to choke her. "Fine, fine, I'll use your bucket. Just the two of you turn around if you would."

"I don't care about the damn bucket, I just want you to shut your mouth. And I'll tell you something lady, you learn to keep it shut because once we're on the trail I'm going to be the only thing between you and a lynch mob that wants you dead, so you learn to do as I say and you could live to make it to San Francisco." If Kendrick noticed his language and tone had lost the carefully cultivated tones of Washington society in favor of the rougher language of the west, he paid it no mind.

"And what makes you think I want to live that long? Because maybe I don't. Not if I have to put up with your arrogant, obnoxious, self-important self. Now, what do you think of *that*?"

"Kendrick, Kendrick." The Sheriff pulled on his arm. "I think you both need to reconsider your thinking."

She watched as the Marshal turned to look at the sheriff before turning and admitting, "Yeah, you're right, you're right."

They stepped away, speaking low a few minutes before Kendrick left the office and the Sheriff walked over to her, pulling his gun just before he unlocked the cell door. "Step out and you can use the privy out back. Don't try anything, just do as I say and nothing should happen."

He escorted her outside and then back into the cell.

"Thank you, Sheriff. That man is simply impossible."

"Parker's not a bad sort and I can't say I find much fault with his feelings. If you did kill that lawman, I don't have any sympathy for you, and you will be hung."

"Sheriff Gromley, is it? I didn't kill anyone. Truly. I've come down from Peabody, Massachusetts for a teaching position here your city. If you will just check with Mr. Pedersen at the school, he will confirm that we have corresponded, and he is expecting me to come teach."

"Maybe so, but anyone can pretend to be anything they want. You head on out to Frisco with Marshal Parker, be honest in your trial and if they find they have the wrong person, you come on back here and I'm sure he'll find a position for you."

"That sounds all well and good, but your friend, Marshal Parker, has already tried and condemned me without even listening to me. Sheriff, he has the wrong person."

"Well, that's between you and him. But I will tell you this, don't rile that man any more than you have. By his reputation he's not too long on patience if he thinks he has a criminal on his hands."

"Thank you. Thank you oh so much." She stated with a sarcastic curtness that surprised even herself. The belated thought entered her mind that she should be a little less caustic to the Sheriff, as he appeared to be her only friend in town.

The Sheriff shrugged and started to walk away. Amanda called after him, "Is there any chance I might have a bath?"

Jim stopped, his back to her and stood for a moment. "You are asking a lot there Miz Barkley."

"Think of it as the condemned's last meal except instead of a meal I'm getting a bath." She sighed, unable to help the sad tone of her voice.

"Suppose you'll want all kinds of privacy while you're at it too."

"I . . . well . . . that would only be proper."

"I'll check with Marshal Parker but I cain't promise you it'll happen."

"*No!* Please. I don't want anything that has to do with that man."

"Have it your way."

With that he turned and left. She didn't see him or the arrogant Marshal Parker again until the next morning; another deputy brought her dinner.

The next morning the Sheriff brought her breakfast and let her outside to use the privy. On the way back inside he stopped and filled a bucket of water, telling her she could use that to wash up some, "but hurry cause Parker's set on you two leaving with the wagon train pulling out this morning."

Grateful for the water Amanda quickly sponge bathed and finger combed her hair. She supposed it would be asking too much for the Marshal to fetch her trunks from her room at the boarding house. Barring that, maybe he would condescend to lend her a brush or comb.

She only got a glimpse of the wanted poster when the Sheriff let her out to use the privy, but clearly the picture bore no likeness to her. "Maybe he's got something to hide and is doing it by trying to put the attention on me. Well, it just might be time to turn the tables on United States Marshal Kendrick Parker, it just might be time."

CHAPTER SEVEN

A short time later Kendrick returned to the jail, a red headed stranger beside him.

"Let's go Bette."

"Who is that man and what is *he* doing here?"

"That's none of your concern. Now step out and turn so your back is towards me."

Eyeing the rough looking red head she decided to comply with the Marshal's directive, at least for the time being. If she played the victim and innocent maybe she could get the other man on her side and he'd help her get away from what she had deemed the presumptively supercilious Deputy Marshal.

He led her towards the edge of town past where the wooden planks served for sidewalks, fear trickling up and down her spine, as it occurred to her that maybe he wasn't going to keep his promise and take her to San Francisco to stand trial, but rather allow the folk of St. Louis to hang her then and there. It was with only a modicum of relief that she saw about twenty Conestoga wagons hitched up to two to four oxen each. His hand on her elbow, the Marshal led her to the last one in line and in one swift movement, lifted her inside. She couldn't hold back a shriek of surprise when he picked her up with the movement so unexpected. Unable to grab on to anything with her hands secured behind her back, she ducked as best she could into his chest, completely unaware of what the simple act did to the man's libido. He climbed up behind her and guided her towards a bench inside the wagon, released one of the cuffs only to reattach it to a bar anchoring the bench. The smell of dusty canvas made her eyes and nose itch. She swallowed in the hopes of chasing the dryness from her throat, this time not from fear but from the stale air of the wagon.

"You'll be riding inside, Bette. At least until we're on our way. If you behave, once we're on our way, I'll see about letting you ride up front with the driver."

"You're too kind, Marshal." She couldn't keep the sarcasm out of her voice or the glare from her look. A look she was sure left no doubt she'd gladly kill Kendrick Parker if given half a chance which was not the best impression to leave him with. Still, Amanda had little artifice to fall back on. If she did, she figured she wouldn't be in the position she was in now . . . an accused murderess on her way to California to stand trial for someone else's crimes. How nice it would be to know how to simper and make a man fawn all over one's self. From what little she'd pieced together from his clipped sentences, a woman called Black Bette had been on a crime laden rampage in the west. There were rumors the woman was headed east, although no one could say why. Although she'd traveled alone by train to St. Louis surely someone had seen her board at the station in Massachusetts and could vouch for her. Unfortunately, the Marshal wasn't inclined to do any investigation and check that or any other part of her story out.

Barring that, why didn't Marshal Parker send a telegram to Peabody or nearby Salem asking after her? A simple telegram confirming her true identity would solve the problem, at least for her. Her neighbors in Peabody knew her well and would vouch for her in a heartbeat. More to the point, why didn't he even question her? There hadn't been one simple question posed to her. He gave orders and everyone seemed inclined to obey them without question. She wondered why the Sheriff didn't notice or ask why a Marshal would jump to the conclusion that she was this Bette person. Why was he so set on bringing her west and not bothering to find out anything at all about her? Fear trickled down her spine as awareness of just what might be going on came to mind. What was his real intent for taking her to San Francisco?

She'd heard stories about unsuspecting women being taken and sold for illicit purposes. Unscrupulous men doing dastardly deeds to them. The question was, would a bonafide United States Marshal be party to such an unprincipled act?

Then again, what if Kendrick Parker wasn't a real U.S. Marshal?

What if the man who had taken her wasn't Marshal Parker at all?

What if *he* was a criminal who killed the real Marshal and was taking her as a hostage? Her head began to ache with the questions that tumbled through her mind.

Still, it seemed the Sheriff and wagon master knew him . . . unless they were in cahoots. Maybe they were part of a gang that kidnapped innocent women for wicked acts. The whole situation just did not make any sense at all. The only surety in the whole situation was that he believed to his bones she was that Black Bette woman.

She didn't miss the care the Marshal took in making sure she was secured inside the wagon before he jumped down and let the flap on the backdrop, sealing her inside. In the dim light Amanda looked around, trying to get her bearings. By the looks of the contents inside the wagon barrels marked beans, dried beef, potatoes coupled with pots and pans, he'd placed her in a supply wagon.

Suddenly she lit upon something that gave her a moment's pause. Her trunks! Someone had fetched her trunks! She couldn't credit the Marshal with such a thoughtful act, telling herself the Sheriff had to have had them brought over. Although how could he have known where she was boarding or that the trunks were indeed hers? No, they were hers. The faded painting of roses on the top could not be duplicated. Amanda herself had painted it on years before. She had no doubt, however, that the marshal had gone through the trunk as thoroughly as he had filled in those forms when he arrested her.

The thought of him going through her belongings, meager as they were, was disconcerting. Her few dresses, while not completely threadbare, were mended several times over. That was not what embarrassed her. No, it was her unmentionables and the thought of him touching them that heated her face, telling her she had turned a deep shade of red. The thought of *that* man with those big hands of his, the long fingers running and fondling . . . yes fondling her unmentionables had her wishing for a deep hole to climb in to and hide away forever.

That thought lasted until she thought about his eyes. Those frigid blue eyes of his. His hands were probably just as icy. "And no doubt he has a rock for a heart."

Deciding that thoughts of Kendrick Parker, any thoughts at all, of the pompous oaf, would get her nowhere, she pulled against her restraints to try in some fashion to reach the trunk.

Of course the man had placed it just far enough from where he secured her that she couldn't reach it, tantalizingly close, but out of reach. "Humph. That man," she told the heavy canvas walls of the wagon, not that they would answer her any faster than Kendrick Parker did. "Well," she told those cloth walls, "when one needs to express one's consternation, one does not care to whom, or what, they express it." In this case, the canvas walls would have to do. She was certain if she even hinted at wanting to pull anything from the trunk, the Marshal would secure her hands ever more tightly and move the trunk even further away. The idea of using a bad word for the first time in her life became very tempting.

She leaned back on the bench, supported by the wooden

plank of the wagon and blew out a breath. If nothing else, she could listen to the sounds of the travelers preparing to leave. Closing her eyes, she let the sounds drift over her . . .

"Are we going to be the fifth wagon the whole trip?"

"Will we make camp early enough to have some light to start the cook fires?"

"How soon before we see Indians?"

"Will we be stopping by water every night?"

"What about baths? I'll get a hot bath every night, won't I?"

The last made Amanda chuckle. "Hot bath," she muttered to herself. "I'd kill for a damp cloth to wash my face."

"And you probably have." Kendrick's voice carried into the wagon as he climbed in beside her.

"I have not." She couldn't keep the exasperation out of her voice. "If you would listen but a moment Marshal . . ."

"To lies? Miz Barkley, you have nothing to say to me that I care to hear."

"Does the truth bother you, Marshal?"

"Nope. A murderer bothers me."

Amanda humphed and looked away from him.

"Thought you might like a cup of water before we start out." He reached behind her and released one of the cuffs.

"What?" She was stunned by his sudden change of direction, taking the cup and sipping lest he try to poison her; she found the waster surprisingly cool and quite refreshing.

She thought he'd turned civil until he spoke again, "We do want to keep you alive to stand trial, after all."

"Am I going to have to hear your taunts the whole way to California?"

"Nope. Just to Wyoming." With that, he rose and moved to leave the wagon before he turned again and looked at her.

It was disconcerting the way his gazed moved from her head to her body down to her feet before rising back up again, slowly, as if he were undressing her with his eyes. Amanda had no doubt the man knew exactly what she looked like without her clothing on. "Why Wyoming?"

He didn't answer her question, merely telling her, "You might want to do something with your hair. Looks like a rat's nest."

She tried to rise in indignation only to be brought up short by the manacle holding her in place. "I might indeed. Someone, however, placed my trunks just out of my reach so you will need to take me as I am. And come to think of it, just how did you get your hands on them?"

He didn't answer her question but asked her one of his own, "Want I should bring them back to the inn, Bette? Cause I can if you don't want them . . ."

"You know I want them you, you . . . humph. Would you kindly release me so I can get to them?"

He grunted, an unintelligible sound, reached over and dragged one of the trunks to her. Tipping his hat, he jumped out of the wagon.

The man confused her. He was made of ice yet somehow managed to be almost . . . human.

Stepping away from the wagon, Kendrick shook his head. For a thief and murderer, Black Bette Barkley had all the appearance and language of a refined lady. He'd gone through her trunks, removing anything that could be used as a weapon. A little doll puzzled him; it wasn't the sort of thing you'd find in a killer's possessions. Bette Barkley certainly was an enigma. Not at all like the wealthy debutantes his grandparents paraded in front of him, but a regular lady. Almost like the schoolteacher she purported herself to be. And damn if that language of hers wasn't entertaining!

"Care to share?" Dusty'd come up behind him just in time

to catch him chuckling over Bette's words.

"Not really." He glanced back at the wagon and motioned Dusty a few steps away. "The less she hears, the better off and safer we'll be."

"Makes sense. So, what's got you smiling like a school-boy?"

"I'm not . . ."

That was the last thing Kendrick Parker wanted to be thought of — a smiling schoolboy. The thoughts he had of Black Bette the night before were bad enough. To have some-one see him as anything but stern and serious about the woman would be wrong. "Just smiling, that's all."

"I suppose if I were on my way to see my brother and his new wife I'd be smiling too."

"Didn't know you had a brother."

"I don't! Jest saying like if I was in your shoes. So?"

"Aw, it's that Bette. Woman has a way with words. Always talking so uppity. Kinda entertaining if you weren't trying so hard to understand what she was saying."

"You mean that bit I heard from her back at the jail is her normal way?"

"Appears so." He smiled, shaking his head.

"Well then, won't be no lack of entertainment on the trail, will there?"

"Please. No!" At that he actually laughed. "She'll uppity talk me to death!"

Dusty headed off, shaking his head.

Kendrick shook his own head at himself. Last night he'd done something he never did. First, he'd lain awake thinking about Brett and his bride. Not just thinking about them or even the fact that his younger brother was married, it was that Brett married a stranger, a woman he never laid eyes on be-fore. Over and over his mind churned on what would possess Brett to do such a thing? Did he talk it over with Rick? With

Wolf? Or, as Dusty intimated in a conversation, did he just up and decide to marry an unknown woman?

And then, just as he was finally falling asleep, he wondered at himself and why he hadn't met a woman who he wanted to spend his life with.

What made it worse were the dreams he had. All night Black Bette walked through his dreams. And it wasn't that she was walking around in them. No, she beckoned to him, seduced him into a kiss, a deep and tantalizing kiss. She lay down in a field, her skirts floating up silky legs, thighs spreading in welcome, causing him to wake more than once with a throb between his legs.

Now, in the light of day, he admonished himself to keep in mind Black Bette Barkley was a dangerous woman, one that would kill him as soon as look at him. Thing was, while in his mind he knew he should feel nothing but disdain for her, the way his gut clenched when he looked at her made him want to do things for her he shouldn't do. Do things *for* her? It was what he wanted to do *to* her that was starting to concern him . . . and he'd only just met her. Was that how it was with Brett? Just met a woman and . . . *Whoa wait a minute there, partner! Brett's wife wasn't a low life like Bette Barkley.*

Clearly all the talk about Brett and the men of Adler Creek's marriages was occupying his thoughts more than they should. All he'd thought about the past couple of days was Brett and his bride. Well that and why he hadn't found a wife himself.

A short time later the wagon train moved out. Dusty and a few of his men in the lead. Kendrick checked on Bette to make sure she was secured in the supply wagon before joining with two other scouts to bring up the rear. The further they traveled from St. Louis, the scouts would fan out with an eye towards Indians or other unwanted visitors. Through the flap opening in the back of the wagon, even from the back of the train, he caught glimpses of Bette. For the most part she was either staring straight ahead — not out the front or back of the wagon to take in the scenery — but at the canvas wall or laying her head back as if dozing. He noticed she had combed out her hair. Rather than the frumpish bun she'd worn since he arrested her, she now had it braided in one long braid. Looking at the braid, about as thick as his wrist, Kendrick mentally undid the braid and the image of her on top of him, her long hair creating a curtain around them while they coupled shot a jolt of pure desire to his groin.

He'd order her to put her hair up in a bun. As soon as they stopped tonight, he would tell her his decision. Plain and simple — she'd wear her hair in a bun, or he'd cut it off.

CHAPTER EIGHT

Shortly before sunset, Amanda became aware of Dusty calling the day's travel to a halt by the stopping of the wagon, followed by it being turned. She guessed it was to put the wagons into a circle as she had heard about.

A few minutes later she heard a woman approaching, "Mr. Parker! Mr. Parker? How is your wife feeling?"

"My wife?"

"Yes! I'm Annabelle Schmidt, Charles Schmidt's wife. I overheard you telling one of the other men that your wife was feeling poorly. Terrible thing to be starting a journey like this when you are feeling peeked. I know how that can be, especially if you are in the family way. Let me tell you! So I thought that I'd stop by and . . ."

"Mrs. Smith?"

"Schmidt. Annabelle Schmidt, from Baltimore. Charles and I . . ."

"Right. Mrs. Schmidt. Thank you for coming by. My wife is just fine. I can assure you she is not in the . . . family way . . ."

"You never know. Just because you're a newlywed doesn't mean you can't have a little Parker on the way."

Listening to the conversation Amanda felt her cheeks heat. Whatever had the cantankerous marshal told these people? What kind of lies was he spreading about her now? And when did he have the time to concoct such a tale? His wife indeed!

The temptation to step to the back of the wagon and set the story straight was overwhelming. The problem with that in

49

the first place, she *couldn't* step to the back of the wagon and in the second, she certainly didn't want the people she was traveling with to see she was being held prisoner. Not that they didn't already know. One never knew what a man as unbalanced . . . because surely he was unbalanced . . . as Marshal Parker would say or do.

"Mrs. Schmidt. I assure you, my wife is fine. She was just a bit tired today and wanted to rest in the wagon. I'd know if she was expecting. Believe me, there are no secrets between us. So, if you will excuse me . . ."

"Well!" She released an exasperated breath, "I brought her some biscuits, the same as I ate when I was in the family way and was going to offer to bring her some soup when it's heated."

"Thank you. I apologize for being brusque. I'm sure you can understand how tired we are all feeling after our first day. I'll be sure to tell . . . Mandy . . . that you were kind enough to send the biscuits. We'll let you know if she needs the soup."

"Apology accepted. We're just in that wagon over there. The one with the little green and white checked flag flying off the back."

"Wonderful. Well, I'll see you later."

He entered the wagon in one surprisingly graceful move. For a man as large as he was both in height and breadth, he moved with amazing feline poise.

"One of the women sent you some biscuits." He carefully placed them on the bench as close to her as he could without touching her.

"So I heard."

After a moment of awkward silence Amanda spoke up, "I'd like to hear just what it is you have told these people about me. However, before that, I need to use the necessary. *Now.*"

It was with pleasure she saw his cheeks take on a ruddy

color that definitely wasn't from spending the day riding in the sun. Thinking to herself that it was only fair she embarrass him after he went through her unmentionables, and she had no doubt he had seen she was pleased at his reaction. She had not folded them with the same precision she found them in.

Without a word Kendrick reached over to the cuffs and quickly released the one holding her in one swift motion. With a grimace he helped her stand while telling her, "You stay away from the other travelers. You don't talk to anyone but me. Understood?"

Amanda nodded and stepped towards the back of the wagon before whirling on him, "And my name is *Amanda!*"

The cooling air of the evening was a welcome respite from sitting in the stuffy wagon the entire day. Despite the cooler temperature outside the wagon, she felt decidedly uncomfortable due to the layer of dust she had accumulated on the trail even though she'd been inside the entire day. With Kendrick at her elbow, she walked to a nearby clump of bushes. He never gave her a chance to look over the camping circle the wagons had formed although around her she heard quiet conversation along with children laughing and playing. After being pent up in or on the wagons all day the children needed time to run and play.

When he stood there staring at her, in frustration at either his rudeness or lack of tact, she reached up to put her hands on his shoulders and tried to turn him around. The way his shoulders tensed at her touch gave her a clue just how strong the man was as well as how her touch offended him. Not that he hadn't appeared strong, it as just that now she had proof. Without a doubt he could kill her in one blow with those big hands of his. "If you won't extend me the courtesy of stepping away for a minute, would you at least turn around?"

His renewed blush told her he had no idea of the predicament he had put her in until she'd asked. Then again, perhaps that was his normal shade when dealing with women. He might look fine of form, but he had no manners or civility to him. No decent woman would want any part of him. If he had any manners at all, he would have listened to Amanda's side of the story before taking her against her will.

"Don't try anything. Just do . . . do whatever you need to do. I'll be right here. You try anything . . ."

"Yes, yes. I know. You'll shoot to kill. Now please!"

He turned and took a few steps away from her.

When she stepped back out a few minutes later he turned back towards her. "Mind if I wash my hands, Marshal?"

His response was only a curt gesture with his hands in the direction of the river.

"I don't suppose you would tell me if this was the Missouri River or not?"

"There a reason you need to know?"

"No." She knelt at the river's edge and wiggled her fingers in it. A fluttering motion with her fingers relaxing her. The water was cool, yet comforting, in its own way, refreshing, while a hot bath would have relaxed. "Just wondering."

"No reason for you to know then."

"You are a most annoying man. I was just curious which route you intend to take us . . ."

"Like I said. No reason for you to know."

From the look on his face it seemed pretty clear he wanted to stomp his feet in a childish tantrum. For some reason, she tried his patience, which was such poor behavior on his part since she was the one who was being taken against her will. And to have him tell people that they were married?

"By the way, don't you think it would have been more prudent to tell people we were brother and sister than to say we were married?"

For a breath his eyes widened, his brows arching slightly upward at the movement, while the pupils seemed to widen in the center of the blue iris. When his jaw dropped open, she had a glimpse of straight white teeth. She wanted to laugh at the expression on his face, like a schoolboy finding the tables turned on him by the girl with the pigtails that he always put in the ink well. Guessing that would only cause his already tenuously held temper to flare, Amanda bit back the laugh that threatened to erupt from her lips.

"The train's following the rivers out west. That's all you need to know."

Amanda digested that. She hadn't paid any attention to just how groups of people, wagon trains, traveled west. She'd gotten to St. Louis on her own and that was as far as she planned to go. In the back of her mind, she'd heard that the wagon trains followed a series of rivers west. Either that or following the Butterfield stage route to the south across Texas to California. It remained to be seen which way he'd take her to get wherever he intended to deliver her.

"Wash up if that's what your gonna do. I don't have all evening to molly coddle you."

Amanda instantly plunged her hands in the water, gasping at the cool temperature, so cool it caused her nipples to harden in reaction. Despite the chill, she also brought up several scoops of water to wash her face, sighing with the pleasure of feeling somewhat clean, if not cold.

"If you promise to behave I'll let you bathe after supper. If you've a mind to do so, that is."

"You're too kind." Realizing once again how sarcastic she sounded, she quickly apologized, "I am sorry. It's been a long, hot day."

"Not needed." He reached for her elbow to guide her back. Stopping after a few steps, he turned Amanda to face him. "There's some things we need to get straight."

"Is that so? I believe I already know the lay of the land. You will grunt out your orders and I am to obey without question.

I will sit, chained in the wagon all day long until you see fit to allow me to use the necessary. Oh and I do have one question."

"I do not grunt out orders. And maybe if you listen for a minute, you will see the wisdom of what I have decided."

"By all means." She gestured her hand in a most regal manner. "Enlighten me."

"As I said, I've told the rest of the folks here you are my wife."

"So I heard. And no one has questioned why I would want to be saddled with an arrogant, obnoxious, foul man like you? And are we a love match or did my parents just off and marry me to the crudest oaf they could find?"

The sharp bite to his indrawn breath alerted her to how frustrated he was before he continued. "As I said, I have made it known you are my wife. We are newly wedded, just before coming to St. Louis. The reason I have given that story is that if the rest of these good people were to know who and what you are, you'd be dead by tomorrow night. These are all God-fearing people, traveling west to make a good life for themselves. The last thing they want is a murderer in their midst. Believe me Miz Barkley, if they know what you are, they will kill you without benefit of a trial. I expect you to behave as I tell you."

"Wouldn't have calling yourself my brother have worked as well?"

"Nope. Brother won't be . . . a husband can keep closer tabs on his wife." She noticed an odd flare in his eyes as he said that. As if his mind was going in one direction while he spoke of another. "Anyone asks, you are my wife. Not that I expect anyone will because you will be keeping your distance from anyone except me. Understood?"

"Well, that shouldn't be a problem with you keeping me locked up in that wagon all day every day. They will just think you are a callous brut."

"That could be an option. What I am offering you, however, is if you do as I say, don't make any trouble, you'll be able to sit up front and converse some with the rest of the travelers. I don't want you seeking them out. If someone approaches you, you don't need to be rude. Just don't be seeking anyone out. If you do as I say here, it will make my job easier and you will be delivered to Frisco safely. Your choice."

Amanda looked up at him, sure for just a moment she saw some warmth in those frosty eyes of his. As quickly as she saw it, the warmth was gone. "You don't expect me to share my bed with you, do you?"

"Lay with you? I'd rather lie with a snake. We'll sleep side by side. Just like any married couple. Either that or I'll cuff you to the wagon. Your choice."

"Throw in the chance to bathe every few days and I will agree."

"Not a problem. I'm not too keen on laying beside a woman who smells foul."

"Nor am I fond of laying beside a man . . . I mean . . . being beside . . . I . . . you need to know. I'm a . . . I've never."

"A virgin, Mrs. Parker?"

"Par . . . my name is Davis, Amanda Da . . ."

"Parker. Mandy Parker. You're my wife and as such you carry my name."

"Fine. Amanda Parker."

"You understand . . . *Mandy* . . . I am telling this story for my own convenience. It would make my job a good deal more difficult if anyone besides Dusty knew the truth."

"Yes. I do understand."

They walked a few steps before Amanda stopped him. When he lifted his brow in question, she told him, "If you decide to tell anyone anything else, you will be certain to share that information with me as well, won't you? That way we can both tell the same story you are concocting."

"Of course. We'll eat by ourselves tonight . . . since you were feeling a bit peeked today."

"Of course."

"And that is the Missouri River."

"I see."

"Only told you in case someone says something so who you really are doesn't come out."

"Naturally." Her tone was dry, clearly indicating she didn't believe for a second that was the reason he told her, although she couldn't divine exactly why he would tell her otherwise.

He helped her back into the wagon, over the gated rear. "Don't even think about trying anything. I expect to find you here when I get back with our supper."

When he returned, it was with two tin plates filled to the brim with a delicious smelling stew of meat, potatoes, and a thick gravy. The scent alone making her mouth water in anticipation of the meal, especially as he hadn't seen fit to feed her or give her any water since leaving St. Louis in the morning. Thick slices of bread with bright yellow butter spread over them sat as far off to the side of the plates as possible without falling off. Amanda enjoyed the look on his face when he saw she'd moved her trunk so it sat towards the middle of the wagon like a table. More than that, he noticed she had pulled out some napkins from the trunk. They'd been a gift from a friend, several years before as a wish for good luck and the hope it would serve as a wedding gift. It didn't look like she'd be getting married now, so she thought she'd enjoy the napkins while she could. Not giving him one had naturally crossed her mind. Amanda wasn't that petty . . . yet. She'd be lucky if she could prove she wasn't the ominous Black Bette.

She noticed he handed her a spoon but kept the forks and

knives to himself. That caused her to shake her head at his precautions. Didn't he realize she knew that if anything happened to him, she'd be in danger? Even if they believed his story about them being married, it would not bode well for her.

Kendrick placed her dish on her side of the table and lowered himself on a nearby barrel to eat. It creaked ever so slightly under his weight but held him well. He filled the small space with both his body and scent.

He was, Amanda decided, like a woven tapestry of contradictions. He smelled of the dirt they traveled over, the big black horse he rode and leather of the saddle as well as his own scent. To look at him he appeared a rugged cowboy yet to hear him speak, he had all the cultured tones of a well-educated easterner. His eyes were a hard-frozen shade of blue, like deep ice on a winter's lake, while at the same time he'd do something considerate.

Despite how hungry she was she forced herself to take only a very delicate bite of the meat and chewed it thoroughly before thanking him for bringing it. The tang of the meat caused her mouth to water a bit more, the flavor playing with her tongue. It was the best meat she had ever eaten.

In response, he nodded and swallowed before answering her. "No problem."

After eating in silence a few minutes Amanda decided that she would at least try to be civil. "So tell me, Marshal, where and how did we meet?"

"What?"

"Where and . . ."

"I heard you. What the hell kind of question is that?"

"One that I am certain at least I will be asked and in the event you are as well, I believe it would be best we both provide the same answer."

"You always talk so formal?"

"For . . . I . . . are you now finding fault with how I speak?"

"Sounds kind of snooty to me."

"Well I will do my best to learn some improper or inappropriate language. Shall I start with calling you a jackass?"

She was pleased when he coughed and almost choked on the mouthful of stew he had just taken. He rooted around for something; she guessed perhaps a drink of the water he had brought into the wagon and handed him the cup he'd given her.

He drank it down and nodded his thanks to her before answering, "That might draw some unwanted attention. As to where we met . . . you were visiting family in Washington and attended a play I was also attending, and I found you . . . acceptable."

"Acceptable? Marshal, you would be most fortunate to have the interest of a woman like me."

"Right. That would be most amusing . . . arresting my wife. And you might want to call me Kendrick instead of Marshal. A loving wife wouldn't be so formal with her husband, newly wedded or not."

"Well, *Marshal*, when you are ready to listen, perhaps I can enlighten you as to why you have the wrong woman."

"I have the right woman. No doubt about that."

She contemplated him while she absently mopped her bread in the gravy. "So what play did we see?"

"Play?"

"You said we met at the theatre. Obviously we were there for a play. What one? What month? Who was with us? Was it love at first sight? Or did I give you the cold shoulder and you had to come calling many times before convincing my uncle to allow you to pay court to me . . . despite my aunt's misgivings you were, and still are, at heart, a reprobate."

Kendrick stood and made to take his unfinished meal to eat elsewhere.

"And when the good people on this wagon train ask why you are not dining with your bride, your answer will be? And, by the way, why would a Deputy United States Marshal be bringing his wife on an . . . what do you call them? Assignment? With him."

Sitting back down he released a long breath. "Of course it was love at first sight. You begged your aunt and uncle to introduce us. You thought I was the most handsome man you ever laid eyes on. Since your uncle knew me from Washington circles, he readily agreed to our courtship which was a short one because when we met, I already had plans to travel to Wyoming to see my family."

She couldn't help herself. Animosity receded as Amanda sat up, leaned forward as if Kendrick Parker was sharing some deep dark secret. "Your family? You have family in Wyoming?"

"Yup. Born and raised a spell there."

"Really?" She couldn't keep the excitement from her voice. "I've never met someone who lived anywhere but in the original thirteen until I traveled to St. Louis. What was it like? Did you see any Indians? Attend any gunfights? Why were you in Washington if . . ."

She frowned at his upturned hand. "Don't you think this is important for me to know so I can play my part in this charade of yours?"

"I guess. I was born in Adler Creek and my mother died when I was pretty young. My father remarried and they had my younger brother, Brett. Before that though, my grandparents had me move back east with them."

"What happened to Brett?"

"He stayed with his mother. She remarried."

"So have you met any Indians?"

"I've already told you more about myself than most people even come close to. Even people I consider friends."

"Well then, if you continue in your singular need to deliver me to California and see to my demise there, I will most certainly be taking all that information to my grave, won't I?"

"Why do I get the idea you just spoke a lot more formally than you would have if you weren't trying to irritate me?"

"Obviously you never met any Indians." She hesitated a moment. "Do you think we'll see . . . be accosted by any . . . in our travels?"

"It's entirely possible." He ran his fingers through his hair. An action she felt seemed quite intimate before realizing the intimacy was in her mind and desires, not in the reality of his actions.

"We'll . . . we'll be safe, won't we?"

"Depends on the tribe and how many. I wouldn't worry about it. Most of them know Dusty and trust him. The ones in these parts know pretty much we are going to keep right on moving and not staying around here."

"Well that's good to hear."

Amanda caught him studying her for a time and prompted, "Yes?"

"You aren't really afraid of Indians, are you?"

"I . . . I'm not sure. I've heard the stories. Then again, before you accosted me in St. Louis, I did see a few men standing around. Of course, they could have been . . . oh what do you call them? Mountain men? To be honest, I've never thought about it."

"Now's not the time to be worrying about it."

"So the play we were attending when we met?"

He thought a few minutes. "How about A Play. By Chekov. I saw a playbill for it before I left."

"Sounds as good as any. So did we have a large wedding?"

"No. Short and sweet."

"Because?"

"Because I needed to leave for Wyoming as soon as I

could."

"Is your family expecting you?"

At that, she noticed his expression closed. It was as if he had brought a curtain down and no one existed in the small space but himself. Rather than answer, he picked up the dishes. "Let's go and bring a towel if you want to wash up a bit. The water will be cold, but at least you can clean up some."

She noted as she went to jump back down off the wagon, he not only reached up to take her by the waist, but he seemed to hold on to her a beat too long when he set her on the ground. It didn't escape Amanda's notice that his hands practically spanned her waist, bringing home, once again, how he could kill her in an instant with little effort on his own part.

Amanda hurried after him to the water's edge. The river flowed thick and freely, perhaps because of the recent snow melt. The air was still fairly chilly, and she made a mental note to dig her long coat out of the trunk as soon as they returned to the wagon. Looking at the sky, seeing few clouds she wondered if it would snow again before they reached their destination.

Crouching down at the water's edge Amanda rinsed off the plates and reached for the silverware which, surprisingly, Kendrick handed over to her without question. It seemed he forgot his decision not to let her have any forks or knives. She was aware of his gaze on her when she ran the towel through the shallow water and began washing off her face. Unable to restrain the contented sigh that escaped her lips she gave into the sheer enjoyment of being able to clean up, however slightly and no matter how frigid the water.

Before she could ask him to turn so she could lower the top of her blouse she heard someone calling, "Mrs. Parker? Mrs. Parker?"

Amanda looked around to see where the other *Parker*

might be only to hear Kendrick answer, "Help you ma'am?"

A tall woman with iron gray hair strode over. "Why yes. I wanted to see how your wife was doing. I'm Zelda Markham, Horace Markham's wife. How are you, dear?"

"I'm fine, thank you." Mandy answered with a slight smile in Kendrick's direction.

"We heard how poorly you were feeling, and I wanted to see if you needed anything. I know you told Annabelle that you were set just fine, but she can be a bit overbearing if you get my drift."

"Oh, not really that poorly and your friend was most kind." Seeking to discomfit Kendrick, she took his arm in both her hands and rested her head on his upper arm. Rather than Kendrick feeling uncomfortable, it was Amanda who felt ill at ease. His arm was like steel. Hard and unmoving, like the man himself. And he was tall. Very tall. She noted her head barely came to his chest. There was no softness to the man either in body or mood.

"Are you sure, dear? I have some excellent tea for an upset stomach if you'd like." Zelda asked.

"Tea? Not right now, thank you."

"For your stomach."

"My . . . oh. Dear. No. I had a slight headache this morning. That's all. All the excitement from the trip. You understand, I'm sure."

"Headache?" Zelda glanced at Kendrick before pitching her voice low, "Have you told your husband?"

Choosing not to lower her own voice, after all Kendrick hadn't told her what ailed her and he certainly wasn't helping her out with Mr. Markham, she said, "Told my husband what?"

"Why that you, errr, that you . . ."

Kendrick cleared his throat, drawing their attention. "I can assure you Mrs. Markham, as I told Mrs. Schmidt, if my bride were in the family way, she would have told me as soon as she knew."

Zelda beamed. "Would this be your first?"

"We are newlyweds," Kendrick dryly informed her.

Zelda's smile grew even wider. "Well then! You both may not know if you will be expecting or not! I'm here to tell you, I didn't know my own signs for sure until my third one."

"Third?" Amanda couldn't keep the surprise out of her voice. Not that large families were an oddity, she couldn't fathom having one child right now let along three.

"Yes. Horace and I have six children, all of them the spitting image of their father."

"I see." Amanda answered. "Isn't that lovely . . . dear?"

"Yes, my love. It is." Kendrick actually winked at her when he answered her. "I can assure you Mrs. Markh . . ."

"Zelda, please. We'll all know each other quite well by time we arrive in Wyoming, won't we?"

"Zelda." Something about the tenor of his voice struck a corc in Amanda she hadn't known existed. It was deep, but mellow. A caress with a certain roughness. If she had to describe how his voice would feel it would match his hands. A bit work hardened with calluses while at the same time, a gentle firmness in the touch. She silently chided herself for giving the man as much thought as she was then and there. He wasn't the type of man she would allow to pay court to herself, that was certain.

"Well, Zelda," Amanda interrupted their discussion. "I can assure you, I am not in the family way . . . and while not proper conversation for mixed company, my husband well knows why we haven't shared our marital bed the past few weeks. Isn't that right, my love?"

In the dimming evening light, Amanda was pleased to see both Zelda and Kendrick blush at her admission, false though it was. This made her realize that it was something she would have to deal with before too many weeks passed. How would Kendrick handle her woman's time? Or could she find a way to conceal it from him?

"However, while you are here, my new friend," she smiled a warm and engaging smile at the other woman, "my husband was concerned about my being here at the water alone to bathe a bit. I'm sure with you here he'd feel more assured as to my safety and can go about his business. Wouldn't you, Kendrick, dear?"

His look of surprise was a definite reward. If he denied her request, he'd look like an unfeeling brute; definitely not how a newly married man would treat his wife. If he gave in, it would mean she'd be free to bathe in whatever water spot they stopped at . . . no matter how cold it might be.

In response, Kendrick brought two fingers to his forehead and saluted her. "I'd be obliged Mrs. Markham if you would keep an eye on my wife. After her spell today I'd hate for something to happen to her if she was alone."

"Of course, of course." The woman beamed. It seemed nothing could keep Zelda Markham down for long.

Amanda sighed as Kendrick strode off, dishes and silverware in hand. Giving a quick glance of the area, she quickly pulled off her blouse and, despite the goosebumps racing along her arms, dipped the washcloth into the chilly water and gave herself a quick sponge bath. Zelda joined her in washing up as best she could, whispering that her Horace would be doing his part to warm her up as soon as she returned to the wagon. The image of a man handing Zelda a warm blanket was quickly replaced by one of Kendrick Parker holding her close against his body, warming her in his embrace. Amanda mentally chided herself for such fanciful and improper thoughts about the Deputy Marshal. Never in her life had she had such lascivious thoughts about a man and why she would have such thoughts about him, of all men, was beyond her reasoning.

As clean as they could be with cold water and no soap the two women hurried back to the campsite. Amanda was surprised when a man, a hair shorter than herself, wearing wire rimmed spectacles and slightly balding quickly approached them. Sliding an arm around Zelda, he looked up with total adoration and asked if she was all right.

"Yes, Horace, dear. I'm more than fine. And this here is Amanda Parker. The Marshal's new wife. Amanda, my husband, Horace."

"Good to meet you Horace. A pleasure for certain."

"You too Mrs. Parker. Zelda, my petunia, the children are all tucked in and with the chill in the air, I think it best we get you snuggled up as well." He winked at her leaving no doubt in Amanda's mind what kind of snuggling he intended. Before she could say another word, she felt something descend on her shoulders. With a start, she realized Kendrick had come up behind her and wrapped her in a warm blanket. If she wasn't mistaken, he had warmed it by the cook fire before enfolding her in it.

"That sounds good to me, too, Horace. If you'll pardon us, I don't want my bride catching a chill." With that, he scooped Amanda up and carried her to the wagon.

Inside, she saw that he had again shifted the trunk and placed some sort of padding on the floor with a bedroll spread out on it.

"Here." He handed her a cup. "Drink it."

Amanda sniffed, and at the telltale scent of whiskey went to hand it back to him. "Thank you, no. I'm not fond of spirits."

"Drink it."

His tone brooked no defiance, but she was still uncomfortable drinking it. "I'd prefer not. I know what happens to women who partake of spirits and it is not a pretty picture."

"No?"

"No. It induces," she looked around as if someone might hear the secret she was about to disclose, "promiscuous behavior."

"Is that so?"

"Yes."

"Bette. You have no concern about me wanting you to be promiscuous. I have no desire to bed you. None at all."

"Errr, well."

"Drink it. I'm not about to have you catch a cold or sick because of a chill."

"Are you going to have some?"

"What? You think I might try to poison you?"

"No. As you said earlier, it wouldn't serve you well to have your wife die on the road."

"I said that?" He scratched his head, trying to remember when he had said such a thing.

"Words to that effect."

"Ah, words to that affect. I was pretty certain I hadn't said anything quite so uppity."

She drank it down before reaching for the brush she'd left sitting on the bench. Pulling free her braid she began to run the brush through the long locks, oblivious to how Kendrick looked at her. Had she seen the heat in his eyes she would have welcomed the coolness she had become used to seeing in them. She brushed her hair until it crackled and then began to rebraid it. "Where do you propose I sleep then?"

"Pardon?"

"Well you've laid out your bed. Where do you plan to have me sleep?"

"Right here." He pointed to the bed he'd erected.

"Then where will you sleep?"

"Right there, with you."

"Oh! Marshal . . . that's not . . ."

"Kendrick." He said it like a caress. She'd never heard a man say his own name like a caress, but this man did.

"What?"

"Kendrick. My name is Kendrick."

"Yes. Of course it is. I . . . Mr. Kendrick . . ." She stammered.

"Just Kendrick. Like I said before, I think it a good idea for my wife to call me by my given name, don't you?"

That did it. She planted her feet about a shoulder width apart, her hands on her hips, "I will thank you to keep that bossy tone of voice to yourself. I have had enough of you and your attitude."

"Good. I'm tired myself. We sleep there, together. Like husband and wife."

"Husband and wi . . . I'll have you know I know just what you are up to you reprobate. I am putting you on notice that as soon as the opportunity presents itself, I'll . . . I'll . . ."

"You'll what, Mandy?"

"Ohhh. And I will not lie with you."

"Sleep. Like I said, without the prissy, uppity talk, I have no desire to bed you. The last place I want to find myself is between your legs."

She gasped. "I have never had a man speak so crudely to me. You apologize this instant!"

"Of course you haven't, Bette. Now get under those covers."

She huffed and instead of doing as he said, reached past him to her trunk.

"What are you doing?"

"Getting my night shift." She pulled a long, white garment from the trunk and told him, "now if you'll step outside . . ."

"No."

"Fine. Then turn around."

For some reason, he did as she wished and turned his back

to her. It was too dark, even with the mellow light of the oil lamp he'd lit, so she could see how he clenched his fists while he listened to the sound of Amanda undressing.

Her nightshift on, she slid under the covers and finally told him, "All right. I'm under the covers."

He turned as she huffed again and rolled on her side away from him. She would have been miffed at best had she seen the smile on his lips.

CHAPTER NINE

For a long while Kendrick lay on his back beside the petite blond. He wanted to call her all manner of names: spitfire, bitch, murderer, shrew. Instead all he could think of was kissing her lips, peeling the heavy cotton nightshift from her body and slide between those legs of hers he'd sworn he had no interest in being entwined with. Women came and went for him. He'd kept a few mistresses over time and in between them there was a certain house of ill repute he visited. Female companionship was never a problem. So how could this woman he'd spent the past few days with be Bette? The woman beside him was intelligent, cultured and a woman, under other circumstances, he would want to know, maybe even to court.

In Washington he had a number of mothers certain their virginal daughters were just the wife for him. One or two of those sweet young things offered their bodies to him. The last thing he wanted was an untried virgin which would, of course, be a problem when he got married. After all, what man didn't want to marry a virgin? To be the one to introduce his wife to the intimate pleasures of the bedroom? To marry one of them though, he'd have to court one of the simpering misses. Then again, maybe there was a good woman in Adler Creek who might attract him. Not that that was the best idea. If they had to bring in a bunch of mail order brides, there weren't many women to pick from there, were there?

And why am I thinking about marriage again tonight? That was the question. He hadn't even considered it before meeting

Black Bette who seemed to be having no problem sleeping beside him. She probably viewed sex as relaxation after a robbery. And what did she do when she killed someone? Something beyond laying on her back while a man pleasured her? *But she sure was embarrassed talking about sex out at the stream.* Then there were the items he found in her trunks. His personal safety transporting a killer at the forefront of his mind he had no compunction going through her trunks. For a woman who robbed banks on a regular basis she clearly didn't spend her takings on clothing or shoes. The dresses, skirts and blouses were definitely hand sewn, but well made. In addition to the shoes on her feet there was one other well-worn pair. Two prissy and virginal night gowns were buried beneath her serviceable undergarments. Not a gun or knife to be seen.

Most confusing of all was the little doll he found nestled between her linens. Was it a remembrance of her past, taken from someone she'd robbed or . . . did she have and lose her own child? For all her prissy talk, it most likely was not the last. The woman was a walking, talking puzzle, intriguing as hell and he needed to stop being so fascinated by her or he was going to lose his edge. That wouldn't do. He sure as hell hoped his telegram reached the office in San Francisco and they had a deputy headed out to meet him in Wyoming and take this woman off his hands. His hands. He didn't want her off his hands, he wanted her in them. He was not going to consider hearing her story about how she was a teacher come to St. Louis for work. No, she was Black Bette Barkley and that was that.

Almost as if she heard his thoughts, she rolled over, cuddling up to him, resting her head on his shoulder, her arm around his waist. She sighed. Contented. As if dreaming about the most wonderful thing.

This, Kendrick Parker, is the worst idea you have ever had. How the hell are you going to make it through two months posing at this wcman's husband and not want more than an act for your fellow travelers?"

He decided that for tonight, he'd stop fighting what he was feeling. Tomorrow he'd put distance between them. For tonight he'd enjoy holding her. With that, he wrapped his arms around her.

Towards morning, he felt her moving against him and not in a manner a woman woke up beside a man she wanted to be in bed with. She shoved against him. "Let go of me, you oaf."

Instantly awake, "Shhhh, Mandy. Shhhh. It's just me. Shhhh, don't wake everyone else up."

"Get your hands off me," she hissed.

"Fine, fine." He raised his hands above his head. "I only did it for your comfort."

"My comfort? How do you think that?"

"It got chilly last night. You . . . ah . . . you shivered and two sleep warmer than one. And I was sure you were used to having a pillow and figured my shoulder was more comfortable than the floor. So I . . . ah . . . I let you slide into my arms. That's all."

God will punish me for those lies. But I sure wasn't going to be able to sleep the other way.

She shifted away from him. "Fine. In the future I'll be sure to have more blankets."

"Fine."

"And while we are discussing our arrangement, Marshal . . ."

"Kendrick."

"Yes. Kendrick. I would like to know how those women came to believe I was in the family way."

"Beats me. You know better how women think than I do."

"Surely you said something to lead them to believe that."

"Not a word. I would guess they drew their conclusion because you were in the wagon all day."

"And whose fault was that?"

"Yours . . . Mandy."

"Of course. It couldn't possibly be because you refuse to listen to reason."

"Exactly." He released a sigh. "Listen, I'm no happier about this than you are. If there were some other way to get you to California, believe me, I'd take it. But I don't, so we do it this way and if you have any sense, you will play the part of a loving wife."

"Fine. And when we arrive at wherever it is you are dragging me, what do you tell people then?"

He looked at her, his shock at the question crossing his features before his expression became guarded and the ice was back in his eyes. "I believe that's information I best keep to myself. Right now, I suggest we make an appearance and get ready to hit the trail."

He escorted her to the water to wash up where they were greeted by Zelda and what appeared to be two of her children. "Mandy, how are you feeling today?"

"Much better, thank you. And who are these two good looking young people?"

Zelda beamed. "This young man is my youngest son, Mortimer and this young lady is my oldest daughter, Christine. Children, this is Mrs. Parker. She's a newlywed."

"Well Mortimer and Christine, I'm pleased to meet you."

"Hello, Mrs. Parker." Christine softly greeted her while Mortimer turned to hide in his mother's skirt.

"Morty, say hello to Mrs. Parker."

"It's all right Zelda, I understand how hard it can be to meet new people. Maybe later Morty and I will chat."

Kendrick listened to the exchange, unable to help himself from admiring the act Bette put on for Zelda. "Well, Zelda, we need to be getting back to the wagon and see what we can get together for breakfast before we take off."

"Say, listen. We have plenty. Why don't you two break your fast with us? I'm sure after the rough day Mrs. Parker had yesterday, she's not quite ready to be cooking. Besides we have fresh bread and newly churned butter."

"Please, call me Amanda and we . . ."

"It would be our pleasure Zelda." Kendrick told her, trying for his most engaging smile. The woman might be a busy-body, but she would certainly keep Bette in hand when he wasn't around.

"Are you sure, sweetheart?" Amanda looked up at him, the expression on her face pure adoration, the look in her eyes, he was sure, pure amusement at the situation they were in.

"I most certainly am, darling. We'll return the favor as soon as you're up to it."

"We'd be pleased to. So tell me, Zelda," Amanda began, "how did you manage fresh butter this far out?"

"Oh." The woman beamed. "A friend of mine who moved to California just last year wrote me with some excellent tips. When you milk the cows you put some of the cream aside in a bucket and secure it in the back of the wagon. The rocking and bouncing of the wagon churns it for you! We do the same thing with the bread, letting it rise while we travel during the day."

"How ingenious. I look forward to hearing more of these ideas on our way west." Amanda assured her.

As they walked back to the circle of wagon, Kendrick wrapped his arm around her waist, bent his lips to her ear and muttered, "Hope you can at least boil water."

Amanda merely smiled up at him, devilish lights in her eyes.

Breakfast was a surprisingly easy event as Zelda talked enough for all of them. Kendrick's head hurt, almost, from her tales of her six children and he gave quiet thanks that he wasn't married and didn't have to contend with such antics.

He was also mighty grateful that Bette wasn't much for talking, at least to him. For some reason he was oddly impressed when, at the end of the meal, Amanda stood and gathered up the dishes to go wash them. Then again, she may have been setting a pattern to make him trust her so that she could wander off when he wasn't paying attention.

Meals done, oxen hitched, Dusty gave the signal to head out. As he rode down the line, he informed each family that they'd need to move a little faster in the coming days. Despite the tolerable temperature, with a bit of a chill in the morning air, they needed to make as much time in daylight as possible. Kendrick hitched his horse to the back of the supply wagon and climbed up in the driver's seat beside Amanda. Telling himself it was just to rile her, he put his arm around her and gave her a quick kiss on the cheek. A few minutes later he wondered to himself just what was wrong with him. With another two to two and a half months on the trail he knew he needed to keep an eye on himself or he'd be wanting to do more than give her a kiss on the cheek for show.

Neither spoke through the day. In fact, the only time Amanda said anything to him was when she offered to find something for him to eat around noon time and later to offer him a drink of water.

When they pulled the wagons around for the evening Zelda again approached them and before Kendrick could make his desires known, Amanda offered to help her make dinner. Shrugging to himself he wandered off to check the area and chat a bit with Dusty. If anyone could keep him from making a mistake of underestimating Bette, it was Dusty.

Chapter Ten

St. Louis, Missouri

"Well dang. I knew I forgot something." Billy McCaffrey entered the Sheriff's office, scratching his head in obvious confusion.

"Got a problem there, Billy?" Sheriff Gromley asked, already knowing full well that just the fact that Billy showed up for work was more trouble than he was worth.

"Crap, yeah, Sheriff. I fergot to give you this the other day." He held a tattered piece of paper, the ink obviously smeared, in his hand, studying it as if it held the secrets of the ancients.

Gromley sighed, "What is it Billy?"

"Aw, jes a telegram. I was by the Western Union two or three days ago and this message came in." He continued to study the crumbled-up paper, its edges shredded from being in his pocket and who knew where else.

"Two or three days ago? Is it a message for you?" He couldn't believe anyone would try to reach the backward deputy, but one never knew.

"Naw. Lyle sed it was fer you. Something about that woman the Marshal was with."

Gromley stood and reached for the paper. "Let me see that." He looked it over. Looked at Billy and read it again. "Aw shit."

"What's it says Sheriff?"

"Billy, stop whining. Where in the heck did you have this the past few days?" He lifted it to his nose thinking to sniff it.

With a glance at Billy with his heavily pomaded hair and stained shirt, he quickly had second thoughts and merely held it up to look at its ragged remains. Finally he laid it on the desk, trying to smooth the wrinkles as if that would change the message.

"Here in my pocket. What's it say?"

"What? Billy, where were you on the days they taught reading in school?"

"Don't need to read when yer the law, Sheriff, and I alays knew I wuz gonna be a lawman. So it sounds like bad news."

"Oh yeah. It's not good, not good at all. You've had this two days?"

"Or three. Whatever day it was that the Marshal took that killer woman with him ta California. That's the day it come."

"I don't believe this. I just don't believe it."

"Bad news?"

"The worst."

"What's it say?"

"Billy, you aren't going to believe this."

Gromley turned and walked out of the office, unaware he'd dropped the telegram.

"What, Sheriff? What's it say?"

The next few days the wagons made steady progress. While the mornings and evenings held a slight chill, the traveling periods through the days were pleasant. Not too warm, just cool enough for a shawl if even that. Close to the river they followed, with the last of the snow melts, relatively little dust kicked up. Rising just as the sun was peaking over the horizon, eating a hurried breakfast of hard tack with biscuits from supper the night before and riding along the trail until an hour or so before sunset, they steadily traveled westward. At times Kendrick wondered how wise it had been to encourage

Zelda to spend time with Bette.

Bette herself was confusing. When he'd first heard about her and then read the wanted posters the woman seemed like a cold-hearted monster. She was unfeeling, rotten to the core, he knew it. He just knew it. The woman he saw now was warm, seemed to care for the children and was intelligent, although there was no law that a killer couldn't be intelligent. While she still used her uppity words around him, she adopted a more relaxed way of speaking around Zelda and the children. Damn woman acted more like a housewife and mother than vicious killer. Of course she could also be a consummate actress in addition to a cold-blooded felon. He told himself he needed to put a stop to her spending time around the children and he would . . . as soon as he figured out a way to have her do so without raising suspicion.

That second night she wasn't too pleased to sleep next to him, nor any other night. He almost laughed to himself when she'd scoot as far away from him as she could when they turned in. Then, when the night air chilled, she unconsciously snuggled up to him. Over the past five days, Kendrick became fairly certain there was something wrong with him when he found himself enjoying holding her while they slept. What was worse he wanted to hold on to her in the daylight hours as well. Fortunately she'd taken to pinning her hair in that ugly bun without him telling her to. The woman was perverse enough that if she knew how that long, thick honey colored hair of his affected him she'd not only wear it down; she'd toss it around to draw attention to it.

Problem was, he was enjoying having her beside him at night.

The days were fine. He rode guard, generally towards the tail of the train, keeping an eye out on any stragglers. Zeke Morgan, a well-known scout, rode point up front. Other scouts spread out early on, sometimes riding for a few miles ahead. The good news was, many of the tribes had gone to winter camps and the trip looked like it would be a smooth passage.

When Kendrick pulled in just as camp was setting up a week into the journey, he took note of Bette helping Zelda with her children and chatting with a few of the other women. Her dark blond hair caught the last rays of the setting sun, making it look more like a riot of molten gold than just plain old brown hair.

It was Dusty who made him aware he was staring at the woman. "You got to admit, she *is* a pretty little thing," Dusty observed.

"Pretty dangerous."

"I dunno. She's always offering to help the other women with the cooking and kids. Got a quick laugh . . . leastways when you aren't around. A few of the single men seem quite taken with her."

"She's a married woman!"

"Ah . . ."

"Shit!" One of those younger men was approaching Bette, Kendrick was sure with adoration in his look. Without a word, he strode away from Dusty, ready to strangle the other man. Fortunately, he heard what turned out to be a very tall, lanky, young man, young enough that he hadn't even started to shave, say something about Bette and his mother.

"Mandy."

His tone was anything but gentle.

"Kendrick. Dinner will be ready s . . ."

"I'd like to talk to you. Now!" Without considering how it looked or what he was doing, he grabbed her arm and practically dragged her away from the circle of women.

"What . . . what are you . . ." It was clear she was going to ask him something he didn't want the others to hear or worse that he didn't want to answer. Desperate, he silenced her the only way he could think of. She barely managed, "Unhand me this ins . . .", before he crushed her in an embrace, one hand holding her head firmly in place, his other stroking down her back, coming to rest just on the upper curve of her posterior while at the same time, lowering his lips to hers. Oblivious to her struggles, Kendrick bent to kiss her. Not a welcoming and light kiss on the lips. Oh no, he kissed her hard, his tongue plunging into her mouth the second she tried to protest, and he plundered her like a man who has been too long without breath. Holding her firmly against him, he couldn't think, didn't want to think. He ground his hips against her belly, insensible to how she gasped at his hardened manhood or that she struggled to break away from him.

She was sugar.

She was spice.

She was heat.

She was a roaring river, sucking him in, possessing him, owning him, taking him to a place he'd never been.

And then she kissed him back. Just a brief moment her tongue danced with his, causing him to groan in sexual need and delight.

That was just before she managed to break his grasp and stomp on his foot. Hard.

"What the? Mandy?"

He felt dazed, as if he were fighting his way to the surface after too long under the water of a deep river.

"How dare you! You . . . you . . . animal." She hissed before turning and running toward their wagon.

Being thrown in an icy river wouldn't have shaken him half as much as the awareness of what he'd just done and in front of who he'd done it. Virtually every member of the wagon train, men, women and a number of the children who shouldn't see such things, had stepped up, eyes wide, mouths gaping at him.

He'd mauled Black Bette Barkley in front of this crowd. He'd behaved like a rutting mongrel.

It was Horace who wryly observed, "Well now, that was a sight to see and an inspiration. Zelda, my dear, take note!"

"Newlyweds. Just a pair of newlyweds folks." Dusty told the travelers. He took a step towards Kendrick and in a stage whisper told him, "Might want to keep it between yourselves from here on out."

"Nothing wrong with a man, k-k-kissing his w-w-ife, now, is there?" From how hot his face felt Kendrick was sure he was blushing deep red and that there wasn't a hole deep enough to crawl into. And where the hell had Bette run off to?

He found her just as he got his own libido under control. For a man who always prided himself on his control and objectivity, he couldn't understand his own behavior, especially now when just the sight of her started his cock getting needfully hard again. Why, he wondered to himself, did his body continue to respond to her when in his mind, he knew she was a cold-blooded killer? What was it about her that made him want her more with each passing day? Was it just because his little brother was married, and he was feeling that he should be, too? Or just the simple fact there was a woman he couldn't, shouldn't, have in his arms at night?

"Mandy?" He blanched at the strain in his voice; berating his body for responding to her once again. She was just a woman!

"Go away you son of a . . . a . . ."

"Best leave my mother out of this, Mandy."

"Had she raised you even remotely proper . . ."

"My mother died when I was a baby."

She stopped backing away from him, big gray eyes softening with compassion. She reached out to him, stopping just before she touched his arm, "Oh! Ken . . . Marshal, I'm so sorry. That must have been so awful for you. What happened?"

It surprised him how quickly her anger at him faded by simply telling her he had no mother. Would a killer react with such a soft heart? "None of your business."

The stiffening of her spine should have warned him. Instead, he was focused on her lips and how even with the brevity of that kiss, a kiss he wanted to go on through the night and then some, they showed just how well kissed she'd been. "I'll thank you to contain your mauling to women who appreciate that sort of maltreatment."

"Mauling? Maltreatment? Thought you'd come up with fancier words than that."

"You bait me? You . . . you . . ."

"Reprobate?"

"Exactly. How dare you accost me in such a public fashion?"

"How dare I? You're my wife. There's nothing wrong with a husband kissing his wife."

"Marshal Parker. Pay close attention to my lips. I. Am. Not. Your. Wife."

With an absent nod he acknowledged to himself that he was indeed paying attention to her lips and he wanted to pay even more attention to them, up close personal with his own and not just with his eyes. That one little kiss shot straight to his groin and his whole body was panting for him to kiss her again and this time not to stop with just a kiss. "You are."

"No. I am not your wife. *You* decided to defraud these good people into thinking I am wedded to you. In actual fact, we are not wed, and I might add I would not consider wedding or even copulating with you if you were the last man on earth."

"Copu . . . now that's the Mandy I know." He was not about to acknowledge how the way her lips moved and the very word 'copulate' itself sent a shard of pure desire to his

groin. He was going to have to do something about this growing lust for her and fast. With another five to six weeks on the
trail he was going to be hard pressed not to touch her again,
even if she were willing, which she clearly was not.

"You mock me. I may be your prisoner, Marshal Parker,
but I will not be your light-skirted doxie. And lest you think
to repeat I am your wife, I am not. *That* is a position I would
rather die than find myself in."

"Look." He threaded his fingers through his hair. "I came
to say I'm sorry. I did it . . . well I did it because of that other
man approaching you."

The look of confusion crossing her features, how she briefly
chewed on her lower lip, the same lip he wouldn't mind sucking into his mouth before their tongues joined made him want
to hold her. "What other man?"

"What other? The tall one with the brown hair."

"Micca? He's only fourteen-years-old. What were you
thinking? That I would fornicate with a child?"

"No. Ahhhh." Damn if her language didn't do something
to his guts. "From, ahhhh, from the sun in my eyes all day,
being tired from riding, it looked like you two were getting a
bit cozy. I ahhhh, ummm, well I didn't want you luring him
in with your questionable charms and convincing him to help
you escape. Yeah, I knew you were going to get him to help
you escape."

"Lure him? Escape? To where? In case you haven't noticed,
Marshal, we're essentially in the middle of nowhere with
miles of flat dry land all around us. Just where would we run
away to?"

"Well, maybe not here, but soon. In Independence or
where the trail . . . look, I don't need to explain myself to you.
You're my prisoner and the only way you have the freedom I
allow you is by going along with pretending to be my wife. If
I think I need to kiss you, to convince people we're a happily

married couple, as much as I hate it, then I will kiss you. Understand?"

"Will that need to convince other people include forcing me to engage in marital relations with you when we are alone in the wagon at night? Because if you think for one minute I would succumb to that argument, especially with the considerable hemming and hawing you are doing explaining yourself at this juncture, you are greatly mistaken. If that is what you intend, make no mistake, I will walk right back into that circle of people and tell them just who you think I am. I'd rather die at their hands, than endure your touch anywhere on my body."

She shocked him. Again! He was still trying to digest what she'd said, feeling his control over the situation slipping.

"Do I make myself clear, Marshal?"

"Yeah. Ahhhh, Kendrick, my name is Kendrick. And just to make *myself* clear, I wouldn't touch you if *you* were the last *woman* on earth."

"Fine."

"Fine."

"Well just fine. Now leave me in peace."

"Thought I'd escort you back to camp. Just so folks know we're still a happily married couple."

"Oh. Of course. We wouldn't want them to think you got all riled about a mere boy."

A boy who looks at you with total devotion in his eyes.

Amanda was relieved when they arrived back at the campsite and no one said a word about what had happened. There were a few looks from the other women, but they were looks of, could it be envy? Gratitude that they now had permission of a sort to be kissed in public by their husbands?

She noticed the men patted Kendrick on the back and shook his hand. With smiles congratulating him on how he'd handled things with his bride.

"Look at them." She nudged Zelda. "Acting like he's some great hero because he humiliated me in public."

"Humiliated? Amanda! Your husband loves you. That's plain as day! You should be pleased he has no fear showing the world how much he does. Any one of us would be pleased to have our husbands show their fondness for us in so public a way."

"He doesn't love me."

"What? I thought you two were a love match. That you couldn't wait to marry."

"Ah. Oh. Yes. Well we are. What I meant was he doesn't love for me to be embarrassed."

"Why would it embarrass you to have him kiss you?"

"We're ahhhh. Well, we're still newlyweds. I'm still adjusting to being married and all."

"Doesn't he kiss you at night when you share your bed?"

"Of course. We, we kiss, we kiss all the time." She knew she'd be struck down for lying. "I'm from Massachusetts though and up that way we are quite private about our marital relations."

"Amanda, there is no reason to be embarrassed by your attraction for your husband or how you two are with each other. Horace and I married for love. Believe me, we have our own passionate moments. And Marshal Parker is a good man. We've talked about what a good man he is."

"You have? Who?"

"A few of the other women and Horace and I. You wouldn't have married him if you didn't think he was too."

"You think that because he's a lawman."

"No. Because of how he is."

"How he is? What makes you think he's a good man?"

"We see he's very private. Keeps to himself, but at the same time, he doesn't miss anything, especially if it could be about your safety. You've seen it, I know."

Amanda thought about Zelda's words a moment. Despite her pique at Kendrick, she was right. In that past few days she'd seen Kendrick do a hundred thoughtful things for the rest of the wagon train. Despite the fact all the scouts were to take turns, he always rode a bit farther out and a bit longer. Even after riding the trail all day he'd gather wood at night and help unhitch the wagons. On occasion he'd wrestle with the younger boys and let them win. All the children liked to run their fingers over his badge.

Of course, he could be doing all those things because he was trying to avoid her.

Then again, if he was trying to avoid her, he would have just had Dusty keep an eye on her and sleep out on the range like a few of the scouts each night. And he wouldn't walk her to the river after supper to wash up or ask her if she were warm enough in bed. He wouldn't ride by their wagon several times during the day to ask her if she were comfortable. When he rode in at night, he always came to her first and then went to wash or take care of his own needs.

He said little to any of the others, keeping to himself. In fact, he spoke almost exclusively to her or Dusty. There were times when she looked into his eyes and instead of the icy blue, there was a glimmer of longing, almost a loneliness.

She debated telling Zelda the truth: that Kendrick had kidnapped her for his own nefarious purposes, whatever they may be.

No, that wasn't true. It was becoming increasingly clear that for some reason the man really thought she was that woman, Bette Barkley. If it came down to it though, who would Zelda and the others believe? A man with a badge or a woman whose image was on a wanted poster?

"You're right, Zelda, he is a good man. I just . . . well I was embarrassed when he kissed me before."

She also was not about to admit just how good that kiss felt or how much she hoped he would do it again.

Deciding that discretion was the better part of valor, Kendrick opted to take his meal with the other scouts. He hoped by giving Amanda a bit more time to cool off, there wouldn't be another row in bed that night.

Mentally shaking his head, he knew it wasn't Amanda who needed to cool off. It was him. And, he needed to find a way to stay cooled off around her. "I'm a man of principle," he told himself. "I'm not the kind of man to force a woman or bed one like Black Bette."

He just wished his body believed what his mind told him.

When all the other men had turned in for the night he contemplated sleeping near the fire or under the wagon because even though he'd gotten his libido under control, it was only just slightly. He looked up at the velvety black sky, the stars sprinkled like diamonds as far as the eye could see. A falling star stirred a remembrance from childhood, something Fallen Leaf had told him and his brothers. What it meant flitted at the edge of his memory, teasing him, yet he couldn't quite place it. He told himself it was the growing chill that sent him to the wagon. Stepping inside the wagon he didn't know whether to laugh or rant when he saw she had slid her trunk to the middle of the narrow space and placed their sleeping mats at either end.

"If you're chilled, I'll take the pallet at the rear," she informed him.

Before he knew it, his hands were fisted, his chest constricting as the flush of anger warmed his cheeks. In just that brief glimpse of the trunk placed dead center in the wagon he felt the war between desire and dismissal rioting through his body. He wanted her, he wanted her more than he'd ever wanted another woman.

At the same time he wanted to run and hide, the pain of rejection ripping through him, cutting him to the core.

How dare she? How dare she try to wall him off? Fighting to control the whirlwind of emotions that wracked him he finally managed, "Don't think so, Bette. I'm not about to let you slip out the wagon and take off in the middle of the night."

"Fine. I only offered so you'd be warm. I'll take the front then."

Warm? The woman made him a lot more than just warm. "Nope. We sleep side by side. Just like always."

"I prefer not to."

"I prefer we do."

"I will not tolerate you accosting me in my sleep."

"Fine, I'll *accost* you now and get it over with. How about that?" He couldn't help snapping. Who was she to reject him? He took a step towards her.

"Ohhh. You . . . you . . ."

He reached for her, "No-good?"

She evaded his grasp.

He reached again and this time caught her and dragged her up against him, making no effort to hide his desire as he held her close, so close he felt her breath caress his throat.

She shoved against him until she realized her movements didn't give her distance, but rather rubbed against his groin, his desire evident with each stroke.

"Humph." She finally managed to break his grip and push him back from her. Unaccountably anger rocked him when she snapped up a blanket, wrapped it around her shoulders, stomped over to the bench and sat down, "I'll sleep here."

"Fine." With more force than was necessary he shoved the trunk to the other side, pulled up the pallet, removed his boots, shirt and pants and climbed between the blankets. "I don't believe for a minute you didn't enjoy that kiss as much as I did."

Billy gazed out the window of the cramped stagecoach, hoping he'd reach the Deputy Marshal before they turned off or whatever the wagon trains did in Independence. He'd never paid much attention to what the scouts or folks traveling west said when they'd come into town. For as dumb as he was, Billy knew that outside St. Louis and without his uncle's oversight he'd never get very far. People did as he said because he was a deputy sheriff, not because they liked or respected him. They respected the badge and his gun, not him, so he didn't listen so well when folks talked about the Oregon Trail. It didn't make sense to him to call it the Oregon Trail when they were going to California. If he caught up with the Marshal though, he'd be a hero. When the Sheriff walked out of the jail those few days ago, dropping the telegram, Billy knew it was a sign that he should go west and make sure the Deputy got the news . . . whatever it was. Whatever was on the paper had to be important to him, otherwise the Sheriff wouldn't have been so angry at him for forgetting to give it to him. So here he was, on a stage west, hoping he'd find the Marshal right soon.

The stage hit another bump, bruising his already sore backside. He should have ridden his horse except that would not have worked out so well because Billy had no sense of direction. Besides, his bum would have hurt from riding in the saddle that long too. At least the stage could catch up with the wagons that pulled out the day the telegram arrived, he hoped. Since they were supposed to be in Frisco in something like twenty to twenty-five days, it seemed there would be no problem catching up with the travelers.

Dang his backside hurt. He didn't know which was worse, the interminable bouncing and jarring on his seat or the smell of the man next to him. The combined odor of tobacco, sweat and old clothes permeated the air. Billy wondered how the two women sitting on the opposite seats could stand the stench until he saw them pass a small bottle between them. It might be girly, but he might consider dousing himself with some of that cologne if the smell got much worse.

Sticking his head out the window wasn't much of a choice either because of the dust and dirt the churning of the wheels caused. Even with the ground still a tad damp from the last snowfall a few weeks earlier, there was still a fine mist of the sandy land blowing in the area.

His stomach growled. Long and low. Reminding him that in his rush to board the stage he hadn't taken time to eat, grab some food for the trip and, short of a change of clothes, he had nothing with him except a few dollars he hoped would get him back home again. At least he ran into Harry Jensen to ask him to tell the Sheriff he was heading out after the wagon train. They'd better find the marshal soon or his stomach would shrivel to nothing. Then again, at the next rest stop, someone seeing he was the law might offer to buy him a meal.

Pulling the paper out of his pocket Billy studied it not for the first time. In fact, it had been an hourly occurrence to pull it out and study it as if maybe this time he could make sense of the words on the page. He wasn't about to ask either of the men he sat between what it said. One thing he had learned was that it was better to keep your mouth shut and let people wonder how smart . . . or stupid you were . . . than to give them proof of it.

At the next stage stop he ventured to what passed for the office and asked the man there if the wagon train had passed through. He supposed it was good news that it had done so, only the day before. By the next day the stagecoach would catch up with them, just outside Independence, Missouri. They'd catch up. He'd give the paper to Marshal Parker and

Billy would be a hero. Whatever it said about that Black Bette woman would prove that Billy was the best man for the job . . . whatever job it was.

Sitting on the hard bench of the wagon, trying to sleep, Amanda shifted. Not so much from the discomfort of sitting on the solid wooden bench, more from the churning in her tummy and the dampness between her legs. Raising a hand, she ran a finger over her lips. Feeling their texture, she wondered if they looked as puffy as they felt. Deep inside there was a longing for Kendrick to kiss her again.

Damn man! He was right. It did feel good. It felt better than anything she'd ever felt before.

The kisses from Charles Hastings back home felt nothing like Kendrick Parker's. Kendrick's kisses took her breath away, made her dizzy, made her want something more. Something much more.

Something she'd never have. At least not with him.

Arrogant man. He kisses her in a public place and when he says he's sorry he doesn't mean it. No. He apologized because it was the right thing to do. Not because he was sorry he kissed her.

Oh yes, he was right. She enjoyed it. Too much.

And she had to make sure it never happened again.

A dark shape formed in front of her.

Before she could move or utter a protest, Kendrick whispered low in her ear, "Neither one of us is going to get much sleep with you up here scooting around and sighing." With that, he lifted her and immediately laid her down on his pallet. He half covered her when she tried to fight him and since she'd seen him remove his gun when he entered the wagon, she knew that wasn't the long, hard object pressing against her belly. "We're both tired and we'll both sleep much better down here. Understand?"

"Yes. Just keep your roaming hands to yourself."

She rolled over, trying to move as far away from him in the cramped space as she could.

When she finally fell asleep, Kendrick wrapped his arm around her, pulling her close, telling himself it was only to keep her from running away in the night.

The following evening Zelda, as usual, invited Amanda and Kendrick to join her family for supper. Kendrick wanted to turn her down until he was sure things had settled down with Amanda. Realizing that Zelda would not let it go and that it would raise questions if they continued to keep to themselves, he agreed to the meal.

"Honestly, Kendrick. I heard you the first fifty times. The last four hundred are a bit overdone." She hissed at him. "I know both the story you have made up about our marriage and about our little tiff last night."

"See what I mean? I may have reminded you a time or two. You exaggerate with the fifty and then some."

"I just wish I had something to bring. You realize, of course, if you allowed me to spend more time with the women, I'd be able to help prepare the meals and we wouldn't be living on handouts."

"We're not living on handouts. Meals are in exchange for my services as a scout."

"I see. And each scout guards someone?"

"No. If we were to be attacked, I'd be at the ready. I'll remind you, at any time I can re-cuff you and just leave you in the wagon."

"A reprobate like you would enjoy that no end."

"How's that?"

"With how you accost me at every turn, having me tied and at your mercy would please you no end."

He felt his cheeks warm, again. Damn if the woman didn't

make him feel like a youngster before bedding his first woman. The feeling of an untried youth was quickly replaced by the image of Amanda lying naked in his bed, her arms secured above her, that long silky hair of hers forming a halo around her, threading down to caress her breasts while she waited for him to join her and bring her to the heights of pleasure. He'd never tied a woman down before. It wasn't something a proper gentleman did. Around Amanda though he had thoughts and feelings he'd never felt before. She did things to his mind and body no woman had ever done before.

He trailed her to the Markham's wagon, enjoying the view of her skirts swirling around her ankles. Amanda chatted with Zelda and the children, Kendrick focused on his meal, excusing himself from conversation by saying it'd been a long day on the trail.

After the meal though, Amanda couldn't help herself when Zelda's youngest, Martin took out a book and asked his mother to read it to him. She'd had enough feeling useless. With a giddy feeling rising into her chest, a slight feeling of light-headedness and without any thought as to Kendrick, Amanda burst out, "Martin, would you like me to teach you to read?"

"Fer real Miz Parker?" the younger Markham asked.

"Can you do that, Amanda?" Zelda leaned closer, her excitement at the possibility clear in her eyes.

"Of course I can. I was a teacher long before Mr. Parker and I met."

"Darlin I'm not sure that's such a good idea. With how delicate you are, your health and all," Kendrick interrupted the women's discussion. "You need your rest and you know how tired you . . ."

"Nonsense, sweetheart." She rested her hand on his arm, giving it a squeeze not in endearment but in warning that she'd do something mean if he didn't go along. "You know how I love teaching and would have loved to have taken such a position in St. Louis. It will be just me sitting with the children in the evening. I know you've been concerned about my earning my keep and this is the perfect way to do it, don't you agree?" She leaned into him, making sure neither Zelda nor the children saw it, and subtly brushed her breast against his arm. It was so subtle and so slight, if it hadn't been for the slight widening of his eyes Amanda would have wondered if Kendrick had felt it. His sudden sharp intake of breath almost made up for his actions earlier, harassing her again about how she was to comport herself. Moving a hair closer, mimicking his actions the night before, her lips almost caressing his ear, she whispered yet at the same time spoke just loud enough for Zelda to hear, "You do agree, don't you, my love?"

Kendrick cleared his throat, obviously struggling to keep the glare from his eyes. "If you are certain it won't tire you out."

"I'm positive."

"If it wears on you, you will stop, right?"

Despite the darkening evening, the glow from the firelight kept her from missing the icy look in his eyes. The grip of his hand on her arm, a telling message back to her — for all appearances a gentle caress was in reality a band of iron — letting her know loud and clear that he intended to quickly, very quickly, put a stop to the lessons.

It pleased Amanda no end to have outwitted the lout.

CHAPTER ELEVEN

By the next morning the women were all buzzing with the news that Amanda would be teaching the children, all of the children, to read in the evenings. Even with the early sunset and the chill of the early spring air, the women were pleased at any learning their children could have. Amanda caught Kendrick chewing his lip, the first time she'd seen any sign of nervousness in the man, after the third woman came by to thank Amanda for setting up the traveling school.

Rather than sit beside her on the wagon, Kendrick pushed her inside. "You knew last night I didn't approve. You refused to listen." He all but spat.

"You didn't say anything."

"I didn't . . . you didn't . . . you knew better. I *showed* you how I felt."

"*I* knew better? Mr. Parker." She chided him.

"Kendrick."

"Marshal Parker, what kind of husband would these good people see you as if you refused to allow me the opportunity to . . ."

"Kendrick and there you go again with your uppity language."

"My uppity language? You grew up in far more genteel . . ."

"You don't know the first thing about how I grew up. Besides, we're not discussing me, Bette." He growled out the *Bette* with such vehemence, she lost her breath. It seemed to strangle in her throat, the air unable to move up or down. For the first time in days the chill of death seemed to encase her heart, making the hair on the back of her neck stand on end. It was the same fear she'd felt when he'd first slapped the handcuffs on her rushing back to the fore. Just that one word . . . Bette . . . was like a death knell echoing inside the small covered wagon. She was certain the wagon had begun to spin around her. She felt like someone had encased her in a dark shroud and was draining the air from around her.

"Mandy? Mandy?"

She looked up at him feeling as if a part of her had fled.

"You all right?" Unaware of what his nearness would do to her, was doing to her, he shifted to put his arm around her shoulders, supporting her. Instead of warmth from his touch, a feeling akin to frost encased her heart, making her shake.

Unable to speak, she only shook her head in the negative. A barely perceptive movement. She prayed he didn't see how badly she shook.

"What's going on here, Mandy?"

"I . . . how can you want me dead? How can you so crave my death?" Her voice broke, the pain she felt with the realization of his plans for her raw and cutting.

"Want? Br . . . Lady, I don't *want* to kill you. If a jury finds you guilty and that's their verdict, someone will, but it's not what I want." He pulled her closer. It felt more like he was pulling a chair closer to him, not another human being. With his other hand, he took her chin between his thumb and forefinger, the contrasting gentleness when he turned her to look at him muddling her ability to think. For a long moment he looked into her eyes. "I don't want to kill you. I don't want to see you dead, I'm just . . . you didn't think before you started this teaching business last night. I wish you would have asked me. I'da, well I would have considered it."

She swallowed. An act in and of itself normal. Routine. Done every day by every person.

"Do you understand why I'm concerned about it, Mandy?"

"Yes." She swallowed again. "I think so. Don't you see though? I am a teacher. It will help me to blend in. I'll be with the children, not the adults and doing something worthwhile. No one will be asking me about myself, my life before," she lifted her arm as if it were the heaviest object and waved it in front of her, as if it flowed through thick molasses. "Before this, before you, I had a life. It may not have been the best or easiest life, but it was mine and I was . . . content with it."

Kendrick dropped his arm from her shoulders, his hand dropped from her chin and he stood. She'd never felt so isolated in her life as she did at that moment. One hand threading through his hair, the other on his hip, fingering his gun, an action she'd come to recognize he did when his thoughts were in conflict with how he saw life should be.

On an exhale he answered, "You're right. You're right. Sorry I blew up at you. I just don't want these people hurt by you."

"They won't be the ones hurt."

"Look, I think we need a . . . some time away from each other for a bit. I'll take some food out on the trail with me and have Dusty check on you during the day. Just don't make any trouble for him, you hear? You have trouble handling the team, let him know and he'll have someone ride with you." He spun on his heel and jumped out of the wagon. Nodding to her once he mounted his horse, he took off ahead of the wagon train.

Realizing she'd be alone almost the entire day, instead of feeling pleased to be free of the irritating man, Amanda felt a loneliness she'd never felt before. Even when Mort climbed up to drive the team for her, she felt oddly bereft.

A short while later, the wagons moving along, following the Missouri River, Kendrick mounted on his horse rode up and down the line. Glancing at the occupants of the wagons but scanning the horizon in the same manner as the scouts did each day. At one point, he took off at a gallop, needing to release some of his pent-up energy. Frustrated energy.

Not frustration from sitting for too long.

Not frustration from the slow pace of the wagons.

Not even frustration from the words exchanged between Bette and himself that morning. No. It was frustration of a kind he hadn't felt since he was in his teens. Frustration at the thought of Bette—Mandy, riding with Mort. Her soft breasts grazing along Mort's arm. Chatting with the other man.

It was that kind of frustration he felt before his grandfather took him to his first brothel. At the not so tender age of sixteen, on that birthday in fact, his grandfather took him to a tasteful house on the outskirts of town. The stately building locked like it housed a senator or diplomat. In fact it was the home to a select group of women for hire. Each one was more beautiful than the one before, at least to his sixteen-year-old mind and eyes. They'd spent the afternoon there. He in one rocm, his grandfather, as he recalled, in another. His initiation into sex had been glorious. And it was after that he first felt true frustration. The debutantes that attended the all-girls school that neighbored the military like all male bastion he was sent to were not only out of reach, but none of them held any appeal to him. He lacked the funds to enter the well-appointed house his grandfather had taken him to on his own and he wasn't about to ask the old man to take him back. Not that he wouldn't go if invited.

He felt that now as he galloped out into the wilds. How could he desire a woman like Bette Barkley? Was it because she was everything he was not? Everything forbidden? Even with those school-marmish and uppity ways of hers he knew was an act. The flashes of heat in her eyes belied the cool exterior she presented to him and the world. And that kiss. Damn, the woman could kiss!

Kendrick Parker was a good man. He told himself he was a Deputy United States Marshal and therefore a good man. He upheld the law. He'd been a good boy growing up. Did all the things his grandparents told him to. The things they wanted him to. Well, almost. They wanted him to go into law . . . as a lawyer, not a lawman, and he did, at least while his grandfather was alive. They wanted him to go into politics, not guard politicians. He was on the side of the law. He was the law.

Bette Barkley was none of those things.

The complete opposite of him. She robbed banks. She killed people.

So why did he want her with an ardor he'd never felt before?

He had to stay away from her. Plain and simple. She was the forbidden fruit in his life, and he had to stay as far away from her as he could.

A few hours later, riding back towards the wagons at a slower pace, Dusty rode up to him, greeting him with, "Don't know which of you is worse. You or your brother Brett."

"Something wrong with Brett you didn't tell me before we headed out?"

"Not really. Just he sure was impulsive about Jenna, deciding he was going to marry her before he even laid eyes on her."

"I'm not marrying that woman."

"Didn't say you were."

"Then what were you saying?"

"That you want her."

"Don't."

"Oh you do. That's no act. When you look at her it's pretty clear. You want her."

CHAPTER TWELVE

Just as they met up with the wagon train, off in the distance, Kendrick saw a large cloud of dust. Pointing it out to Dusty, the two kicked their horses to a faster gallop, trying to make it back to the wagons before whatever was approaching it could get there. They slowed only when Dusty was able to make out the shape of a covered vehicle. "Looks like a stage."

They road on past the wagons with a word to the lead wagon to keep on going.

"Hank." Dusty greeted the driver as the stage came to a halt, the dust surging around the carriage causing the occupants inside to cough.

"Dusty Hendricks, good to see you. Musta missed you when we pulled into town the other day."

"'pears so. You know Marshal Parker?"

Hank shook his head, "Cain't say as we've met. You got buizniss out this way, Marshal?"

"Of a kind," Kendrick answered. "I have family in Adler Creek, Wyoming. Heading out to see them."

"So yer traveling with this fella, huh? Won't meet a more fair or honest man, 'cepting myself that is."

"That is a certainty." Kendrick assured him.

By unspoken agreement Kendrick and Dusty turned their horses around and began moving towards the wagon train with the coach. "You on deadline to hit Independence before tomorrow?"

"If we can. You need sumpin?"

"Nope. Just thought you might be interested in taking

supper with us before you continue on tonight."

Before Hank could answer Billy hung out the window. "Marshal Parker! Marshal? Mr. Parker!"

Kendrick turned at the sound of his name, squinting an eye at the young man leaning out the window of the door. His head level with the bottom of the window's ledge as if he were kneeling on the floor of the coach.

"I know you?"

"Yeah! It's me, Billy McCaffrey. You know, Sheriff Gromley from St. Louis' deputy."

"Billy? Geesus boy, what are you doing out this way?"

"Got a message for you. A telegram came jes after you left town. I been tryin to find ya until the Sheriff tole me you was headin out this way."

"He sent you after me?"

"Ah, after a manner of speakin, yeah."

"You have a message for me?" He extended his hand in the hopes Billy would be a bit more forthcoming.

"Sure nuf." The wagon lurched forward, throwing Billy backwards to the floor.

The other men grumbled and yelled at him to just sit down, one of them telling Kendrick they could talk when the wagon stopped. Impatient as he was, he let the stage move on. What difference could a few more minutes make?

Puzzled at why Billy would be traveling west, looking for him, wondering what kind of message the sheriff would be sending to him, Kendrick rode on in silence. His thoughts running back and forth between whatever Billy might have to tell him and Dusty's words about him and Bette. Was his attraction to her that evident? Did she see it as well? Feel it? Did she want him? If she did, wouldn't she let their kisses go on? Not fight against sleeping beside him each night? What if he didn't deliver her to the Marshals meeting him in Adler Creek? What if his telegram to them went astray?

No. They'd show. He'd turn her over and she would be out of his life. Maybe he'd stay in Adler Creek. Build a life for himself there with his family being there was no one left he cared about in Washington. Maybe he'd even send for a mail order bride of his own.

Dusty and Kendrick caught up with the wagons a short while later. With growing impatience Kendrick waited for a moment to pull Billy aside. When they made camp for the night the wagon's travelers were pleased to stop, stretch, and have a decent meal rather than the tepid water and salt pork that waited for them at the stage stop.

Billy's feet barely hit the ground before Kendrick grabbed his arm and pulled him aside. "What is it you have for me?"

"Kin a man have a minute to get his bearings? Maybe a drink or something?"

"Sure." Kendrick looked over his shoulder, past the dust swirling around the wagon, calling, "Dusty, grab us a cup of water, huh?"

"Listen, Marshal, I'd 'ppreciate something mor'n water."

"Water's what we got. So while Dusty's bringin it, what do you have to tell me?' Kendrick stood, legs braced apart, hands on his hips, riding just above his guns. His badge glinting in the fading sunlight, his expression barely unreadable by the brim of his Stetson set low on his forehead. Even without meaning to be, he was pure menace.

"This. I got this." Billy pulled out the tattered, worn telegram and handed it to Kendrick.

Taking it gingerly between his thumb and forefinger, Kendrick examined the paper or rather what was left of it. With his other hand he pushed his Stetson back on his head. He was not pleased. Turning it over, turning it upside down, holding it up to the quickly fading sun he studied it. Clearly less pleased than he had been a heartbeat before.

Squinting his eyes he was able to make out a few words:

Bette, isco, STOP, stagec, woman, STOP and some miscellane-
ous letters.

The message made no sense.

"Billy, you have any idea what this . . . said?"

Dusty approached with the water which, after a wince,
Billy drank down and handed the cup back to Dusty. "Something important?" Dusty leaned in to look at the frayed and
torn page.

"Apparently. But since I can't read it, I'm hoping Billy here
will be able to fill me in on what it said. Billy?"

"You kint read neither?"

"I read just fine. It's how mangled this telegram is that has
me asking."

Billy looked at the page, his face scrunched up as if he were
in great abdominal pain. "Wellll," he turned his head to better
see the page. "The Sheriff sed it weren't good."

"Billy, what exactly did he say?" Kendrick probed.

"Ah, let's see. He sed." Billy chewed on his lower lip, hand
on his hip while he scanned the sky as if some answer lie between the deep purple evening and gray clouds that would
soon cover the night sky. "He seeedd . . . .he didn't believe it.
That I wouldn't believe it."

"And what was it he didn't believe, Billy?" Kendrick struggled to hold his patience and, if Dusty hadn't put a warning
hand on his shoulder, Kendrick would have most likely
grabbed Billy by the collar and shaken him good.

"Wellll, I'm not exactly sure. Seems whatever was on there
was something mighty big."

Suddenly Billy's statement about Kendrick not reading
made sense. "Don't you read?" Kendrick was incredulous.

"Nope. Like I tole the Sheriff, no need to. I'm a deputy, not
a lawyer nor nothin like that."

"So you have no idea what this message says . . . said and
the Sheriff didn't tell you?"

"Naw, he don't tell me too much. He just kept saying he didn't believe it."

Kendrick slapped the hand holding the letter to his side and heaved a long slow breath. His gaze scanning the sky in much the same manner as Billy had except it seemed Kendrick was more like praying than looking for an answer. "When exactly did this telegram arrive?"

"The day you all left St. Louis."

"You mean I was still in town when it arrived?"

"I think so, but you were all busy like and, well gettin' too close to that Black Bette, well you know. Being how she's such a dangerous criminal and all I figured you'd need to have at least one lawman standing back to take over. You know, if things went bad."

"No, I don't, Billy. You're a deputy sheriff and you were . . . what? Afraid of the woman?"

"Never know. She kilt a lawman or two and well, she was yer prisoner and all sos me getting close didn't seem all that smart. See what I mean?"

"So you knew I was in town, you knew this was about her and . . ."

"No. No." He slapped his hat on his thigh and paced a step back and another forward before speaking again. "You was packin up the wagon, she wuz still in the cell and I was by the Wells Fargo office, jes walking by you see? And Ben, the owner, called me in and tole me he got a telegram fer you and to get it to you. Well by time I got to the jail you was leadin Black Bette . . ."

"Shhhh. Billy, before you go on there's something you need to know?" Kendrick spoke low, leaning towards the young man.

"Fine. Listen though, kin I get myself some food and somethin to wet my whistle afore you do? I'm mighty hungry and thirsty." He looked past Kendrick at the folks milling around the cooking fire.

"In a minute, Billy. This is important. You got this before we even left St. Louis? And didn't give it to me or the Sheriff until later?"

"Dang, Marshal. You jes got it, even you cain't be that stupid. And the Sheriff, well, that was a couple-a mornins ago."

"Did he send you here?"

"Nope!" Billy grinned, clearly pleased with himself. "I decided all by myself ter come and make sure you got the message."

"Shit! Which is it, Billy? What happened and why are you here?"

"Well, like I said before, he did. In a manner of speaking. I don't know what yer all upset about, Marshal. You got the message, don't ya? So what's the problem?"

"Problem is, Billy, whatever you have done with this message since you got it, only a few words can be made out. I don't know if it says she's guilty or . . . innocent."

"So? Send a message to the sheriff when we git to Indipindince. Kin I go eat now?" Billy whined.

Kendrick pulled his Stetson the rest of the way off and ran his fingers through his hair, the other hand back on his hip, resting near his gun. "Yeah, sure. And Billy, Bette is answering to Mandy. Folks think we're married, and I want to keep it that way. You stay away from her and you don't say anything about her when you meet her, understood?"

"Sure, Marshal. No problem. Don't want nothin' to do with a killer anyways."

"Billy." Kendrick's tone gave clear warning. "You say nothing about her. Nothing at all."

Kendrick watched the younger man walk away, shaking his head in disbelief.

"So what's going on Kendrick?" Dusty asked, squinting not from the light but in apparent confusion.

"I'm not sure." He held the telegram a short distance from his body. Scanning the contents as if suddenly the words would appear again. "You heard what he said. This arrived while I was still there and from what I could see of the words, it was something about Bette, Mandy. When I arrested her, I telegraphed to San Francisco that I had her and they needed to have someone meet me in Wyoming to take her back there. I didn't expect an answer, but they had one. We just don't know what. Even though Sheriff Gromley read it, it seems he didn't tell Billy or Billy doesn't remember what he said."

"So the problem is?"

"The problem is I don't know if they were saying to hurry west and bring her back that way or," he paused, swallowed and blew out a breath he hadn't realized he was holding.

"Or?"

"Or that the woman I've got isn't Black Bette."

"You think she's innocent? That she's really the school-teacher she sez she is? Mandy?"

"I don't know. I just don't know." Kendrick shifted back and forth from foot to foot, took a few steps in each direction, his agitation evident in every tense move. He'd always seen things in black and white, right and wrong. This situation with Bette . . . or Mandy . . . didn't fit into any of the neat packages he lived his life. "I gotta. I gotta err on the side of caution. I gotta take it that they want her there and want her there fast."

"So you gonna take the coach on the southern route? You'll get there in about three weeks instead of almost two months to get to Adler Creek."

"I don't know. My family needs me. I got to get that infor-mation to Brett about his wife. There's a trial going on and the man at the root of it is just about a worse sort than Bette. The information I have on Julian Carlman could put him away for life, if not have him hang. More likely than not, Bette is going to hang no matter what."

"They'll hold Carlman till you get there."

"Yeah, but they expect me in a few weeks. They got a traveling magistrate waiting for the information which will hang up the circuit court for awhile. Don't know who or what he's going to be hearing cases on, but there could be other miscreants waiting for trial. If I take Bette direct to San Francisco and then go to Adler Creek, it could be four, maybe five months till I get there. That's a long time for Brett to wait for things to square out for his wife."

"I gotta ask. You think the rest of the folks are safe from her?"

Kendrick looked back towards the wagons. He could only make out shadows in the dark. Was she even there? Or had she run off and was already making her escape? Would she try to climb on the stage and make her way to California that way and evade standing trial?

"What?"

"Bette. Mandy. Do you think the rest of the folks are safe from her?"

"I believe so. She knows that if they suspect who and what she is, they won't want her traveling with them. They may well take justice into their own hands and it wouldn't be a quick or easy death. She won't hurt anyone."

"So you gonna stay with the wagon train?"

"I don't know, I don't know. I'll decide by morning when the stage pulls out. We'll either be on it or moving out with you."

"I gotta say, I don't envy you the decision, Kendrick. Which is best for you, your family and the families of her victims. Not a good place to be in."

The sound of a stone scuffing along the ground drew Kendrick's attention, his hand going immediately to his gun. He cleared the leather of the holster before the stone came to a rest.

"Mr. Parker? Kendrick? Is that you?" The soft feminine voice carried through the night air to him.

"Mandy?"

"Yes." She stepped into view, a worried look marring her features. "Are you all right? Is everything all right?"

"What are you doing away from the wagons?" He stepped over to her, roughly taking her arm. In the darkness he still didn't miss her wince of pain at how he gripped her.

"I was worried. About you. I saw the stage pull up and saw the young man from the jail. I saw you walk off with him and in the distance you seemed upset. When he came to the circle and you didn't, I became concerned something happened to you."

"And what if it did? Wouldn't that suit your plans?"

"I beg your pardon?" She glanced at Dusty to see if he heard the exchange and understood it better than she.

"If I was dead, you could just go off on your own, couldn't you?" His voice came out strained, almost a growl, filled with bitterness and a tinge of anger.

"If you were dead, I believe I would be in a none too pleasant situation. I believe I would be perceived as a widow, a sad state to be sure. But what would they do with me? What would you, Mr. Hendricks, as wagon master do with me? Would you tell them I am who this man," she jabbed her finger in Kendrick's direction, "claims I am? That I am a murderess? Or would you continue the tale that I am his widow? Would you send me back to St. Louis to fend for myself after this man," again the pointed a finger at Kendrick, "has besmirched my reputation, or would you deliver me to the nearest town to fend for myself there? Or, perhaps, deliver me to his family and tell them that it is their duty to provide for me and to make amends for the wrong he has inflicted on me?"

Dusty chuckled. "She sure does have a way with words,

don't she?"

"Don't encourage her. She gets more uppity with them if she thinks she is bothering you with them."

"Oh! Oh you arrogant, mule-headed, despicable, reprobate!" She stomped on his foot and turned to leave.

Before she was two steps away, Kendrick reached for her again, this time gripping both arms and pulling her hard up against him. With her back flush to his torso and hips, he felt her buttocks through their clothing. Try as he might, the image of grabbing her posterior instead of her arms raced through his mind, down his spine to settle in his groin. Damn if the woman didn't make his body react in a way he could not control! And damn himself for his inability to get her out of his mind. When she gasped, he knew she felt the hardness of his shaft and rather than being pleased at his reaction—perverse woman that she was, she was affronted by his desire for her. Well he was too! The last thing Kendrick Parker wanted was to want this woman. And now she knew just how his body reacted to hers. It was just a physical reaction. That was all. If she dared to say anything about it, he'd tell her it was just physical and that any woman's body would do.

Thing was, no other woman's body would do. He was starting to want to slide between the sheets and between the thighs of this woman and only this woman.

He shifted back ever so slightly so that their torsos were no longer in contact.

He glared at Dusty grinning at him.

"If something happened to me, Dusty has instructions to deliver you to the Sheriff in Adler Creek who will then make arrangements to have you transported to San Francisco. Should something happen to me, he would continue the charade that you are my wife so as not to disrupt anyone else's journey to Wyoming and on. Understood?"

She wriggled out of his grasp and slid her hands down the

sides of her long gray skirt. "Understood. And," she looked at Dusty, her eyes widening at his grin, "I trust you to uphold the Marshal's promises."

"Oh I do. Trust me . . . Miz Parker . . . I do."

Back at the circle Amanda surprised Kendrick yet again when she pushed him towards their wagon and returned a few minutes later with a plate for him. "I should let you serve yourself, but that wouldn't be keeping with our appearance as a loving couple." She huffed and sat beside him.

They ate in silence for a few minutes before Amanda broke into Kendrick's thoughts asking, "So what did the deputy want?"

"Seeing a bit of the country."

"Seeing . . . don't you find that odd?"

"Why would you think it odd? People want to see the country all the time. If war comes in the east, no one will be doing much traveling. Best to do it now, don't you think?"

"Then why hasn't he come to sit with you and talk?"

"Because Billy knows I'm not very fond of him and if you are smart, you will keep your distance from him as well."

"He's the man who started the problems, well the other problems for me in St. Louis, isn't he?"

"He is the one who let some folks know who you are."

"Who you *think* I am."

Kendrick looked down at her, brow raised. "He won't bother you and if something should happen to me, Dusty won't let him near you either."

"I assure you he is not someone I wish to associate with. Thank you for that consideration."

"What happened tonight, when we were out past the wagons . . ." Kendrick began.

In the fire's light he saw Mandy turn to him, her eyes wide before she averted her head and interrupted him, "Do you really think war will come?"

That brought him up short. He was about to explain his body's reaction, to dismiss it and she cut him off. Obviously she didn't want to know. "I don't know. Like most folks I hope not. It does seem though, with all the vitriol it will. You like that word, Mandy? Vitriol?"

"You mock me."

"No, just trying to keep conversation light. Guess that's not the best thing when talking about war, huh?"

Before she could answer, two of the children came running up, "Is it too late, Miz Parker? Can we still do some reading and learning?"

"No, children, not at all. In fact, I have a book all ready for us and, what about sums? Do you think we should do some sums too?"

"I don't like sums," one little girl told her.

"I do." Another spoke up.

"You don't know what they are." A third put in.

"Well, let's see about some sums for a bit and then we'll take turns reading until your parents say it's time for bed. How about that?"

Kendrick noted she was so immersed in her talk with the children, she lost all interest in him and their talk of war. It was as if he did not exist when the children came around her. He found her smile for the children, enchanting. That was not a good thing.

For the next hour she went over sums with them, teaching the younger ones what the numbers looked like and helping the others learn simple addition. They then took turns reading from a children's book she had, the older ones doing most of the reading while Amanda held a younger one on her lap, showing him or her the words in a second book. If he remembered right, he had seen three or four copies of each book in her trunks and wondered why. Now he understood — they were for students. Her students? Or were they just to hide be-hind the role Black Bette Barkley had taken?

The next morning while Amanda washed off their break-fast dishes and gave herself a short sponge bath at the river's edge Kendrick sought out Dusty.

"I decided. My family has to come first. We're going to go on with you to Adler Creek. I'll just keep a close eye on her. She won't be any trouble."

"And Billy?"

"That's up to him. He can either go on with the stage to wherever he wishes or return to St. Louis."

"Not go to Adler Creek?"

"Absolutely not." He saw Dusty wanted to laugh but managed to hold it back.

A short while later they pulled out; Billy apparently decid-ing to stay with the stage until the next stop and then planning to catch the next stage back to St. Louis. Kendrick again pon-dered the contents of the telegram. Was he making a mistake going forward to Wyoming? Should he be on the stage getting her to San Francisco as fast as possible?

Or, did he have the wrong woman?

Chapter Thirteen

Mid-morning the next day the wagon train, with the stagecoach trailing, pulled into Independence, Missouri. It was not quite the bustling city St. Louis had become but the travelers were still able to purchase some items they found missing.

Leaving Amanda with Dusty, Kendrick headed towards the general store in search of the telegraph. In his anger at Billy the night before, ignoring most anything the boy said, coupled with wondering if the telegram was a warning about Bette or confirmation he had the wrong woman, he'd completely forgotten Independence might have a telegraph. The solution would be so simple. Send a telegram to San Francisco and see if in fact he had Black Bette Barkley.

Or it could have been.

While they had the equipment, they had no operator. He asked if anyone in the town had even rudimentary knowledge and there wasn't a soul.

Striding back along the wooden planks that made up a variation of a sidewalk, his boots clunking on the thin slats, he silently cursed his luck and then amended it to Brett's luck.

He'd heard about Brett's rejected courtship several years earlier. Whatever the story was with his bride, there were complications. What were the chances she would be related to someone who his office had been keeping an eye on? Actually, things had gone relatively smoothly until he laid eyes on Black Bette Barkley in St. Louis. His younger brother, Wolf, would tell him it was fate, that the woman was his destiny.

Maybe they were just supposed to meet, and this was how it happened. And what? Was he supposed to ignore her crimes, hope she didn't kill anyone else including him and go about their business?

He told himself Wolf didn't always know what he was talking about.

"Any luck?" Dusty stepped over to him, speaking low as Mandy had no knowledge of the message or what concerned Kendrick at the moment.

"No. No operator in town. Any idea if anyone on the train knows anything about the damn things?"

"Don't think so."

"Well, it's not worth the risk asking. All that would do was raise questions I don't want to have to answer. Especially from Mandy." At least that was what he told Dusty and in his mind, he believed what he said. That was except for that small voice that was starting to tell him he wanted to spend as much time with the petite woman before he sent her on to San Francisco or back to St. Louis. He clamped down on the voice. Told it to shut up because there was no way he was going to feel anything but disdain for a woman like that. Wide hazel eyes, soft lips, sweet voice, plump bosom and, even dirty, a pleasing scent. No. He was not going to care one iota about her.

He was relieved he didn't see any sign of Billy. With any luck, that one would be on the next stage back to St. Louis and out of his hair for good. Pity the poor sheriff to have to deal with him.

A short while later the wagons began their trek out towards Wyoming, Nebraska territory their goal in the next few days. Looking up at the sky, a cerulean blue, Kendrick gave thanks that the late March weather was mild. It wouldn't do for them to be caught in a late spring snowstorm.

Over the next few evenings the children eagerly came to their wagon for Mandy to go over some lessons with them.

They gathered round her, each one vying for one of the special spots sitting next to her.

It kicked his gut when he'd see her during the day pulling out some of her books, looking at different passages, earmarking the pages and looking off into the distance. At night she added small talk and questions about what the children had seen during the day, spiced up with her own observations. As stars began to fill the night sky, she would point out the different constellations. One evening one of the Indian scouts traveling with them told a story about the stars. Even the adults sat awestruck by the telling of the long-ago tale. Those were not things a ruthless killer would do. They were things a schoolteacher would do, things he wanted his wife to do for their own children. Things he wanted Mandy to do with their children. Children that would never be because one day soon Mandy would ride out of his life.

The little voice in Kendrick's mind started to grow louder. The woman who sat with her back to the wagon wheel, soft tendrils of dark blond hair framing her face, a face that glowed with excitement at the children's questions, no longer formed the image of a killer in his mind. The woman who sat beside him on the wagon and made sure he got his meals just didn't seem like the kind of woman who would kill a man in cold blood. The voice chided him, not so quietly that he had arrested the wrong woman.

With everyone raptly listening to the scout, Black Bear's tale, Kendrick pulled out the wanted poster and studied it, not for the first time. The woman on the poster was, without a doubt, the same one whose face shone in the campfire's light. If he told himself that often enough, he'd eventually believe it himself.

Dusty approached him as he was saddling his horse the next morning. "Mornin, Kendrick."

"Dusty."

"Seems Billy decided to stay in Independence to catch the next stage back to St. Louie."

"I don't care where he goes or stays as long as it isn't with us. Boy's more trouble than he's worth. Idiot almost got Mandy killed back there and sure as hell would start something here."

"Starting to sound like you care about the woman."

He caught himself just before jerking up the cinch harder than was necessary, forcing himself to slowly draw in a breath before answering. "I could care less about Bette Barkley. What I do care about is making sure the letter of the law is followed without anyone meddling and Billy McCaffrey would do just that."

"Uh huh."

Kendrick turned, slowly, towards Dusty. "I mean it. The Barkley woman doesn't mean squat to me. The law will not be broken on my watch."

"Oh I know you don't care one way or the other about Black Bette. It's Mandy Parker that's got you acting like a schoolboy."

Kendrick turned, gaping, fists clenched as he took in Dusty's retreating form. It was clear from the movement of the other man's shoulders he was having a good laugh at Kendrick's expense. "Don't care about Mandy Parker, either," he muttered.

"Yes. Well that is not exactly news, Marshal." Mandy's soft voice sounded from behind him.

He drew in a sharp hiss as he turned towards her, "Don't be sneaking up on me woman. It could get you killed."

"Tell me something new, Marshal."

"Kendrick."

"What?"

"Kendrick. It's not seemly for a wife to call her husband

Marshal."

"I'm not your . . ."

He glanced around him, "I thought we agreed you'd stop arguing with me about that."

"You stated . . ."

He pushed his Stetson back on his head, "What do you want, Mandy?"

"Amanda."

"You come over here to argue with me? Because if you did, I'm not in the mood."

"I came to give you this." She thrust a napkin, warmed by whatever was inside, into his hand. "I thought you'd like some warm bread out there this morning. Sorry I bothered." She spun on her heel and started to walk away.

"Oh no you don't." In one movement he thrust the package into his saddlebag and reached for Amanda, pulling her into his arms and lowering his lips to hers. Ignoring her struggles, he kissed her lips, across her cheek and when she started to struggle and speak returned to kiss her lips, twisting his tongue inside, silencing her with his kiss. A battle that was becoming all too familiar raged through his body—the need to rub against her, to push her to the ground and settle between her legs warred with his need for control and propriety. Suddenly she leaned into him, resting against him, her hands tangling in his hair, now grown to crest his shoulders. A soft, sweet whimper broke from the seal of their lips, her own need evident in how she welcomed him into her embrace. It wasn't until Kendrick heard the thud of hooves fly past him along with Dusty's call to mount up that he regained a semblance of control over himself.

Hands on Amanda's shoulders he took a step back without releasing her from his grip. "You need . . . when you . . ."

"Marshal Parker, it is uncalled for, for you to accost me, to maul me in such a public . . ."

"Told you before, I'll kiss my wife when and where I want." With that he hauled her back up against him, one hand on the back of her head, tangling in the silken locks, unmindful of the hair pins stabbing into his hand. The other rested on her bum, holding her firmly against him. He'd never forced a woman before, never stole a kiss, but it was all he could do not to pleasure his wife in front of the entire train. His wife. His wife. The phrase played over and over in his mind. His wife. Mandy wasn't his wife. Mandy didn't even exist. She was a woman made up to hide the fact there was a wanted killer in their midst. He forced himself to relax his grip, to let her step away. When she brought the back of her hand up to her lips, he wanted to shake her, to yell at her how dare she try to wipe his kiss from her lips.

But it wasn't a wiping motion she made. Rather it was as if she meant to imprint the feel of his lips against hers so the memory would never fade. Eyes wide, a mixture of fear and desire in the pewter depths, she stepped back from him and stepped back again, putting herself out of his reach. "Please . . ."

"Please what, *Mandy*?" He couldn't help it. Something drove him to goad her, to make her react in some way. To react with emotion rather than her uppity words.

"Please refrain from accosting me in such a public fashion again."

"Fine. I'll wait till we're between the sheets at night. Then I'll *accost* you right proper."

"Huh?" Her mouth opened in shock. She blinked in disbelief. With a huff she spun on her heel and ran towards the wagons.

From deep inside a primal need to chase her down wove its way through Kendrick's body. "Damn woman turns me upside down just coming near me." He muttered angrily to himself. With brusque, efficient movements he finished saddling his horse, mounted up and hightailed it out towards the front of the wagons. Today he would ride scout. He'd ride himself to exhaustion so that tonight even the idea of touching Amanda . . . Mandy . . . would seem impossible.

For over an hour Kendrick rode, and rode hard, giving the horse his freedom to run as he needed. The rhythmic pounding a panacea to how Kendrick's blood ran hot in his veins over the woman with the honey colored hair. Miles from the wagon train he reined in. Common sense telling him if he rode much further out, he wouldn't be giving them the safety his job promised. Turning back, letting the horse walk at a cooling pace he decided it was time to give himself a hard look. The man who stood there kissing Mandy — Black Bette — this morning was not who he was. Shaking his head, he gripped the reins so tightly his hands ached. In the distance he saw a single rider approach and in a few minutes saw it was Dusty who approached.

"You okay, Partner?" Dusty asked when he caught up with Kendrick.

"Yeah. I don't understand myself these days."

"You mean since you met Mandy?"

He sighed. "No. If I'm honest with myself, it happened before then. Brett. You know, growing up he had it the hardest of all of us I think. Most of the kids knew he was half white and they picked on him till he was big enough to fight. After that they may have thought it, but no one was going to say anything because he'd beat the tar out of them. Wolf, both his parents were Indian, and I know he never doubted their love. I think . . . I think if my ma lived, she and my pa would have had a good marriage. I like to think she would have adjusted to life in Wyoming. Or maybe they would have moved back east. I didn't grow up there. I didn't hear any taunts. With my grandparents raising me a lot of my life was sheltered and I only really saw the upper crust of society. When I heard Brett married though. I don't know. It's hard to say. I guess . . . it seemed . . ."

"You jealous he married first?"

"Not jealous. I'm happy for him. Don't know much about her except what you said back in St. Louis and a few lines he wrote me. I figure he wouldn't marry just anyone. She'd have to be someone special. There he is, in the middle of nowhere and the perfect woman for him just shows up. Me. I live in a metropolitan city; I travel between the best cities and never meet a woman who I'd even want tea with. Then I stop off in St. Louis and run right into a woman I can't . . . Dusty, I can hardly keep my hands off of her!"

"I noticed."

Kendrick shook his head. "You know my reputation?"

Dusty shrugged. "I hear things. They say you have ice in your veins. That the reason your eyes are as blue as a mountain lake in winter is because there's no warmth to you at all. I've heard when you've had to kill someone you are like a machine. Completely methodical. You do your job and walk away."

"That's how I've done my job. No emotion. I meet that Mandy though and . . ." he shook his head again, confusion evident from the slump of his shoulders. "I just don't understand myself. If I feel anything for her, it should be disdain, not want. No matter how many times I tell myself she's just a woman and a rotten one at that, my head can't seem to control my body."

"There's a word for that, partner."

"Yeah. I know. Stupid. One of these nights I'm going to let my guard down and the woman will put a bullet between my eyes."

"That's not how I see it."

"No?"

"Nope. The way she looks at you, well it's about as hot as

119

you look at her."

Dusty spurred his horse, leaving Kendrick to think on his words. To the open air, Kendrick declared, "I don't give her hot looks. I don't." With a silent vow to himself that he would feel nothing for Black Bette he headed back towards the wagons. He was Deputy United States Marshal Kendrick Parker, the cold-hearted, methodical federal officer known for his levelheaded thinking and actions. That was the man who would greet Bette when the train stopped for the night and the man who would escort her to Wyoming. There'd be no more stolen kisses and letting her get under his skin.

Chapter Fourteen

Following that too potent kiss, even days later, each night Amanda, as she made up their bed, tried a different arrangement to keep Kendrick at a safe distance. She told herself she was relieved he rode out early each morning and kept away from the train during the day. He took his supper with the men and kept his distance while she taught the children each night. Oh she'd feel his gaze on her each night. But he never approached. When it was time to turn in, he'd enter the wagon after she was snuggled under the blankets.

As usual, tonight, she told herself it was because he was a disreputable rogue that he had kidnapped her against her will and stolen her livelihood from her, not because she was starting to want more than those kisses, kisses she was finding herself missing. "Poor excuse for a gentleman," she muttered under her breath. "I can't wait to see his face when he finds out what a mistake he has made. Of course, brute that he is he probably won't even apologize let alone make reparations."

"You say something, Mandy?" he asked as he climbed up in the wagon and took in her latest design to keep her distance from him. He startled her because he entered before she had turned in.

"No. Until you listen to what I have to say about who I really am, I have nothing to say to you."

"Fine. So, that line of pots gonna keep you warm when the chill sets in tonight?"

"What do you care if I'm warm or not?" She turned and in the soft glow saw he had shaved the beard that had been growing over the past few days. Whether it was for his own comfort or the fact that this morning, when she woke, chest to chest with him, she grumbled when his beard abraded her cheek she didn't know. And, she reminded herself, she didn't care. She was strong enough to admit to herself that the real reason she groused at the beard wasn't so much because it scratched her. No, the problem was it felt good. Too good. His beard was soft and made her wonder what it would feel like to run her fingers through his hair and know she was doing it. Not the unconscious entwining she engaged in when he kissed her. She wanted the freedom to do it the way he often threaded his own fingers through it. The blond locks crested his collar — shorter than many men of her acquaintance wore. He also eschewed the thick sideburns most eastern men sported. Kendrick Parker was definitely his own man. A very potent man from what she'd observed as he rode, gathered wood for the fires and strode about the camp. Taller and broader than most, he was a force to be reckoned with.

And stubborn as a mule.

No. He was more stubborn than a mule. You could pull a mule or kick it in the posterior and it'd get moving. Kendrick Parker just dug in and stayed there till he was good and ready to move.

"I care. Don't want you getting sick and holding things up or making anyone else ill."

"You're too kind. I'll be just fine without you accosting me in my sleep."

"I don't," he paused for emphasis, "*accost* you in your sleep."

"You most certainly do."

"Lady, I can't stand what little touching I have to do for appearances. I'm not about to touch you when I don't have to."

"That's why you constantly paw at me in public before you

force your kisses on me."

"I don't paw at you. And if I do touch you, it's purely for appearances."

"Well good. Which side of the pots do you want?" She huffed, hands on her hips, her stance defiant. For all the good it did. The man still made her feel weak-kneed.

Lord help her if he ever realized how she would watch for him during the day, drinking in the sight of him mounted on his horse. Sometimes she imagined herself sitting between his thighs on the big stallion. He was always there to help out the other men on the trail setting up camp or bringing buckets of water for the women. When it came to the children, especially when one of the younger ones would get cranky after a long day on the trail, he always spoke to them with fondness in his tone. A few days out of St. Louis he had begun to allow one of the children to ride a bit with him while he rode scout. When it came to Amanda, at least outwardly he treated her as a gentleman would. It was becoming increasingly necessary for her to remind herself what a troublesome man he was.

Amanda rolled over and glanced out at the dark gray visible through the wagon's flap. Shivering she was sorry she'd made such an issue over the pots and touching Kendrick. She wasn't just cold. She was freezing. She huddled deeper into the blankets and listened to the sounds or rather the lack of them, surrounding them. The stillness, the peace was unlike any other she could recall. She'd always lived in or near cities. There was always some sort of noise, even the clump of horses moving down a street. The stillness, the sheer peace surrounding them was akin to a din in its lack of sound.

She shifted.

A pot rattled.

She tried to shift away from it.

Another pot rattled.

The harder she tried to quietly move away, the more sounds the pots made.

"Dammit!" Kendrick exploded just before he shoved the pots and pans towards the foot of the wagon. Without another word, he reached for her and pulled her up, hard, against his chest.

"I beg yo . . ."

"Shhhh, go back to sleep."

"I will not. You let go of me this instant or . . . or . . ."

He cracked open an eye. Even in the dim, dark, gray of the night she could see that icy shade of blue. Like a rare gem, the blue of his eyes beckoned to her, Amanda told herself it was an unnatural shade. That was better than thinking it was the most beautiful blue she'd ever seen, or that it wasn't ice she saw but heat.

"Or what?" It was almost an animalistic sound. Almost. There was something in it Amanda couldn't quite identify. Yet at the same time it was a sound she wanted to hear again. To her very core, she wanted to hear it again.

She managed to wedge her hands up against his chest and tried to push him away.

"Just be still or I'll do something a lot more unpleasant than keep you warm with a soft place for your head."

"I doubt there is anything more unpleasant than your hands on me." She struggled against him and wondered why he was wearing his gun in such an odd place. Why on earth would a man position his weapon dead center of his groin?

She got her answer. At least the one of what was more un-pleasant than his hands on her when Kendrick lowered his lips toward her. Before she knew what was happening, his lips touched hers. He brushed them, ever so slightly, a whis-per of a touch, back and forth against her own. Not the pas-sionate taking that first kiss was. This one was softly sensual, meant to seduce and entice.

In the back of her mind she noticed how his lips were slightly rough. Chapped. Like his hands. Hardened, calloused in their own way, from the days on the trail. Yet so gentle, so warm. He increased the pressure ever so slightly when he wrapped his arms around her, bringing a hand up to cradle her head, holding her just so. With his hand, he caressed her head. She couldn't shift away from him. The same as the other morning, yet different. She didn't want to move away from him. Lord forgive her she didn't want him to stop. There was more. There was no doubt in her mind . . . there was more to the kiss.

A moan escaped her lips. A sound so different from any she'd ever heard Amanda couldn't credit it as coming from herself.

And still he continued that soft, slow, sensuous motion, grazing his lips back and forth along hers.

With his other hand, he pulled her closer and pulsed his hips against hers.

Her hands seemed to find a mind of their own because she certainly didn't control them when she slid her arms out from between their bodies and slid them down his arms, feeling the muscles there . . . his biceps and his forearms. This was no Washington dandy. Oh no, this was a man, a solid man who brought heat to her in places she didn't know could feel such warmth. She wanted more. Something more. Something she didn't know she could want.

Almost as if he heard her innermost thoughts, he shifted his mouth to her upper lip and pulled it between his own lips. The same whimper escaped her lips, in the most primitive way asking for more. And he gave it to her. He stroked the seam of her lips, not with his own, but with his tongue. Warm, wet, delicious . . . the taste of the coffee he had drunk before bed on his breath, coupled with a hint of the mint he had chewed on after. She didn't realize she'd opened her mouth, welcoming him, until her own tongue connected with hers.

Even then, in the ages old dance of stolen kisses she didn't realize what she was doing, didn't hear her own sighs of pleasure until she felt a pooling between her legs. That and grinding his hips brought to her consciousness the knowledge that it was most certainly *not* his gun that rested against her belly.

She pulled back, hard, shoving away from him. She would have slapped him if she had the sense to take her hands from his arms. "You arrogant . . . you miscreant . . . you . . . you."

"Damn good kisser there, Bette. Warmed you up a bit, didn't it?"

That did it.

Her hand connected with his cheek in a loud crack.

"Where do you think you're going?" Kendrick reached for Amanda, as she scrambled for the foot of the wagon.

"Away from you, you miserable excuse for a . . . a . . ."

"What's the matter? No uppity words to describe me? Rogue? Brut? Darling?"

"D . . . Ohhh."

She had just pulled back the flap when he grabbed her by the waist. The two of them gasped at the same time when they saw the layer of snow covering the ground. As if their minds were joined through the kiss they'd just shared, at the same moment they both said "ohhh."

Amanda sat back, unable to help herself from landing on his lap. So stunned by the blanket of white covering the ground, she didn't seem to notice his hands on her waist. "What do we do now?"

He pulled one hand off her hip and scrubbed his chin with it, "Don't rightly know. Guess we continue on. That's gonna be Dusty's choice."

That wasn't the question she'd asked. It was the answer she'd take. She wasn't about to let him know that she meant with the snow on the ground, how would they manage to stay in such close quarters and not touch?

Kendrick shifted around her, still holding on to her waist with one hand, pulling back the flap with the other. "No one else is up and moving around. Maybe it will melt by morning."

"Do you think so?"

"No. It was just a maybe."

"How did this happen?"

"You know," he sat back pulling her to lie in his embrace, "for someone as smart as you are, I'm surprised you don't know that."

She squirmed to get away from him and realized that all it did was cause her to rub up against him in a manner she wasn't quite sure was the best way to rub up against a man she didn't want to like. "I *know how* snow happens. I just didn't think it would happen now. It's almost April. There should be . . . the ground should be turning green. Some rain maybe . . . but snow?"

"It happens. Guarantee you the pass over the Rockies will still have snow when you get there."

"Can the wagons continue?"

"Like I said. That's up to Dusty." He looked out the flap again before reaching over to pull it closed. "So since there's nothing for us to do at the moment, how about we get back under those blankets and . . ."

"That, Marshal, is not a good idea. It is a very poor idea. I'd like to know why you felt you could take such liberties with me? How dare you . . . you . . . kiss me!"

"Just an accident Bette. I was dreaming about a woman I found desirable and you happened to be there. Although, I'm pretty sure that was your willing tongue dancing with mine."

"Ohhh. You are a jackass. You have no manners at all, you . . . you . . ."

"Shut up, Bette, or I'll kiss you again."

She scrambled up off him and headed back towards the blankets. After scrounging around in them for a few minutes she pulled out the skirt she'd worn the day before and began to dress.

"Where do you think you're going?"

"I need to use the privy if you must know."

"Fine." He stood and reached for his coat.

"What are you doing?"

"Taking you out."

"I can find it myself."

"Don't want to take the chance you'll fall in the water and freeze to death out there."

It was, in fact, Kendrick who slipped and fell, landing in the river.

"Kendrick!" Amanda yelled as his head went under the water. It looked to Amanda as if he'd hit it on a rock barely visible beneath the surface. Not that he could have avoided hitting it. In panic she watched him slide through the ice and into the water.

"*Kendrick*!" Amanda screamed again. "Oh my God, *Kendrick*!" She rushed to the river's edge. "Kendrick! Someone! Help! I need help."

She managed to grab him by the shoulders and began to tug him out of the water. A thin gash poured blood from his temple. Despite the cold from the chilly water, the blood seemed to flow unabated making her think there was a much deeper cut somewhere on his head. "Help me! *Someone please help me!*" She screamed.

What seemed like hours later, several men came running. She'd gotten his head out of the water but struggled to pull out his body. In seconds, they were able to pull him the rest of the way out.

"Is he alive? Is my . . . h-h-husband alive? He's all right, isn't he? Someone, please, tell me. Kendrick is all right, isn't he?" Amanda hovered behind the men holding Kendrick. "Please, let me see him."

Dusty ran up along with another man who said he had some medical experience. The other man felt around Kendrick's throat for a pulse. When he nodded his head that there was a pulse, Amanda released a breath she hadn't known she was holding. "Why isn't he moving?"

She grabbed Dusty's arm, "Help him. Can't you help him?"

"What happened? What did you do?"

"I . . . Mr. Hendricks, I needed to, well we needed to go outside. We were both surprised to see it had snowed. He . . . he slipped and fell in the river. He'll be all right, won't he? Please, make him be all right." She couldn't hold back the sob in her tone.

He wrapped his arm around her. "He's mighty hard-headed. He'll be just fine, Mrs. Parker. Let's get him into the wagon and get you both out of those wet clothes, okay? We don't need no hypothermia setting in."

It took three of the men to carry Kendrick back to their wagon. Another man running ahead, calling for someone to start heating some water and to bring extra blankets. As they got to the wagon Amanda tried to climb in to make room for the men to bring in Kendrick. Instead, Dusty called to one of the other women to take Amanda to her wagon and get her into some dry clothes. He assured Amanda they'd get Kendrick undressed and start getting him warm.

"Mr. Hendricks, I can't leave him. I need to be here. To help. To be sure he's all right."

"You'll be no good to him if you're sick yourself Mrs. Parker. Go with the ladies, get warm and dry and then you can take care of your husband."

"But . . ."

"*Mandy*. It's what he'd want."

With reluctance she went with the other women. By the time she got to the Schumaker's wagon, her teeth were chattering uncontrollably, and Zelda told her that her lips were turning blue. Mary Patterson told her they were about the same size and while Zelda and Felicity helped her remove her dress, Mary rubbed her arms to help her warm up. What seemed like hours later Amanda was dressed in one of Mary's wool dresses, had a coat on and a hot tea in her hands.

"Drink it down now," Felicity told her. "You need to get warm both from inside and out."

"Kendrick. Are the men giving him something warm to drink too?"

"I'm sure the men are doing what's necessary," Sally Ann told her.

"Oh my God! What if he's . . . d . . . d . . . hurt! I need to get over there. Now!"

The other women saw there was no arguing with her, and she rushed back to her own wagon as soon as she could. When she got there, Kendrick was grousing about the attention he was receiving and demanding to see Amanda while Dusty held a cup of whiskey to his mouth. She didn't need to be all the way into the wagon to smell the spirits one of the men had poured for Dusty. In the glowing lamplight, she saw Kendrick had been stripped naked and her breath caught when she saw his chest.

If her imaginings about his kisses did things to her body that had never happened before, the site of his almost naked body inflamed her senses more than she thought possible. In the lamp light his skin appeared golden. A fine sheen of blond hair seemed to caress his chest, a chest that rivaled those she had seen on the Greek statutes in a museum exhibit she had seen a few years past. His stomach looked like a washboard it was so muscled. There was no fat on the man. It was all firm muscle and sinew. She had a glimpse of his thigh when he pulled up the long johns someone had handed him. It stunned Amanda when she realized she was more interested in admiring Kendrick's body than finding out how he was feeling. *When did I become so unfeeling? And, so wanton? When did I start to care for this man who brought me here against my will?*

"Kendrick? How do you feel?"

He looked up at her.

She was surprised that there was no ice in his gaze, rather his look was warm. Approving.

"Like I hit my head on a rock and I'm freezing."

"Let me get you some more blankets." Amanda turned to the woolen blankets one of the men had carried in, while one of the men helped him into a thick flannel shirt. As soon as she could, she sidled close to Kendrick, putting an arm as far around his shoulders as she could reach. He spared her a glance that showed her his surprise at the caring action.

"What happened out there?" Dusty asked him now that the furor had died down and it was clear Kendrick would be fine. That he watched Amanda, as Kendrick answered letting her know the trail master had little trust in her.

"My bride didn't want me venturing out to take care of business alone so she went with me. Good thing she did, too."

Amanda struggled to keep back the gasp that threatened to erupt at Kendrick's lie. Then again, was it what he said or the glimpse she had of his chest? She couldn't quite figure out why he would take the responsibility for their outing. When the blanket she'd placed around his shoulders slipped, she reached to bring it back up around him, gently telling him, "Here, sweetheart, let me help you." If someone would have asked her what she was thinking, Amanda would have not been able to explain herself. When she moved to help him button his shirt, her fingers seemed to have lost all function and she had a more difficult time buttoning up his shirt than Kendrick had been having. This, after her heart had just stopped racing from seeing him fall into the river and almost drown.

She gave in to her fancy and allowed her hand to accidentally on purpose caress his chest. The hair there was soft, feathery, his skin a contrast to the roughness of his hands in how satiny it felt. It seemed incongruent, a man with skin soft as satin. Then again, she hadn't touched that many men's skin. In fact, Kendrick Parker's was the first.

The dry flannel shirt finally buttoned up to his chin, Amanda again fussed with the blanket she'd wrapped around him. Her left hand around his shoulders, she alternately patted his back, while sliding her right across his chest, completely unaware she was making clucking sounds, very much like a mother would make to a sick child. She started when Kendrick reached up to take her right hand, surprised at the warmth in it after he'd been in the cold, snow-covered river.

"Gentlemen, thank you. We appreciate your help, don't we darling?"

"Yes. We certainly do! I would have lost Kendrick had you not come. I don't know what I would have done if I'd lost him." She ducked her head, unable to look the other men in the eye over her lie or Kendrick to see the smirk of a smile she knew would be there.

The last man who jumped off the wagon turned briefly towards the couple and told Amanda, "You need anything more tonight, you give a holler. We'll be right here."

"Thank you."

The flap closed, Amanda shifted to help Kendrick settle in. "Are you sure you're all right?"

"Yeah. I've been hit by harder."

She couldn't help the small smile that spread across her lips. "I bet you have and enjoyed it too."

"Didn't take you long to get to know me, did it?"

"No." The smile faltered. The truth, that she was getting to know him, hit her hard. She wanted to hate him. This was the man who had taken her from a job she dearly wanted. She had a future planned for herself and he took it away. "They say, that is, I've heard, that after someone has been rendered unconscious they need to stay awake for an hour or two."

"And?"

"Well it's hardly been an hour. We need to keep you awake."

"I see. How do you propose we do that?"

"I don't know. It seems to me you would have an idea of it."

"Oh I have an idea. Just not sure you'll be interested in what I have in mind."

"What do you . . ." she couldn't miss the look of heat in his eyes. "I hardly think that's proper."

"It'd definitely warm me up."

His grin began to irritate her.

"We have more blankets."

With a long sigh he acceded, "You're right. Blankets it is."

Kendrick lay back, still feeling a bit cold, but warming up, as Amanda set their makeshift bed to rights. "Don't need the pans, Mandy. I promise I'll stay on my side."

"Are you sure you're all right?"

"I'll be fine. It's not the first time I've slipped into a river."

She finished bustling about with the bed, bending towards his feet to be sure they were encased in the blankets before tucking the top in around his chin just before blowing out the lamp. In the remaining darkness she slipped under the covers and released a sigh. "Do you fall into rivers that often? In the cold?"

"No. Not really. Mostly I swim in them. 'Preciate your concern, Mrs. Parker."

In the silence he thought she'd fallen back asleep and was surprised when she whispered, "As you said, if anything happened to you I'd be at the mercy of the other travelers. I believe without a doubt you will feel like the cad I know you to be when you discover I am not this Bette woman." She fell silent again.

He finally spoke, "If it does turn out you are who you say you are rest assured, I will make amends."

"In that case you have powers beyond this world because I fail to see how you can restore me to the position I would have had if you had left me in St. Louis."

Kendrick thought on that. The last thing he wanted to admit to her was that the past few days he'd been thinking about what it would take to make things up to her, if she was the woman she asserted she was.

He listened as her breathing evened out, cursing himself for his thoughts. How could he desire her the way he did? What was possessing him to want to know her, to . . . what? Share his life with her? One of the reasons he had been so successful as a marshal was because he approached each case with cold hard facts. No emotion. Solid, objective investigation. What was it about this woman that had him throwing all that made him the lawman he was away?

There was no doubt who she was the day he saw her in St. Louis. Kendrick's gut had served him well through every case he'd taken on. Even coming upon two men arguing over something, instinctively he knew who was the victim and who was the suspect. Each time the arrests played out in court, it proved over and over again that he knew who was the wrongdoer. That was how he felt when he first saw Bette. Not the poster. The woman in the store. It was a perfect match.

Gromley's telegram bothered him. What was the message? That she was innocent and let her go or that they'd tied yet another crime to her?

He rolled over on his side and despite the darkened shadows of the wagon he was sure he could see her face. The soft skin, pert nose, those hazel eyes, her frown when she looked at him. Her smile when she forgot to hate him.

Thoughts of those frowns and smiles led him down the wrong path. To the kiss they'd shared before she'd bolted from the wagon. He'd kissed many women. Never one that left him feeling like that.

"Are you sure you're all right?"

Her whispered question startled him. He'd thought she'd been asleep or would have at least pretended to be. It had to be because he was tired and his senses dulled from the spill in the river, not because he was attracted to her. "Yeah."

Her hand on his arm, sliding up his forearm to rest on his bicep sent sparks of desire to his groin. A simple touch had never affected him like that before. It shouldn't with this woman. "Your head doesn't hurt too badly?"

"Head's fine."

"Good. Well good."

She didn't remove her hand. He wanted her to. He didn't want her to. He needed her to remove it. He wanted her to leave it there and . . .

"Do you remember, Marshal . . ."

They were back to "Marshal".

" . . . the first night here, in the wagon. You had taken hold of me. I was certain it was because you were afraid I'd try to leave. You assured me it was only because two sleep warmer than one."

"I remember."

"Are you still chilled?"

What did she mean by that? What was she getting at? "Any

reason why that would matter to you?"

"No." For some reason it pleased him that she sounded unsure.

Whatever it meant, it had to be . . ." Stop it. Stop it now. Kendrick Parker you are losing your head over the wrong woman. She sounds unsure because she thought you were lying. That's it! She thought you were lying and hated being in your arms as much as you hated holding her.

"I just thought," she faltered. "I thought that if you were still cold that the body heat, our body heat . . . well only because I don't want you to take ill so I'd be at the mercy of . . ."

Despite his own wise counsel to the contrary Kendrick cursed himself for lying when he told her, "Well actually, I am a bit chilled. I'm not sure the blankets will . . ."

In an instant she was snuggled up to him. He hadn't even felt her toss her blankets over him and slide under his. Mentally shaking his finger at himself, he couldn't resist his own sigh as she snuggled up to him. It felt right. Not just the warmth that began to seep quickly into him. It was holding her that felt so incredibly good and right.

"There's one thing that might help me warm up a bit faster?"

She shifted as if to rise and find whatever it was that would make him feel better. "What?"

"Come here." He reached behind her and pulled her halfway down on top of him. Bending his head up towards hers, he caught her in a kiss. Slow, sensuous — a kiss neither one of them wanted to end. When Kendrick finally pulled away, just before he lost control of himself, he whispered, "Now that warms me up just fine."

"I . . . I'm glad."

He needed to keep his guard up. Keep it up? How about get it up? Because if he didn't, she'd outwit him and escape. The last thing he wanted right now was for her to escape.

Chapter Fifteen

Next morning Kendrick caught Amanda looking him over, stirring up warring emotions that seemed to sit far too close to the surface these days. Never in his whole life had he been this confused and within days . . . no . . . hours of meeting Amanda his world had turned upside down. *That* did not happen to Kendrick Parker. He was in control at all times. No surprises, no being hurt. "I'm fine, Mandy. No need to worry."

"I wasn't . . ."

"You were. And while I appreciate it, I'm fine." He smiled and as awkward as it felt pulled her into a quick hug. For the first time he craved contact, human contact, for the sake of companionship. It wasn't a greeting or prelude to sex. It was simply the need for comfort from another person. Surprisingly, she hugged him back, warmly, and patted his back.

A few of the women came by to check on the couple, Zelda clucking as she brought warm oatmeal. Amanda was surprised to find she somehow felt reassured when Kendrick decided to ride in the wagon beside her that day. Normally she kicked up a bit of a fuss when he did. Today she welcomed his presence and supposed to herself that it was only because he could have died the night before. It couldn't possibly be that kiss they shared. Or how disappointed she'd been when he didn't kiss her again in the darkness of their wagon.

Within a few hours of pulling out of the camp the thin layer of snow that had caused the near disaster the night before melted, assuring the travelers that the storm the night before had only been a fluke and summer was just around the corner. By noontime, coats were being removed with the coming heat of the day.

With a few moments to reflect Amanda realized she'd been more than pleased when she heard that troublesome Billy McCaffrey said he was going to head on back to St. Louis. It was with relief when he did in fact stay behind in Independence. The boy was trouble of a different kind than that of Marshal Parker.

A few days later, Kendrick, a slight sniffle in his nose, told her they'd reached the Platte River. After his initial orneriness about telling her which river they were following he seemed to relent and tell her where they were. Lately when he'd ride beside her in the wagon, he'd point out the different plants, few that there were, that they passed. He made the seemingly never-ending trek through the dry land almost enjoyable. When he'd talk about journeying to Adler Creek as a boy his whole demeanor would change. It would soften just a tad and his eyes would crinkle up when relaying a mischievous prank. Not that he was the one doing them. It seemed it was always one of the other boys who would start it, Kendrick standing on the sidelines, almost like an outsider looking in.

The night after his misadventure in the river, pulling into the evening's camp site Amanda couldn't help but notice dark rings under Kendrick's eyes coupled with an odd pallor underneath wind ruddied cheeks. She automatically uttered "bless you," when he sneezed and then took a closer look at him. He didn't look well. Without thinking she reached up and laid the back of her hand against his cheek. Hot. Painfully hot. Kendrick was running a fever. "You're fevered Mr. Parker."

"I'm fine."

"No, I'm certain you are fevered. Here, come into the wagon and lie down. I'll make you up some soup."

It irritated her when he shook off her hand telling her, "I'm fine."

"Annoying man. I'll not have you taking ill on me. Into the wagon."

Grumbling he climbed in, moving as if he ached from head to toe.

Amanda glanced at the sky. It seemed to be taking on the same iron gray cast they'd seen the night of the storm. Concern for Kendrick had her cancelling the children's class that evening. Rather than abating as the night wore on, Kendrick's fever spiked even higher. Someone said they were near the settlement of Lancaster in the Nebraska territory. If she remembered correctly, it was last year that the people of the Nebraska Territory voted, in a close race, to not take on statehood. Still settlers came and Lancaster seemed to attract many of them. The day before, the wagon train passed some settler homes, the occupants stepping out to wave. A few approached for news about the war brewing in the east. Walking or riding their horses beside the wagons the settlers hungrily listened to the talk of war and happenings they clearly hoped to be removed from.

By morning Kendrick was in the full throws of the illness and travel beyond the first homestead they came upon was simply not possible. Even Kendrick, in his fevered state, agreed that he and Amanda should find a place to stop rather than go on. Better for them to stay put than infect the other travelers if what he had was serious. At a homestead they could stay in a barn until his fever broke and they were assured of his health. There were stories of too many settlers who died on the trail because they pushed on. If he took a turn for the worse, well hopefully it really was Amanda Davis who traveled with him and not Black Bette.

When Dusty came to check on them, he managed to tell Dusty his plan that they would find a homestead to take them in. There was no way he could travel further as ill as he was. If Kendrick and Amanda didn't catch up with the wagon train in a few days, when he got to Adler Creek, Dusty would send his brother, Brett, back to get them.

"You listen to me, Bette. You listen good," Kendrick grit out, clearly fighting the fever that was bit by bit winning, "You don't tell whoever takes us in the truth about who you are. You tell them you are my wife, Mandy. I need you—I need you to promise me you won't run. You promise me something happens to you you'll wait for my brother to come get you. Will you make those promises?"

"Kendrick Parker, you are *not* going to die. Do you hear me?" Her vehemence surprised even herself. The fear of losing him almost overwhelmed her. Was it just a few weeks ago she wished the man dead? And now, suddenly faced with the prospect of him dying for the second time in a matter of days, she couldn't imagine life without him. Her momma had once told her love and hate were close emotions. But her hatred for Kendrick Parker could in no fashion turn to love. The man was an arrogant, despicable, hateful despot. No woman could possibly want him for a husband. None at all.

So why did the thought of him dying or her losing him hurt so very much?

"I'll take that to mean you won't run."

Dusty agreed with Kendrick's thinking, muddled as it was, and by early afternoon they found a family willing to take them in.

"Oh you poor dears." Annabelle Haynes' warm and caring voice assured them that they could stay until Kendrick was at least able to travel again. "We'll have your husband right as rain in no time."

The first homestead they came to was typical of the few

well-to-do families that Amanda had come to see on the trail. The family had chosen what Kendrick told her was the classical style of house with a columned porch, windows made of real glass and painted white rather than leave the wood natural. She was relieved when it wasn't the more often seen log or frame-type house. Not that there was anything wrong with a house like that. After all, people built what they could afford. It was just with him so ill, the better the shelter the better chance he had. Those log houses, Kendrick told her, were mostly twelve foot by twelve foot and hurriedly constructed because the families had to use the time to start their farms up before starving in the next winter. His description of the cold and bitter winters on the plains left her wondering why anyone would choose to live there. Then again, Massachusetts didn't have the most temperate of climates. The house they pulled up to though seemed, at least from the outside, to be the kind that would have what she needed to help Kendrick. They would definitely have a well-sheltered barn where she and Kendrick could stay.

"Are you sure you wouldn't feel better if we were to stay in the barn?" Amanda asked after introducing herself and Kendrick. "We don't want to make any of your family ill."

"No. Not at all." Allan Haynes assured her. "We're made of pretty solid stock. Besides, if that badge on your man is real, we don't want to be turning away the law. Settled as Lancaster is, having a Marshal abouts is a good thing."

"Truly. Mrs. Parker, believe me, I've cared for my children through enough colds and influenzas to know when it's serious and when it's not. Mr. Parker's just gotten himself a bad cold." Annabelle seconded what her husband said.

She bustled them off to a bedroom towards the back of the house, her husband helping Kendrick to the comfy room. "I think this room will do you best. Since its wall is shared with the kitchen, you'll be able to enjoy the heat from the kitchen.

Now, while Allan brings in your trunks, let me fetch you some tea and start up some soup for Mr. Parker." Both the Haynes left Amanda to settle Kendrick in.

Kendrick staggered to the bed, clearly exhausted. Amanda watched, mesmerized, as he struggled to bring his fingers to his shirt. He fumbled with the buttons a few moments before his head slumped to his chest, one hand falling to his lap while the other tangled in the buttonhole. Transfixed by this virile man's seeming sudden descent into helplessness, Amanda took a step forward. The noise of her foot on the floorboard drew his attention. When he looked up, her heart broke. Gone was the coldness from his gaze. Instead she saw fevered blue eyes laced with what could only be fear. Fear of what? Incapacity? Abandonment? Death?

The need to comfort him, to ease his aches, pains and the overwhelming sadness in his gaze replaced the fascination of watching him try to move. In a heartbeat, Amanda knelt before him where he sat on the bed. Cupping his feverishly hot cheek she murmured, "It's okay. Kendrick, I'm here. Let me help you." Gently she reached for the buttons, speaking in a soothing tone as she would a little child or a wounded animal. "I'm right here, Kendrick. I promise I'll take care of everything." Quickly, yet with the distance felt by one caught in an emotional storm, she undid the buttons and pealed the shirt off him. She bent to remove his boots; he laid back, the strength to sit long gone. Tossing the shirt to the floor she hesitated only a moment before placing her hands on his belt buckle.

"My guns."

"I'll take care of them. Don't worry. Let's get you into bed, shall we?" Before the words were out, she'd undone the buckle and pulled apart the placard holding his pants. Drawing in a deep breath, she began to tug them down, closing her eyes while she fumbled with the pants. The deep red flushed her cheeks at the most intimate act she'd ever performed. Not even the kiss several nights before in the dark of the wagon was near as intimate as peeling off this man's pants. Only his raggedly indrawn breath, forcing her eyes open, spurred her on. "Oh, Kendrick, Kendrick, we need to get you under the covers. I need you to help me, help me pull off your long johns."

He struggled to pull the sleeves down his arms, the fabric falling to lie across his torso before his strength ebbed to a new low.

Amanda bit her lower lip. She had to get the long johns off. Taking in another breath and closing her eyes as if that would give her strength, she tugged at them. When he grunted her eyes flew open to see she'd been twisting the fabric around his hips in a way that could only be uncomfortable. Trying her best to avert her eyes, yet at the same time drawn to look, she caught a glimpse of what she could only define as male perfection. The Marshal was indeed perfectly made. Even with the fever taking his body, he was a gorgeous specimen. Not even the statues in the museum or pictures in her text-books rivaled his physique. Struggling she managed to pull him up on the bed and tuck him in. "There we are. We have you in bed. In no time you'll feel better. I promise."

"Mandy." Her whispered name was a plea.

"What is it?

"Water."

"I'll get you some. Right now. Hold on."

She rushed from the room, found the kitchen where Anna-belle already had started the promised tea and soup. After telling the woman who had taken them in what Kendrick needed, she returned to him a few minutes later with the cool drink. "Here, drink this. Try to drink all of it. I read in a book once that it's best to keep a fevered person hydrated."

He didn't appear to hear her use of the term *hydrated*,

missing the opportunity to call her uppity but he did manage to drink it down before falling into the sleep reserved for those who can do nothing more than give into the sandman's call.

CHAPTER SIXTEEN

For the next few hours, Amanda sat by Kendrick's side, at first oblivious to what was a charmingly appointed room. When Kendrick's breathing deepened in a restful sleep, she gazed about the room. Annabelle Haynes had clearly put her heart into making the room comfy and cozy with a sturdy looking table and chair that would serve as a desk, a couple of shelves holding knick-knacks that were probably tucked away in small little crannies of their belongings when the family moved west. Homemade quilts covered the bed where Kendrick lay. When he suddenly moaned and struggled to rise, she turned to calmly hold him down on the bed. In between his tossing and turning he rambled from the fever. He called her name, Bette's name, muttered words of endearment — probably to some eastern lady he intended to one day wed, a thought that, for some unknown reason, hurt to her core.

"Want you. Want you under me . . . in you . . ."

"What? Kendrick, what did you say?"

"Mine. You're mine! You belong with me. Can't you see that?"

He sat up, his eyes rimmed red with fever, making the blue appear almost purple. He grabbed her arms, a surprisingly strong grip despite his illness. "I can save you. Don't you see that? Just let me . . . be my . . . gotta get to Brett . . . got to save his wife . . . then can save you, Mandy, my wi . . ."

He fell back, unconscious. His breathing was surprisingly ever, especially after his outbreak. She couldn't make sense of his words. Or rather, didn't want to. His ramblings were almost too intense, especially when he insisted she was his, that she belonged to him. She didn't want him . . . she didn't want to want him.

Sitting beside him, holding his hand she watched him sleep. Sometimes restless, sometimes tossing and turning when the fever spiked. She found that if she stroked his arm with her fingers, a slow and easy up and down motion, he quieted.

"What is wrong with me?" she whispered to the silent room. "How can I feel anything but anger at this man?"

Her thoughts drifted back to when she first met Kendrick, or rather when he first rumbled into her life. She hadn't had much chance to see St. Louis having just arrived in town the day before, getting a room and hoping for the coveted teaching position. "I know I could have had the job. I just know it."

But that was before Kendrick Parker barreled into her life. She had no doubt she could have done him serious bodily harm at any time those first few days. And then somewhere along the way, her feelings changed. She saw that now. Clearly. He may be a loner, keeping to himself but that didn't mean he didn't care about other people. It was as if somewhere deep inside was a hurt that no one had been able to mend. Maybe it was because he'd lost his mother so young. Maybe it was something else. Watching him, being with him day after day, night after night, she saw a part of Kendrick she was sure no one else had even a glimpse of. A part he didn't want anyone to know was there.

"Well, soon we'll be in your Adler Creek and you'll turn me over to your friends and we'll go our separate ways. Still, I wish I could see your face when you learn I'm not who you think I am." She smoothed a lock of hair off his still warm forehead.

Annabelle came in several times the first few hours

bringing Amanda tea or soup. Kendrick finally settled into a fairly restful sleep, his muttering seemingly done. "You look worn yourself, dear. Would you like a hot bath and to get some rest?"

Unconsciously Amanda poked her fingers into her bun, trying to primp and secure it, wrinkling her nose, "That would be divine." She examined her fingers. They were clean. Her hands were clean from bathing Kendrick. "I have to admit, with my hu . . . Kendrick . . . being so ill I completely forgot about myself. Yes. A bath would be just the thing."

"And then we'll set you up in bed for a nice long sleep."

"I'll think on the sleep. Actually I have dozed on and off the past few hours. I hate to leave his side, you know?" She didn't want someone to hear his ramblings if they began again. Didn't want the Haynes to know Kendrick thought she was the notorious Black Bette.

"You're newlyweds, aren't you?"

"Y-y-y-yes, we are."

Annabelle chuckled, "Your blush may not be showing on your cheeks, but I certainly can hear it in your voice. How long have you been married?"

That caught Amanda by surprise. "Um, well let's see." She'd have to remember to tell Kendrick what she said when he woke. "Three months thereabouts."

Annabelle laughed, "I don't know too many women who don't know down to the exact date!"

"I suppose that's true. I have to admit, my time with Kendrick has been such a whirlwind. And the weeks on the trail, I have lost track of time to a point . . . It's been quite a time since meeting and marrying him, rushing on our way, heading out to his family in Wyoming. Why I've just lost track of the time passing!"

"I believe I would have as well. So! Let's get you that bath."

Amanda turned to Kendrick one last time. While fussing

with the blankets, making sure they were snug up to his chin she quietly told him, "I'll be back soon. I'm just going to take a little bath. A *hot* little bath." She couldn't keep the smile from her voice. "You rest, I'll be right back soon."

He slept on, despite her words.

Before she fully stood, Amanda reached over to brush a lock of hair off Kendrick's forehead, noting to herself how his blond hair had grown over the past few weeks. Even in the cool weather, riding out in the sun, his hair had bleached to a pale blond. She made a mental note she'd see about shaving him as his beard was growing and he'd shown a definite preference to being clean shaven. It struck her as odd that she would know so much about a man she'd just met and was not at all fond of.

"He'll be just fine, Amanda. I promise you. And, if nothing else, you won't be able to take care of your husband if you yourself aren't fit."

"That's what Zelda, my friend from the wagon train, said. You are right. You are so right."

A short time later, with a long, relaxed and purely self-indulgent sigh, Amanda settled into the warm tub. The Haynes certainly seemed to have everything well in hand, especially in such a rough and unsettled part of the country. Opening her lids, after having lowered them to enjoy the luxury afforded by the bath in total peace, she looked around the room. Yes, the Haynes certainly seemed to have just about everything a body could want. The bathing chamber was set just off the kitchen. There was a vanity with brush, comb and more colorful knick-knacks that looked like they held creams or some such. The windows all with glass, were framed by white curtains with little red roses on them. A most appealing room. One she wouldn't mind having in her own home. In the relaxing warmth of the tub she allowed her mind to drift, imagining a life with Kendrick. Through the fog of her imagination she pictured herself, standing on a porch, pretty flower boxes dotting the edge, a sliding chair, large enough for two against the railing to the side, kissing Kendrick good-bye as he rode off to work in the morning. Indulging her fantasy she could swear she heard herself tell him "Goodbye, sweetheart, I'll see you tonight."

"You surely will, my love. I'll miss you all day."

"Just be careful. I love you."

She shot up in the tub. *What* was she thinking? Imagining telling Kendrick Parker she was in love with him. "I've probably got a touch of that influenza myself." She raised her wrist to her forehead, feeling for fever.

Still . . . her own home. She leaned her head back against the rim of the tub. If Kendrick Parker had his way her "home" would be a jail cell until they put her to death.

Annabelle surprised her by entering with a bucket of steaming water just as the bath was starting to cool. "I thought maybe you'd like a little fresh, hot water, to rinse the soap from your hair."

"Oh Annabelle! You are too kind. Especially to someone you just met."

"Nonsense. Out here anyone could be your neighbor and it just helps to be neighborly. I just feel so bad for you and Mr. Parker with him taking ill and all. Especially when you are only about two weeks from his family. You must be so excited to meet them."

"I . . . to be honest I hadn't thought much about it. I've been so absorbed in spending time with Kendrick, getting to know him, our journey out here. I hadn't thought that far ahead. Now that I think about it, yes, I am. It will be a pleasure to meet them."

"Now! Let's see about getting some food in you."

"I'm fine. The soup has been quite filling. Really. And I should be getting back to Kendrick." She didn't want to spend too much time with Annabelle and end up saying something that would come back to haunt her. More than that, she hated lying to the kind woman. As soon as Annabelle bustled out of the room Amanda rose from the tub and quickly dried off. Just in time she pulled on a comfy robe as two little children ran in at that point, "Mommy! Mommy! Where are you? Mommy?"

"Here she is!"

The children came up short, eyes round, looking at Amanda wrapped up in their mother's robe, her long honey brown hair snaking down her back and around her shoulders while it dried. "Who are you?" The little boy asked.

"Children, this is Mrs. Parker. Mrs. Parker, these are my children, Michael and Sarah."

"Well hello there." Amanda greeted them.

Annabelle continued, "You know how mommy asked you to be quiet?"

The children nodded in unison.

"Well, that's because her husband, Mr. Parker, isn't feeling very good. Mr. and Mrs. Parker are the two people staying in the guest room for the next few days. Since Mr. Parker is still feeling poorly, we need to be quiet a little longer so he can sleep, okay?"

The little girl stuck her finger in her mouth, grabbed on to her mother's skirt and nodded while the little boy assured, "Yes, mama, we'll be good. Can we have some cookies?"

"And milk?" The little girl murmured from beneath a fold in Annabelle's skirt.

"I think that sounds splendid. Don't you agree Mrs. Parker should join us?"

Both children nodded in the affirmative.

"Well then, that is an excellent idea," said Amanda. "Let me just check on my husband and slip into a clean dress."

Quietly entering the bedroom, Amanda was relieved to see

Kendrick lying peacefully, his chest rising and falling slowly and steadily, his color less flushed. It seemed the fever had indeed broken. She checked the blankets and when he didn't stir, quickly changed into a fresh dress, brushed her hair and, deciding to let it hang loose went in search of Annabelle and the children. Stopping at the door, she returned to her trunk and rummaged around until she found a volume of children's stories and made her way to the kitchen. Offering to read to the children for a bit was the least she could do.

The kitchen was warm, cozy and much appreciated on the chilly day. Entering the kitchen Amanda took note that the same white curtains with little roses dotting them graced the kitchen window. The big black stove with not the usual four but six burners. Brass pots and pans decorated the walls around the stove along with some homey drawings. A cold box sat near the sink and a pipe of some sort that Annabelle told her brought running water into the house covered one counter. Annabelle already had thick sandwiches made and sitting on the table. There was milk for the children and, from the enticing aroma, hot coffee for the women. Taking the seat Annabelle indicated, Amanda set the book down and sank into a sturdy wooden chair with a plump cushion on the seat. She reached first for the coffee and, after a long swallow, she leaned her head back and let the liquid slide down her throat. "Mmm, that has to be the best coffee I have ever had."

Annabelle laughed, "Probably because it's been awhile since you remember having one that was hot and freshly made when you drank it!"

"Could be. But I will definitely cherish this cup." Reaching for her sandwich, she took a bite and took her time chewing, enjoying the flavor of the fresh baked bread.

"What's that, Mrs. Parker?" Michael asked pointing at her book.

"Why, this? It's a children's book by the Brothers Grimm. I

thought maybe in a bit you'd like to hear a story."

That got little Sarah's attention, shyness quickly dissipating. "I would please, Mrs. Pawka."

"Excellent. I'm so glad to hear that."

"Let's let Mrs. Parker eat her lunch first though, okay children?"

They nodded solemnly.

"Well, Mrs. Haynes . . ."

"Call me Annabelle, please."

"Then you will call me Amanda!"

"Amanda it is!"

"How long have you and Mr. Haynes been settled her in, Lancaster, is it?"

"Yes. Lancaster. We made our journey out here approximately ten years ago. We grew up together and my husband always wanted a cattle ranch so when the opportunity arose we headed out this way. We are fortunate his family supported our decision and assisted us in so many ways."

"Does it get lonely out here?"

"No. Not really. Lancaster proper is only about seven miles away and in the past few years supplies from the east have arrived with more regularity. I can't imagine returning to the east, especially with all that talk of the war. What did you hear before you left?"

"Before I left, that is, before we left, there was some talk. There was posturing on both sides to be sure and some bits of fighting. I'm sure cooler heads will prevail and the union will be preserved."

"We can only hope. Mr. Haynes and I do not believe if war happens it will find its way to our doorstep. Mrs. Parker? Are you feeling unwell? Are you concerned if there is war your husband will need to return?"

"I don't know. I hadn't considered that. I still have friends back east. With all the changes in my own life I hadn't thought of them caught in a war. War would be horrifying. However, many of the people I spoke with didn't seem particularly concerned."

"Then it does not seem as if it is a possibility."

"No. No it doesn't. I . . . I don't expect to return to the east."

"So are you and Mr. Parker planning on staying in Wyoming?"

"I . . . well we haven't decided exactly where we will end up. He is most anxious to see his family and I'm looking forward to it as well." The talk of war reminded her that if Kendrick had his way, before long she would be dead and buried. She'd never know if it came to a division of the country or not. Shaking off the morbid thought, she turned to the children, "Well! Shall I read you children a story before I go check on my husband?"

Not long after she finished reading a tale to the children she returned to the bedroom to find Kendrick just opening his eyes.

"Where were you?" His voice came out in a rusty growl while he struggled to sit up.

Amanda blanched at his nasty tone. "Well after seeing to you, I had a bath, thank you very much and had a bit of lunch with the Hayneses."

"Haynes?"

"The family that has kindly taken us in. Kind even to you, when I offered to have you stay in the barn."

She watched as he continued to struggle to sit up in the bed and so angry at his attitude, that she fought her own impulse to help him rise.

"I expect you to stay close by me. Not go off on your own. What did you tell them?"

"Humph. Did you want them to bring the bathtub on to the bed beside you? Were you hoping for an illicit look at me while I bathed? You obnoxious . . ."

"Reprobate?"

She gaped at his use of the word and couldn't quite bring her lips together when she saw laughter instead of the usual chill in his eyes. "Yes. Reprobate. I told them we were wed a short while ago, about three months and we were going to visit with your family in Wyoming. Annabelle, Mrs. Haynes, wanted to know about the war and I told her only what I knew."

"And that was?"

"That the men are busy with their bluster and posturing, as men do, but with luck it will all die down."

He shrugged a shoulder out from under the blanket and picked at a piece of lint on it. "We can only hope. That is for certain."

Forgetting her resolve to keep her distance from him, Amanda crossed over to the bed and sat on the edge. "Kendrick, what if we do go to war?"

"Then we will fight."

"We? Will you return east to fight?"

"I don't know. That will depend on my assignment."

"What about me?"

He turned to gaze at the wall, studying it as if the answer lie somewhere in the knots and panels. "You won't be returning to the east, Mandy. Surely you know that."

At her sharp intake of breath he turned and grabbed her wrist before she could stand. "That came out the wrong way. I'm sorry. I didn't mean to be so blunt."

She glared at his hand, still a warm brown next to her own pale wrist. His hand was so big, the strength there obvious despite how ill he'd been, making her fine bones seem even finer. She had to harden herself against him. "I'm sure you did."

"No. No I didn't. Listen, I haven't told you this because I didn't want to get your hopes up. But I'll tell you now, I'm of a mind to go with you to 'Frisco and speak on your behalf. Maybe get you a life sentence instead of death. I just want to clear up the mess my brother got himself into and then, well, we'll see."

Forcefully pulling her hand from her grip she told him, "You are too kind." Her tone belied the words. She rose and started for the door.

"Mandy?"

"What?"

"Could you hand me a glass of water or at least hand me my pants so I might get one?"

She stalked over to the bureau and poured a glass from the pitcher and brought it to him. His hand shook slightly as he lifted it to his mouth, giving away the fact he still felt weak. Before she knew what she was doing, she placed her hand on his cheek and glided it up to his forehead Amanda felt the fever that still clung to him. "You're still a bit fevered. Are you up for some broth? It may help a bit."

He sagged back against the pillow. "I need to . . ."

At his hesitation she ventured, "the privy?"

"No. I . . . I need to keep . . ."

"You're afraid I'll leave you here? That I'll tell them you kidnapped me and forced me to go with you against my will?"

"You could."

Releasing a breath, her lower lip caught a moment between her teeth, "Don't you think I would have already done that if I meant to? Did you forget the promises you asked me for and I agreed to? Listen, why don't we call a truce you and I? For the next few days at least. Until you can travel. Once you are well, we'll continue our mutual hatred of each other."

"I don't hate you, Mandy."

"Oh no?"

"No. I did. Or I hated what I thought you did. What you've

been accused of doing. Now. Well it's kind of hard to hate someone who . . . never mind. Yeah, a truce will do."

"Fine. Would you like some broth then?"

"Yeah. I would."

Dinner with the Haynes was one of the more enjoyable meals Amanda had had in some time. Perhaps even years. Kendrick had fallen back asleep after he'd had his soup and seemed peaceful while he was at it. She thought about his reaction if he woke and found her gone again. Most likely he'd be angry and then, remember their truce and that she promised not to leave him. It remained to be seen if he believed her or not. Even if she wanted to, even if there were a way to escape the odious man, she promised she would stay, and she was a woman of her word.

Returning to the room for bed, Amanda found him tossing and turning, the fever back in full force. She managed to get some water into him, tucked the covers yet again and deciding that sleep could wait, pulled a chair over to keep watch, hoping it would once again break. Annabelle told her the doctor would come the next day; the fever needed to be broken tonight.

"C-c-c-cold."

"What?" She'd dozed off. "What did you say? Kendrick?"

"C-c-cold. S-s-s-so cold."

Sweat poured off his brow and down his cheeks, he was burning up with fever, shivering so hard from the chills the bed shook as if he would rattle off the floor. The blankets didn't begin to warm him. She was desperate to help him, feeling there was no way she could until Kendrick's words came back to her; Amanda muttered to herself, "two sleep warmer than one . . ."

Quickly doffing the nightgown she'd put on, she climbed

between the sheets and hugged Kendrick to her.

The fevered chills had him trembling so hard, the bed shook as if the very ground beneath them would open up and swallow them. His teeth chattered so hard she thought he'd bite his tongue in two.

"B-B-Mandyee, so-so-so c-c-cold."

"Shhhh, it's okay. I'm here. We'll get you warm. It's okay, Kendrick, we'll get you warm." She wrapped herself around him, holding him in her arms while throwing a leg over his for stability. The intimacy of their position went unnoticed in her worry for his health.

He gripped her. Hard. Almost choking the air from her lungs. "Hurt."

With one hand Amanda smoothed his hair off his forehead while with the other she drew him closer. "Where? Tell me where."

"All over. Hurt. So cold."

"Here. Hold on to me, okay? Can you hold on to me?"

Kendrick shifted, moving upward until his head was aligned with hers, his chest grazing her breasts. Their hips were so close, Amanda couldn't tell where his ended and hers began. She couldn't keep back her sigh of pleasure when he shifted so she lay on her back, the leg she wrapped around him parting. Then he slid one thigh over hers bringing them so very close . . . so close as if they were one, she couldn't ignore the throbbing in her groin.

"Mandy." A whispered breath just before he brought his lips to hers. Despite how his body shook, he had no problem caressing her lips, kissing her, making her want to open to him.

The soft brush of his lips against hers, the barely there touch, sent sparks of delight racing through Amanda. She never wanted the moment to end, while at the same time, the ache she'd felt when he'd kissed her on the trail returned. A sweet pressure between her legs, a feeling she never imagine existed.

When he began to plant soft, gentle kisses against her lips, her jaw, down her neck, softly murmuring her name, all rational thought left. Try as she might, sensation overrode anything and everything, except the feelings the man evoked. Opening her lips to welcome him into her, was a coming home. A sense of rightness. She belonged here, with Kendrick. All anger at him for taking her against her will from St. Louis, of his refusals to listen to her side of the story, fell at the feelings this kiss from him evoked.

His shivers dwindled from the warmth they created, he pulsed his hips against hers in a steady motion. She should have stopped him then and there. Amanda told herself she had to stop there. But she wanted more. The ache grew to a need, a need for more from him, with him. A small voice told her he was sick, too sick to exert himself in any way. Another part told her to ignore the voice, to let him be for her what no other man would ever be. She tried to tell herself if he knew what he was doing, it would sicken him to be doing this with her. The feelings he evoked in her while he stroked her body, the unintelligible murmurings from his lips while he kissed her overrode the increasingly smaller voice.

"Kendrick."

The sound of her own voice, pleading for something more, was somehow erotically overwhelming to her.

As if he heard that need, he rasped her name, "Mandy, my Mandy."

Memories of the kiss, that first kiss flooded her mind. His lips on hers, his tongue tangling with hers. How it felt to be in his arms, rubbing up against him.

That feeling of wanting, needing more rose again to consciousness. There was something Kendrick and only Kendrick could give her. A need that no other man was going to ever be able to fill.

He was hot. And suddenly, as only a woman can know, she knew that his heat was from want, not fever.

Hot. From growing passion rather than illness that took him.

Hot. From the way the two moved together as if they had done so time and again.

"I want you, Mandy. I want you so much."

"Oh, Kendrick. Yes. I need . . . I want . . ." She didn't know what she wanted, just that he knew she wanted him as much as he wanted her.

His mouth, an inferno from desire rather than fever, melted her resolve and fueled her passion. The liquid heat of his mouth traveled across her shoulder to her chest, seeking the peak of her breast. He traced patterns up, down and around the globe, taking her nipple into his mouth. He sucked with a warm, wet pull, the pleasure so intense it almost hurt. Sharp shards of pleasure shot through her. Each nip created a pulse between her legs.

Not content to bring pleasure just to one breast, he shifted them so he lay covering her. His mouth worked his special magic, while one hand stroked, kneaded and delighted the other breast. His other hand threaded through her hair. When he groaned from the pleasure of her body his hips bucked against hers.

Impossibly, he slid closer to her. Her mind told her he couldn't be any closer; her heart demanded he become one with her. She'd never wanted anything as much as she wanted Kendrick Parker to join with her.

They kissed and sighed and kissed again. Soft whimpers mingled with sensual groans.

"Mandy, tell me you want me. Tell me." His whisper clearly one of passion, not pain.

"Kendrick, yes. Yes. More than anything. I want you. I

want to be with you."

Without another word, he rolled her completely on to her back as she parted her legs to welcome him to her innermost core. Inch by exquisite inch Kendrick slid towards his goal, inching into her most intimate essence. Amanda didn't know which was hotter, Kendrick's body or her desire for him.

He pushed. He pulsed. He stopped.

He met with her intimate barrier, the most special gift she could give her husband.

With his mouth, his cheek he nuzzled hers, "Mandy." A whispered promise. Desire laced with need.

Lifting her hips she met him, the momentary sharp pain there and gone as he pushed through with her help. The fullness of him inside her both satisfied her need and left her wanting more at the same time.

His hips pumped in short, rapid, strokes, teasing and tormenting her in a way she hadn't known could exist. Tiny shards of pleasure accompanied the tiny pulses until he groaned and pushed himself to the hilt. With his mouth on hers, his tongue dancing with hers, the pain of his breaching her intimate barrier came and went with the beat of her heart.

She didn't need to think. No one needed to tell her. She knew as only a woman can what to give, what to take.

Wrapping her legs around his hips she drew him deeper inside, causing him to groan with the pleasure of having his balls beat against her, his manhood buried to the hilt. She couldn't help herself. There was no thought, just feeling, just needing and wanting the man she was joined to. With her hands, racing along his back, over his buttocks, up his ribs and over his shoulders she demanded he pump harder, faster. She had to touch him everywhere at once. It was as if she stopped touching him, stroking him, she'd break apart. Their breaths mingled in with their kisses until the two found their ecstasy in one final thrust of his hips.

He rose above her, a brief moment in time while he filled her with the evidence of his desire.

A pleasure-filled lethargy carried her to a dreamily dazed state. She belonged to him. With him.

"Love you, Mandy."

In the darkness she froze. Not from the chill of a fever but from the words the man beside her said.

CHAPTER SEVENTEEN

A short while later, Amanda woke from her passion in-
duced slumber, a deep, yet short sleep, a more restful
sleep than she could remember having. Her body ached in
longing for more of what she had just shared with Kendrick.

With a start she realized Kendrick not only still lay on top
of her, part of his manhood rested still embedded inside of
her. Semi-soft, yet still so potent. Sliding her hand up over his
biceps she stroked his cheek. She told herself it was not the
caress she wanted to share with him, rather to test if the fever
had broken.

Finding the fever had in fact broken, embarrassment
flooded her. *Oh dear Lord, I've copulated with a man who is not
my husband!* Worse, it was the man who took her against her
will and was dragging her halfway across the country. It was
the man who could very well be the cause of her death.

And he'd said he loved her. The sound of his voice when
he told her he loved her echoing in her mind. He couldn't. He
wouldn't. She didn't. It wasn't possible. Then the naughty
side of her, a side that seemed to show itself more and more
since meeting Kendrick, asked, *Will he make love to me again?*

Galvanized into action by the thought, Amanda wriggled
out from under him, surprised that with her movement he
didn't wake. Oh he tried to hold on to her, but she evaded his
grasp and managed to pull herself from the bed, pull on her
long, flannel nightgown, cross the floor and sink into the pad-
ded rocking chair that sat near the window. Drawing her feet
up under her, the edge of the nightgown covering her toes,

she rested her chin on her knees. Thoughts whirled unbidden through her mind.

He said he loved her.

Surely he said that to anyone he was intimate with.

Of course he didn't love her.

She certainly didn't love him.

He said he loved her.

Amanda looked out the window. It had snowed while she lay so intimately with Kendrick. Snow, the reason he was ill, the reason they were here at the Haynes', the reason she'd given her maidenhead to the man who would be the instrument of her death. There was just enough to blanket the ground in pure crystalline beauty. The bright light of the moon cast its light across the snow-covered field. So white. So pristine. Like she had been just a short time ago. The shadows cast looked like little streams and rivers across the landscape, darkening here and there. Like having sex with Kendrick . . .

"No." She whispered. "That wasn't darkness. Amanda Marie Davis, it was the most wonderful thing you have ever felt and the one thing you will never again feel. He couldn't love you."

"Mandy?"

Kendrick watched her wake to his soft call.

"Kendrick!" She rose stiffly from the rocking chair and stepped over to him. There was something about the gentle way she placed her hand on his forehead. This was not the brusque Mandy who fought him at every turn, not the woman who hated him. There was something vaguely intimate about her touch and a sliver of a memory, a caress, slipped through his waking state.

"What are you doing?"

"Just checking."

"For?"

"You had a fever. A bad one. Don't you remember?"

"I . . ." He looked around the room. "We're . . ."

"At the Haynes'. A family near Lancaster here in the Nebraska territory. You took ill on the trail and just as you were getting worse you and Dusty decided that it would be best to find a place to stop. We came here. They took us in just as your fever was getting worse."

"And?"

"It spiked and then . . . then, well it broke last night."

She dipped her head, looking down and drew in a quick breath. If he wasn't still so tired, he would have thought it was a sharp breath. A nervous one as if she were hiding something.

Fussing with the blankets, a scent at the same time familiar yet oddly out place drifted up to him. He thought he caught a glimpse of color and then it was gone. With the blankets pulled up around him Amanda told him, "We need to keep you warm. Don't want the fever coming back. Ahhhh, are you . . . hungry? Thirsty?"

He studied her a moment, taking in the fullness of her lips. He told himself he must still have the hint of fever because her lips looked like someone had kissed her thoroughly. Why that thought should rankle him, made no sense. Mandy didn't know anyone here and surely she wouldn't have shared any stolen kisses with the man of the house. Even less likely was that she would have kissed him. Yet something about the set of her mouth, the fullness of her lips . . . he mentally shook himself, "Thirsty. Yeah. If the Haynes' are up I wouldn't mind something to eat. I can wait though till everyone else is up and about."

"I'll go check. You just, um, you just keep these covers bundled up around you, okay?"

"Sure. Mandy, you'll come back, right?"

Amanda got to the door and stopped. She looked down at her nightgown and turned, blushing back towards him. Ignoring his question she told him, "Seems I'm still dressed for . . . sleep." Picking up a clean dress from her trunk she told Kendrick to shut his eyes so she could change.

He wanted to honor her request. He really did. He didn't know if he could. Something felt different. It wasn't anything he could put his mind on. It just felt different. The soft cotton didn't do a very good job hiding her curves and curves she had in all the right places. With her hair down, flowing around her shoulders and down her back, she looked delectable and at the same time, like an angel. His groin tightened in what had become a familiar way around her. Pretending to close his eyes, he rolled ever so slightly to the side. While it gave the appearance of giving her privacy, in actually it put him in the exact position to watch her pull off her nightgown and stand in all her glory in front of him. The view lasted less than a minute. In fact, she was pulling on her chemise and pantaloons before he'd even begun to drink in the beauty of her body. Round in all the right places, trim waist and that long honey blond hair. His groin wasn't just tight. He was hard. Damn hard.

"Okay. I'll be back in a few minutes. Just keep those covers up tight there."

When she left, he brought his one arm out from under the covers and wrapped it around the back of his head, propping himself up. He felt a certain lassitude. A restful feeling just like after having sex. "Odd what a fever can do."

He sniffed. The air smelled like sex. The scent of a sexually satiated woman and a happy man filled the air and his body felt just as it did when he'd spent hours pleasuring one. Amanda was the last woman on earth who'd take him to her bed. And she was the last one he'd want to share any intimacies with. So what was going on? "Must be the fever. Gotta be the fever." *So why is she acting like she has something to hide? Because she does. Because she's . . . she's not Bette, she's not Black Bette!*

Kendrick let his gaze roam out the window at the icicles dripping their filmy water down from the eaves. The snow covering the ground would be gone before long. If she were in fact the despicable criminal he wanted to believe she was, she wouldn't have gotten him to this house. She wouldn't have cared for him when he was so ill. Bette would have left him as soon as she could. No, Bette would have taken his gun, the very one he could see lying on the table across the room and killed him the moment his back was turned. Amanda stayed by his side. His mind drifted back to the telegram. His heart told him what his mind didn't want to know.

He'd arrested the wrong woman.

When Amanda returned a short time later, she had a tray filled with food. The scent of griddle cakes, eggs, bacon, a tall glass of milk and a cup of coffee wafted over to him, causing his stomach to growl long and loud. Clearly he hadn't eaten for a spell.

She made a bit of a to-do about helping him sit up before he told her he needed to use the privy. For some reason the deep pink of her blush pleased him. She handed him a sheet to wrap around his waist and directed him towards the privy. When he returned a few minutes later she had the bed stripped and was putting down clean sheets.

"What're you doin, Mandy?"

"Changing the sheets."

"Why?" He watched her finish tucking the blankets in before pulling the top sheet back and directing him to get into the bed.

"Err, ahhhh, my grandmother always said you need to stay in bed a good twenty-four hours after a fever breaks so you ge: yourself under the covers. Since you sweat pretty hard when the fever was breaking they were, well, not exactly tainted, but just not healthy for you to lie in. Now, back to bed with you."

"Really. I'm fine."

"And what if you aren't and the next time we can't get the fever to break? Humor me and climb back into bed."

"Fine. Fine. What about my breakfast there?"

"You can eat it in bed." She tucked the covers in around him and pulled another blanket around his shoulders before placing the tray on his lap.

"So why was it you needed to change the sheets? I'm gonna feel really awful if I get crumbs in the bed."

"Like I said, the others were sweat-soaked. Not at all healthy for you. This way you can eat and then rest a bit and everything is fresh."

"And this didn't bother Mrs. Haynes?"

She hesitated. He might have missed it had he not seen her gaze shift back and forth across his lap. "Why no. She understood and agreed with my reasoning completely."

Despite the fact Kendrick noticed she wouldn't meet his gaze, he couldn't bring himself to rile her. There was something different, softer, about Mandy this morning. Maybe the sex scent had affected her as well. Maybe it made her want him as much as he was wanting her. That couldn't be though. Just because she was kind and took care of him, if his suspicions were right that he'd arrested the wrong woman, she'd never forgive him.

To Amanda's relief, Kendrick's fever stayed broken and in a few days he was fit as ever and ready to travel. The days with the Haynes' were one of the most delightful times in Amanda's life. Despite Annabelle's insistence that Amanda stay with Kendrick while he continued to recover, Amanda insisted on helping. When Kendrick tried to caution her to keep to herself, she asked him, "Don't you think it would be rude to partake of their hospitality and do nothing in return?"

Grudgingly he agreed with her. The women spent their days spinning wool, baking bread and trying to keep up with the laundry made by four adults and two active children. Amanda regaled Annabelle with stories about their trip on the wagon train.

Two days after Kendrick's fever broke Amanda helped him into the kitchen so they could join the family for dinner. Mr. Haynes suggested to Kendrick they might want to stay as the town was looking for a second lawman and having Amanda there to teach would be a wonderful addition to the town.

Despite the Haynes' entreaties to stay in Lancaster, Kendrick insisted they needed to be on their way. Annabelle assured Amanda that they would be happy there.

"That's a mighty tempting offer, but my family is expecting me. That is, us."

"Still getting used to having a wife, huh?" Mr. Haynes joked while patting him on the back.

"It seems so. I know they are eager to meet my bride."

So, with the snow melting or almost completely melted they headed west. Neither seemed inclined to speak which was fine with the other. Only the most cursory conversation passed between them.

It was Kendrick who finally tried to break the ice by observing, "Pretty land out here, huh?"

"I suppose. It's so big. It's like the land goes on forever."

"It does seem that way. Not as many trees like back east."

"Kendrick, what will you tell your brother?"

Her question surprised him and seemed to come from out of thin air, "About?"

"About me."

He'd really wished she hadn't asked because he really didn't want to answer. Without a doubt he'd handled things badly and now he only had a matter of days to set things straight without losing her. It crossed his mind that he could point out to her a husband couldn't testify against his wife and that if she married him, he'd have to keep quiet about her, except that wasn't true and she'd probably know that. He chewed the inside of his cheek, angry at himself because he had always told the truth. It had gotten him cuffed by his grandfather more than once, but he clung to the truth. Now, for days he'd deceived Mandy, dragged her across the country when in fact he could have made some inquiries about her in St. Louis. Plain and simple he could have gone to the head of the school and asked if he'd corresponded with her. He could have waited to hear back from the San Francisco office instead of tossing her into a jail cell, treating her like dirt and humiliating her into pretending to be his wife.

"Kendrick? Are you feeling poorly?"

Startled he turned to her, "What?"

"Are you feeling poorly again?"

"No. Why?"

"Your silence and the expression on your face."

"What's wrong with my face?" He scrubbed a hand across his lips, feeling the beard that was growing in but otherwise nothing out of place.

"The look on it. You look like a boy who's just drank a whole bottle of castor oil before he realized he had. You don't look well."

The idea of telling her he was still sick had a certain appeal. They could stop, spend a few days out here in the middle of nowhere and maybe he'd find a way to convince her not to be too angry when she found out he was becoming increasingly certain he had the wrong . . . or rather the right woman. In a tender moment he could tell her he loved her, that he'd fallen in love with her That, however, would be yet another dishonest act heaped upon the number he'd also committed where Mandy Parker, make that Mandy-whatever-she-said-her-last-name-was, was concerned. "No. I'm fine. Just thinking."

"You mean you haven't considered how you'll explain me to your family?"

Maybe he could cut her questions off with a simple answer, one that might scare her, just a bit, into being quiet so he could think out how to handle this situation. "He knows I'm bringing you out. That and that some Marshals are coming from San Francisco to escort you out to your trial."

"Kendrick, you've shut me out every time I've tried to tell you I'm not that Bette person."

Now he felt like a total brute, "Mandy, it's not for me to say. You'll have to prove it to a jury."

She refused to speak to him again after that.

On the fifth day out the silence finally got to him. He'd thought about the situation from every angle and still wasn't close to finding an answer. To break the silence Kendrick observed, "I woulda thought Dusty'd made it to Adler Creek by now and my brother would be on his way."

Amanda swallowed and gripped her side of the wagon before answering, "Perhaps he felt we'd be following rather quickly behind."

"Don't know. Don't mean Brett or the sheriff, Rick, won't be on his way any time now."

"The land is so vast. So empty. It's been days since we passed a homestead. Are you sure we're going the right way? How would they even know which route to take to find you?"

"That's true. Either way, we should be there in another day or two."

"It's hard to believe we've been traveling over two months. At times I can hardly remember St. Louis."

Kendrick had no answer to that. How could he tell her he was glad she wasn't remembering St. Louis because that meant maybe she didn't remember how they met. He lost count of the times he started to tell her that he had begun to realize he had the wrong woman . . . or the right one . . . before they arrived at the Haynes'. Or that he knew without a doubt while at the Haynes' he was certain it wasn't Black Bette he was bringing west.

Thinking back, a few days out from St. Louis, he first knew that she might not be Bette. Now it was the true knowledge that he arrested the wrong woman that had his gut clenching. The realization hit him, hard, when he sat in their room at the Haynes' homestead the second day after his fever broke.

He almost told her then, but he didn't. Kendrick knew if he did, she'd demand to be sent — taken back east. Even with the talk of looming war he knew she'd want to return to St. Louis. It bothered him to lie to her now about her future. She wasn't going to go to San Francisco. There was no way she could be Black Bette. More important there was no way he was going to let her go. He was sure of one thing and that was that he had fallen in love with Amanda. Well, he was sure of two things: the other being that somehow, some way, he was going to make her fall in love with him before they went further west. Maybe even before they arrived in Alder Creek.

Thinking back on when he first knew his suspicions were right, it was as if the events unfolded once again before his eyes. The afternoon his fever broke at the Haynes, he knew . . . Amanda'd moved the cushioned rocker over to the window and bundled him up in blankets with one wrapped around his feet. She'd fussed over him being out of bed. Told him she didn't think it was a good idea and then grudgingly helped him up before snuggling him into the blankets.

"There!" She'd said, pleased with how she'd arranged him. "That should keep any chill away from you while I help

Annabelle."

He reached for her hand, stroking it, a vague memory of a woman's breast cupped in his hand flitting through his memory, "I'd rather you stay here, Mandy."

"Why? It would really be rude if I didn't help out after they've been so kind to us."

"You sure that's all you're about?"

She was furious at his question. Even if he hadn't seen the look in her eyes, the way her shoulders hunched up and she gripped her fists, it was evident he'd angered her.

"You are the most insulting man I have ever met. What do you think I'm going to do? Massacre them and steal a horse?"

He couldn't answer her. It took all his power not to hang his head in self-disgust.

Watching her help Annabelle hang the laundry, he thought over the weeks leading up to their stay here in Lancaster. Images raced through his mind—Mandy bringing him his meals, Mandy reading to the children and giving them lessons, Mandy washing his shirts at the river, Mandy caring for him when he was so ill.

His conscience pricked at him. There was no way a woman who did things like that could be a killer. It just wasn't possible.

Out in the yard she'd pulled a sheet out of the laundry basket. Watching the large white square flap in the wind a memory tickled just beyond his recollection. When he woke, a glimpse of the sheet, a mark . . . the scent of sex in the air when his fever broke was unmistakable, as was how he felt. Satiated with a sense of completion and peace. No, not peace. Just a lack of tension in his body. The tension he'd been starting to feel just being near her.

But if they'd had sex, if he'd made love to her, wouldn't she have said something? Most women demanded marriage for less. Mandy acted no differently than she had before.

Perhaps a bit more distant but that could be because they were nearing the end of their journey together.

Was it because they were close to their destination? Or because he'd done the unthinkable and forced her to lie with him and now she didn't know how to tell him it had happened.

"Dear Lord!" Kendrick startled even himself.

"What?" Gray eyes flashed in a combination of panic and surprise.

Kendrick tried to collect himself, "Nothing."

"Nothing? You don't speak a word to me for days unless it's to grunt to a question I ask or to order me around and then when you speak it's to blaspheme and you tell me nothing?"

"So it seems."

"Humph."

Admonishing himself to keep better control of his outbursts Kendrick returned to his thoughts. Did I force her? Oh my God, if I forced her! Would she tell me? Is that why she's kept to herself? She's afraid if I know what I did, if I did it, that I'll expect to share her bed again? Over the next few hours Kendrick warred with himself. What would a better man do? Take a chance and ask her? Would she tell him the truth? Probably not.

" . . . family? Kendrick? Are you feeling poorly again?"

"What? Did you say something?"

"Yes. I've been talking to you. Are you feeling poorly again?"

"No. I feel fine."

"Are you certain?"

"Yes. Unlike you I don't need to rattle on and on for no reason."

"Then what about your family?"

"What about them?" His family. What would Brett and Wolf say when they heard he dragged an innocent woman across the country, through a snowstorm? What would Brett's wife say? Would she be so offended by his actions and refuse him entry into her home? Maybe the woman beside him really was Black Bette.

" . . . me."

"What?"

Amanda slapped her hands on her lap. "Kendrick Parker, if you are feeling poorly, tell me now while we can do something for you in daylight. I don't want to find you delirious again when it falls dark and no way to find help."

"I told you. I'm *fine.*"

"Then what *is* the problem?"

"What problem?"

She heaved a sigh that sounded like pure despair. "If you don't want to speak to me just say so."

"I don't want to speak to you."

"Fine."

"Not right now anyway. Later I will or I might. Look, right now I just need to think." Damn if the woman didn't muddle up his thoughts again.

"Is that what you've been doing the past few days? Thinking?"

"Yes."

"I see."

"You do?"

"Yes. I knew you were thick headed and dense as a stone mountain. I just didn't realize how thick headed you were."

"I'm not thick headed or dense!"

"Are you certain? If you must spend over two days thinking you must surely be slow of mind."

"I'm not! I'm trying to think about what to say . . . I'm just thinking. That's all."

"Fine."

"Fine."

For the next several hours they rode in silence. He could tell from the rigid posture of her shoulders, held so taunt he thought she'd snap that things were not fine. From the way she held her lips, drawn so tight the skin around them was white, things would not be fine for some time to come. It occurred to him that maybe if he kissed her things might be fine. Then again, it would probably make matters even worse. What woman lay with a man and didn't demand marriage or even talk about it?

A woman who hated the man she was with.

CHAPTER EIGHTEEN

Next morning, after breaking camp and still barely speaking a word to each other, they soon came up on the first homesteads outside Adler Creek.

"We're almost there." Kendrick told her.

"How . . . how can you tell?"

"Those houses. I recognize them from my last trip out."

"Have you decided what to tell your family?"

"About what?"

"About me."

"I'm not sure there's anything to tell them, Bette."

"So we're back to Bette?"

"Seems so. Listen, there's something I need to tell you."

A shot rang out. In the distance Kendrick and Amanda could make out two riders approaching.

She turned and gripped his arm, alarm making the gray of her eyes look like tempered steel. "Indians? Is it Indians?"

Concentrating on seeing the riders he didn't have the time to think about how good it felt to have her hand on his arm, even in fear. "No. Don't think so. If it was, they wouldn't have sent a warning shot. Looks like White men."

A few minutes later two men, both wearing a pair of guns, their Stetsons set low on their brows, reined in beside the wagon. "Ain't you the ugliest thing I've ever seen." The dark-haired man mounted on a tawny colored stallion, its black tail and mane giving the horse a regal look, commented low while he extended his hand to Kendrick. When he tipped his hat towards Amanda, she immediately noticed the startling blue of his eyes. Like Kendrick's only so much warmer. Not that Kendrick's eyes hadn't been warmer the past couple of weeks. At times they'd been so hot she thought her skin would melt at his look. The other rider, a big blond wearing as she now saw, sheriff's star, moved his palomino closer to the wagon to shake Kendrick's hand commenting, "Yup, almost as ugly as you, Parker." He, too, tipped his hat to Amanda, "Ma'am."

"Kendrick, we got a telegram . . ." The dark-haired man started.

"I know. I know. This is Black Bette Barkley. Hope you got a cell all ready for her." The words rushed from his mouth.

"That's the thing," the blond started.

"I know who I have, Sheriff. We'll just get ourselves into town, settle Black Bette here in, and I'll contact my office and the San Francisco office." Kendrick cut him off.

The other two men exchanged a glance Amanda couldn't begin to read, grinned at Kendrick and turned their horses to head back into town alongside the wagon.

"In case you're wondering," Kendrick looked at Amanda, "the ugly black-haired fella is my lit . . . younger brother, Brett. The really repulsive looking one is Sheriff Rick Hansen, a friend of my brother's and mine."

The one called Brett looked at her, smiled, and winked as if he shared some special secret with her, "Not that it matters to Kendrick whether or not we know who you are, isn't that right, big brother?"

"Right." He glared at his brother a moment before asking, "How's your wife, Jenna? And Wolf?"

"Wolf's good. Due in town in the next few days if he's on his regular schedule. And Jenna, Ah. That. You sure you want to be discussing my family in front of the country's deadliest killer? I mean, you don't know what such a black-hearted criminal could do to an innocent family."

Mandy humphed and folded her arms over her chest,

refusing to look at either Parker brother. The Sheriff's chuckle from the other side of the wagon didn't make things better either.

"She won't be hurting anyone."

"Sure now?"

"I am. I've got the situation under control."

"Good to know you have the situation under control," the sheriff smiled at them.

"Well then," Brett answered, "my bride is just fine. Seems there was a misunderstanding about who and what she was . . ."

"You're right." Kendrick cut him off. "We'd best wait till we're in town and I've got my . . . prisoner secured before we talk. Long as Jenna's all right."

"She is. Your telegram arrived just in time. The whole situation, including the mistaken identity has been resolved. Mistaking someone's identity can create a passel of trouble, let me tell you." Brett tipped his hat to Mandy again and finished, "Still, I'm mighty glad to see you."

The sheriff only smiled at the two men, like cats that had eaten a canary.

With the sheriff riding on one side and Kendrick's brother on the other, Kendrick drove the wagon into what Amanda believed had to be the town of Adler Creek. While neither of the Wyoming lawmen spoke to or even really looked at Amanda, they cast frequent, amused, glances at Kendrick. Kendrick, meanwhile, sat looking straight ahead, practically refusing to acknowledge either of the other men.

For Amanda's part, she fought her concern for Kendrick doing too much too soon after his illness. At the same time she wondered why he wasn't catching up with his brother on what he'd been doing. She wanted to hate him.

Unfortunately, that was becoming more and more difficult with each passing day.

After being in St. Louis and seeing what she had of Lancaster, Nebraska, the town of Adler Creek should not have surprised her. Like many easterners she thought of the west as wild and completely uncivilized. With wood-planked sidewalks, glass in the windows, cleanly lettered signs on the windows and doors of the various shops, it was a town reminiscent of St. Louis and one that under other circumstances, she might have enjoyed visiting. In the first few minutes of arrival she took in the women in their multi-colored poke bonnets, the same as the women on the wagon train wore. Men in cloth and leather vests ambled down the street, most with guns strapped to their hips. A slight breeze caressed her cheek while she took in the buildings and spied what had to be Indians walking down the street, oblivious to their arrival. A buggy, sitting on high wheels, barreled by as if racing against several men on horseback.

Some of the buildings stood two stories high, a surprise from what she'd heard of the west. They stopped in front of the building marked *jail* and Kendrick helped her out of the wagon. Taking her elbow he led her into the jail and towards a cell.

The Sheriff, who Kendrick called Rick, stepped over to open the cell with Kendrick escorting her inside. "I'll bring your trunks in a bit. I need to . . . I gotta telegraph 'Frisco and let them know we've arrived."

Rick shook his head. Brett smirked. Kendrick pulled the door shut and started for the door. "You two might want to join me." He sounded definitely put out and, if she wasn't mistaken, a tad nervous.

"We just might," Brett told them, his grin growing bigger by the minute. "We just might." When the door to the jail shut, Amanda paced to the cell doorway and sighed. "I can't

179

believe those two are actually enjoying this," Amanda told the empty jail. Pacing the tiny cell, rubbing her hands up and down her arms Amanda had nothing but her thoughts to keep her company. The same thoughts that had run through her mind every waking minute since she had woken up in bed next to Kendrick Parker after she'd allowed him to take liberties with her body.

"No, he didn't take liberties, Amanda Marie Davis, you gave yourself to that man of your own free will. You wanted him, you wanted to be with him, and you gave yourself with no thought for the future. What if you are pregnant? What then? You certainly can't expect him to honor you by giving you his name. Besides, his fellow Marshals will probably arrive here soon if they haven't already come. And what will they do when they learn you are with child? Force you? Humiliate you?" She mentally shook her finger at herself.

She'd heard stories about how women in prison were allowed to give birth before being executed, their children given to strangers to raise. Would Kendrick want a child he fathered out of wedlock to someone he thought a heinous killer?

"Probably not. Maybe I'm not. It was, after all my first time and the only time." She shivered and moved to sit on the small cot in the cell. So many questions and *that man* wasn't likely to answer any of them.

Outside the jail, a few doors down, a laughing Sheriff Rick Hansen turned to Kendrick. He'd stopped so fast Kendrick and Brett almost ran into him. "You got yourself a problem, Kendrick."

"And what would that be?"

Rick reached into his pocket and handed him a slightly yellowed piece of paper. "We got this almost two months ago.

You got the wrong woman."

"I know."

"*You know*?" Brett yelled at him loud enough to cause heads to turn in their direction.

"Shhhh." Kendrick tried to hush him.

"You know? If you knew, why did you drag her out here?" Rick asked in the same low, almost disinterested voice Kendrick himself used when interrogating someone.

"I didn't know when we left St. Louis." He studied the message Rick handed him even though he already knew what it would say. Black Bette Barkley had tried to rob a bank in Sacramento, California the very day he'd met . . . make that found . . . Mandy. The woman was shot and killed as she left the building. Mandy was an innocent woman. The San Francisco office of the Marshal's service gave clear instructions that, in the event he hadn't gotten the telegram sent to St. Louis or realized his mistake before, to return her immediately to St. Louis with their apologizes. As if an apology would make up for dragging her a thousand miles from where she wanted to be and a job he now knew she wanted and desperately needed, if her worn yet well-kept clothing was any indication.

"So when *did* you know, big brother?"

Kendrick's lips flattened as he expelled a breath through his nose. Squinting his eyes while looking down the street, not seeing the Adler Creek, but St. Louis. "I don't know. I suppose when we were a couple of days out."

"What was it that happened to get you thinking about that?" Brett asked.

"The way she was. How she is. She read to the kids on the wagon train, started teaching them. She tried to tell me she was a teacher when I arrested her. When I checked her belongings, you know, after the arrest, she had a considerable amount of school supplies in her trunks. Amanda knew just how to draw the children out. And even though I knew she wasn't fond of me she made sure I had food and when she washed her clothes, she took mine, too. Domestic type things.

"Just outside Independence Billy McCaffrey, a deputy in St. Louis, caught up with us with part of a telegram that arrived the day we pulled out. I had a feeling it said I had the wrong woman. By time he got there it was pretty tattered and only a few words could be made out."

"Didn't he know what it said?" Rick asked.

"No. Idiot doesn't read. All he knew was that the Sheriff said it wasn't good. I tried to tell myself that they were warning me she was more dangerous than we thought, but deep down I knew that wasn't so."

"Then why didn't you go back and check it out?"

"Why? I had to get out here with the evidence clearing your wife."

"It wouldn't have taken that long and you could have telegraphed me. You'da probably made better time traveling alone coming back out this way."

"Maybe. It's easy to say what I shoulda done now. At the time I had to go with what I thought."

"And when this Billy showed up you still thought she was guilty?"

"I didn't know. Then just outside Lancaster, Nebraska, I took ill and she could have run. She could have just left me and run off. But she didn't. She took care of me. Nursed me back to health. She's a good woman." He wasn't going to tell his brother and friend he suspected he had violated her. They already thought him beyond redemption with his behavior. No way was he going to confirm their suspicions.

"So let me ask you this." Rick drew his attention. "Why is she sitting in my jail if you know she's innocent and you dragged the wrong woman halfway across the country?"

Kendrick chewed the inside of his mouth and looked down

as if his boots held the answer. "'Cause I want her."

"You *what*?" Brett's shout caused several other people to glance in their direction.

"Because I . . ."

"I heard you. I can't believe you. Damn, Kendrick, you're a Deputy United States Marshal! You don't drag a woman around the country because you *want* her. I can't believe I have to be the one to tell my big brother this. You let her know you are interested in her. If you thought you wanted her you could have told her so in St. Louis and asked her if she'd wait a bit for you to return and court her proper. Then you court her and when the time's right you go down on one knee and you ask her to marry you." Brett bit the words out.

"Yeah, Kendrick. That's the way you do it. Just like your little brother here did. Yup, bide your time, let her know in subtle little ways for oh, how long, Brett? A few months at least, huh? Yeah, all that flowery stuff wins every time, don't it Brett?" Rick couldn't hold back a chuckle as he taunted his friend.

Kendrick couldn't miss the glare Brett sent Rick's way. "Something I should know about you and your bride?"

"Nope." Brett answered at the same time Rick answered, "Yup."

"Sure now?" Kendrick studied his younger brother.

"Look. Maybe Jenna and I had a few little ruts on the road to where we are now. I love my wife and she loves me. That's all that counts."

"Oh I don't know, Brett. Those ruts were more like caverns. Jenna wasn't very interested in marrying anyone and your little brother here was bound and determined . . ."

Brett cut him off, "We can discuss my courtship later. Right now *you* have the problem of having a woman in our jail who doesn't belong there. What are you going to do about it?"

Kendrick pushed his Stetson back on his head and pursed

his lips. "I don't rightly know. I care for her. I want to be with her. Shit. I want to marry the woman and spend the rest of my life with her. I suppose I could ask her to return east with me when I bring Carlman back to stand trial and court her on the trail."

Rick ignored the part about Carlman and mildly asked, "You told her any of that?"

"No. Haven't quite gotten around to telling her that. She . . . ah . . . she has a bit of a problem with me. I have a feeling if I tell her I know she's innocent, that I got . . . that the right woman's in California, that the problem will be a tad bigger and she won't take too kindly to me."

"I can see that. Especially when you get around to telling her that Bette's dead and you had a feeling all along she wasn't the right one."

"Or that she *is* the right one," Rick chuckled.

Both Parker men glared at him.

"Well, if the way she looked at you when you put her in that cell is any indication, she already doesn't take too kindly to you." Brett informed him.

"I know. Believe me, I know. So what do we do?"

"Uh, what do you mean by 'we', big brother? Some example you set for me."

"Surely you have some idea?"

"Why, because I'm a happily married man?"

Rick coughed, making Kendrick wonder not for the first time just what the story was with his brother's marriage.

"Okay, how about this? How about we take her on out to your place and she has a nice hot bath and change of clothes and a good meal and when she sees how you and Jenna get along I ask her if maybe she wouldn't like a life like that?" Kendrick looked hopefully towards his brother.

"Huh?" Brett looked him over. "Do you think that a few niceties are going to make her think what you did is just fine?"

"I don't know. It's a start."

"Well I'll agree with one thing." Rick interjected. "Getting her out of that cell is the first thing you need to do. I've had enough trouble with the women in this town having an innocent woman spend her time in jail."

"Shit! I almost forgot! With all this around my Amanda it slipped my mind. Brett, your Jenna, everything is okay there, right? You said she was okay out on the trail, but seriously? Everything is settled for her? I mean since I didn't see her in the jail my telegram helped and all's well."

"Yeah. I'll fill you in later. You should know, however, Carlman's dead."

"What? How?"

"In short, he tried to kidnap Jenna and fell on his partner's knife. Just from what your telegram said he got off easy."

"Damn." Kendrick thought for a few seconds then smiled, "So looks like I'll have some time here to court Miss Mandy."

"Would that be before or after you tell her the truth?" Kendrick saw Rick could barely restrain the smile that threatened to bloom.

The three men walked back towards the jail. Kendrick stopped Brett just before they entered. "So we can come stay with you, right?"

"Hey! Do you really think you need to ask? Stupid as I think you are right now, it's still your home. Anytime you want to move out this way and stay, it's your home too."

"Thanks."

Without waiting for the Parker brothers, Rick strode over to the cell and unlocked the door. "Miss . . . Davis?" At her confused nod he continued. "Seems there has been a little mistake. Marshal Parker . . . that would be Deputy United States Marshal Kendrick Parker, would like to tell you about it." Rick clearly was enjoying rubbing his mistake into him.

Amanda stepped from the cell. Even covered with dirt

from the past two days, tired from caring for him, her hair mussed, she was the most beautiful woman Kendrick Parker had ever laid eyes on.

She gazed at Rick, "You called me Miss Davis. You know? You know my real name?" Anger replaced the bewildered expression she'd had when speaking to Rick; her voice hard she glared at Kendrick, "Something you want to tell me, Marshal?"

"Uh. Yeah. Um, Brett, Rick, you two want to go get some coffee or something?"

"Oh no. Not me," Rick chuckled and went to sit behind his desk.

"Me neither. I got nothing better to do than be right here." Brett added as he planted his hip on the edge of one of the desks.

"Okay." Kendrick swallowed. "How about some coffee, Mandy? Would you like some coffee? Rick and Brett could go get you some."

"No, thank you." She sighed. "And once again it seems I must remind you, my name is, as the kind Sheriff here addressed me, Amanda. Amanda Davis."

"No coffee. Well how about some tea. I know you like tea. I've seen you drink it." Damn if he didn't sound like some wet behind the ears twelve-year-old with his first crush.

"No, no tea. Thank you. What is it you wish to tell me, Marshal?"

"Fine. No coffee, no tea. How about water? They could go . . . leave us and get . . . well, would you like . . ."

"Tarnation, Marshal! What is it you have to say to me?" He didn't like how very much like a schoolteacher correcting her student she sounded.

"You need to know . . . well actually, you see . . . ah, Rick here got a telegram and . . . Well Brett saw it . . ."

"Could you please spit it out, Marshal?" She was back

calling him *Marshal* instead of Kendrick. Not a good sign at all.

"Sure. I can do that. Well you see. Out in California, Sacramento to be exact, there was an incident and well it happened at a bank, if I recall what I heard — errr — read correctly and well, wouldn't you know it . . ."

"For a man of few words, except to order me around, it appears you have lost your ability for coherent speech. *What* is it you are trying to tell me, Marshal?"

"Ah, well, it appears you aren't Black Bette Barkley."

The sound of her hand hitting his jaw in a resounding crack echoed through the jail.

CHAPTER NINETEEN

"Well," Rick dryly observed. "Guess that tells you what the lady thinks of your admission there, Kendrick."

Kendrick fingered his jaw, looking at Mandy with renewed interest. "I knew she was feisty. I just didn't expect anything like that."

"*She* is standing right here so I'll thank you to stop speaking about me as if I'm some useless object or too dim-witted to understand you. As I previously stated, you, sir are a pompous jackass and reprobate. If you had just once . . . *just once* . . . bothered to listen to me, you would have seen I could not possibly have been the woman you accused me of being. But *you* had to be in charge, didn't you? *You* had to be all mighty right and the *big* hero, didn't you? It had to be your way. Just what do you propose to do to make things up to me? *What*?"

"Well I was thinking . . . ."

"You were thinking. Now isn't that a novel concept. Kendrick Parker can think. Or so he thinks he can think because that's what he said he was doing for *days* on the trail." She tapped her chin as if discovering a new theory.

"Now, Mandy . . ."

"Don't you dare *now Mandy* me." She shook her finger at him before she turned, oblivious to her general state of disarray, and faced Rick. "Sheriff, arrest this man."

"Arrest him? Well now, Miss Davis is it? You know, Parker men take being slapped in the face as a part of their courtship. Seems you just let him know you're amenable to being courted. Isn't that right, Brett?"

"Jenna slap you, Brett?" Kendrick asked.

Brett chuckled until he caught Amanda's glare. "I have no idea what slapping Parker men has to do with courtship and I have no desire to find out. At least you, Mr. Parker the younger, have the good sense to listen when someone speaks to you. Yes, Sheriff, I'd like him arrested. He has kidnapped me, defamed me, taken my sole source of income from me. And that is just for starters."

"Ma'am, I'm not sure . . ."

"Not sure? What? Are you in cahoots with him?"

Unable to hold back his laughter any longer Brett burst out with loud guffaws, doubling over from how hard he laughed. "Ken . . . Kendrick . . . cahoots? You really did it this . . . this . . . *ouch*! What'd you stomp on my foot for? I'm not the one who took you against your . . . w-w-will!" Laughter shook his entire big-boned frame, his bright blue eyes twinkling with mirth.

"Of course, since he is the elder brother making a mockery of this, some of your behavior can be excused. You had to learn such reprehensible actions somewhere and no doubt it is from this miscreant. And as for you!" She turned to Rick, "Do not think for an instant you are innocent of any wrongdoing. The lack of response to my request on your part indicates complicity in his actions."

Rick's jaw dropped and he stared at Amanda a good few breaths before turning to Kendrick. "What did she just say?"

"Basically that you are as bad as I am. Mandy kinda gets a bit uppity with her words."

"You oaf!" She stomped on his foot and marched towards the door to leave.

"Whoa, whoa!" Kendrick grabbed her arm.

"Despite my appearance, no thanks to you, you hardheaded bully, I am not a horse. Now release my arm."

"Mandy." She fought the feeling of warmth as he pulled her closer to him. "I'm sorry. Really I am. I'll make it up to you. Somehow. I promise. Listen, I've already made arrangements for you to stay at Brett's place. He's got this big ole ranch and his wife, Jenna, will love to have the company until we can make whatever arrangements . . ."

"Arrangements? Marshal Parker, I am not a piece of furniture to be arranged. If this mule headed clod," she gestured toward Rick, "will not do his duty and arrest your sorry carcass, I will await the magistrate and have him deal with the hoard of you."

"H-h-h-hoard. Oh my God. Kendrick, she's . . . *ouch*! Lady you got to stop stomping on my foot like that. My wife won't take kindly to . . . ouch, now you stop it." She walloped him again, this time above his ear just before she pulled on it while she reached for the letter opener on the desk. Before Kendrick could stop her, she was rapping it on Brett's knuckles.

"Well if that don't prove she's a schoolteacher, I don't know what does." Rick managed between chuckles.

"Rick, shut up. Brett, you're only making things worse. Mandy, please, listen to me." Kendrick all but pleaded.

"Listen to you? Why do I always have to listen to you, but you never have the presence of mind to listen to me? Do you realize if you had, just once listened to me, I would be happily teaching in the school in St. Louis and would never have had to endure your infuriating presence?"

"That's enough." Laughter completely gone from Rick's tone that was pitched low yet brooked no defiance. "Brett, Kendrick, out. Now. This is my jail in my town and I'm not about to have the peace disturbed because you two have no sense when it comes to a lady. Out!"

"Rick . . ." Brett started.

"Out."

Rick watched the Parker brothers leave, the movement of

Brett's shoulders as he walked out the door indicating he was still laughing, irritating both Amanda and Kendrick no end. At least they had that in common.

Amanda's "Well, I see how it is. You will allow that miscreant to depart while I am detained here with you" almost had Rick laughing again as well.

Raising a brow, Rick took two steps back towards his desk, leaning against it. His one butt cheek half sitting on it, arms folded, he waited for Amanda to speak.

"Well, Sheriff. Have you something to say to me?"

"Damn if you don't sound like a schoolteacher. It defies my comprehension how Kendrick didn't pick up on that."

"You mock me?"

He blew out a sigh. "No, ma'am. I'm not mocking you. I'm trying to figure out how to make this right. The Parker boys, they . . . well they are a bit different. For all their . . . civilized appearances, they can be a bit wild and impetuous. All but Wolf that is. For some reason he's the only one of them that thinks before he acts. Then again, growing up with those two around, especially Brett, guess he learned from their mistakes."

"Wolf? There is another brother? Did his mother dislike him so she named him after an animal?"

"No. Actually his mother loved him a great deal so she named him after the bravest animal she could think of. Her own . . . totem."

"He's . . . why that sneak. That deplorable sneak."

"Kendrick do something else that has you . . . perturbed?"

"Yes, indeed he did. I asked him in the very beginning if he'd ever seen an Indian and it appears his brother is one. Surely with that piece of information you can see the man isn't to be trusted."

"Sorry, no. I don't. Miss Mandy, I know you are upset. Anyone would be. You have to understand I can't arrest him for doing his job. Kendrick, Marshal Parker, believed you were Black Bette Barkley. You do resemble her, and you were in an area it was suspected she might go to. You can't bring charges against him for doing his job. The problem is, how do we make it right for you? In the long term he'll get you back to St. Louis or wherever you want to go. The Marshal's service will write a letter or issue a statement that you were arrested in error and your record will be cleared. I'm sure Kendrick or his boss will intercede in your behalf with the school you were supposed to teach at and have your position given back to you. That's in the long term.

"Meanwhile, we have to get you to wherever you want to go and find you a place to stay until we can make those arrangements. I'm sure Kendrick'd take you back east this minute, but I don't think you care to be in his company right now."

"No. I don't. If I ever see him again, it will be too soon."

"Yeah, well, Adler Creek isn't that big of a town, so more likely than not you will see him. Don't mean you have to talk to him and if you want, I'll tell him to stay away from you and not talk to you."

"I'd appreciate that."

"So, our first problem is for you to decide where you want to go. Our second is getting you there. Dusty's already headed back to St. Louis and it will be at least four months till he's back this way again. Brett could probably take you, except his wife, Jenna, is expecting and would be on her time more likely than not before he got back. That leaves me and I can't exactly leave town for a few months, so that means you are going to have to stay here for a spell."

CHAPTER TWENTY

"Stay? Here? No. I . . . can someone take me to Lancaster?"
"Lancaster?"

"Yes, Lancaster, Nebraska, where we stayed when Marshal Parker took ill."

Rick considered that, it wasn't the solution Kendrick wanted. Not by a long shot. His whole choice of options was merely to give Amanda some time to calm down so Kendrick could press his suit with her. "I'll ahhhh, I'll have to see if someone can do that. That's a long-term solution. Meanwhile, we need to find a place for you to stay here in Adler Creek. Now we do have a hotel and I'm sure Kendrick will be more than happy to pay for your board there."

"Absolutely not. I will not be beholden *that* man or perceived a kept woman."

"Okay. Well, then, as you know, Brett offered to let you stay at his place. His wife, Jenna, arrived here about a year ago from New York. She had her rough times before marrying Brett. You might like her. In fact, I'm sure you would. In a way, you two have a lot in common."

"And what would that be? Knowing one of the loathsome Parker brothers?"

"Yeah, that too. And dang if you don't have a way with words." He shook his head. "So, what will it be? The hotel or the Parker ranch?"

"I'll stay here."

"In the jail?" He couldn't believe how his voice squeaked when he asked her. "No, ma'am. Absolutely not. Like I told

Kendrick, I've had enough problems lately with innocent women staying in the jail . . ."

"You detain women here on a regular basis, Sheriff?"

"No. Jenna . . . well when you meet her, give her a little time to know you and I'm sure she'll explain. Trust me, she went through a rough situation. It was pretty bad for awhile there."

"Did Brett do something to her?"

"Brett? No. He protected her. From the outset he would have laid his life down for her. No. I've already said too much. Wait till you know her a bit, but you can't stay here."

He watched as indecision followed anger which was followed by confusion crossing her face. Getting her to Lancaster, if that was where she wanted to go, wouldn't be that big of a problem. No, the problem was he was trying to help his childhood friend out of the mess he'd gotten himself into and to give him a chance to court the woman he was so set on having.

"Might I have a glass of water?"

That surprised him "Certainly. Just water? Don't want some coffee or tea?"

"What I would really like is a shot of whiskey, but that would not be a very lady like request so that water will be fine."

Chuckling to himself Rick went into the back where the jail had a little kitchenette and returned with the glass of water, which Amanda drank down before handing him back the glass.

"So? Short term?"

"I suppose Mr. Parker's house will do. That is, if you are certain his wife will not mind, not that you can speak for her or him but . . ."

"Not a problem. Brett offered and I can assure you, Jenna will be more than happy to have you there." At least he hoped so. When Brett said he had sent for a mail order bride and Jenna showed up Rick was certain that it was the ultimate in Parker Brother Folly. This business with Kendrick far out ran any of Brett's idiocies over the years.

"Can't believe he threw me out of my own office," dark hair, blue eyed Brett Parker groused.

"He wasn't too happy, was he?" Kendrick commiserated.

"No. You really did it this time."

"I did? Listen, I was just bringing you what I promised — the documentation to absolve your wife from any wrongdoing. So what happened?"

Brett gestured towards Milly's cafe. "And went and arrested an innocent woman and then dragged her all the way out here. How about a coffee and something to eat?"

Kendrick scrubbed his jaw. "What I need is a bath. Hell, Mandy needs one too."

"You saying she smells?"

"No. Just thinking how neat she is. She's one of those women who has a place for everything and everything in its place. You should have seen her tru . . . Yeah, something to eat would be good."

In the café they settled into seats far from the few other late afternoon patrons, ordered some sandwiches and Kendrick once again prodded Brett. "So?"

"Well, a little over a year ago Henry Bascom, the banker, got this idea to send for some mail order brides."

"And you sent for one?"

Brett studied his older brother, knowing if he lied Kendrick would know because Jenna would eventually spill the beans. "Not really. Before the wagon train with the women arrived one of Dusty's men, Zeke, rode into town and mentioned there was one woman who seemed kind of troubled. I spoke up and said she was my bride. To this day Rick hasn't stopped buggin' me about my making that up."

"So you didn't plan to have a woman come on out, but there was a spare one and you just up and claimed her?"

"That's not exactly . . ."

"And how is that different from my escorting Mandy out this way?"

"Escorting? Kendrick, you arrested her!"

"Yeah, well, why did you pick Jenna?"

"Just a feeling. It's hard to explain what it was like. I just had a feeling about her. Something I couldn't ignore. So I rode out with the men who had sent for brides and knew which one was Jenna right off. I didn't think it was possible until I met her but I'm sure I fell in love with her then and there. She didn't want to get married. It wasn't just me. She didn't want to marry anyone. I knew she was hiding something, but she wouldn't tell me. I had this feeling that if I didn't marry her right off, I'd lose her, so I pushed it and we got married almost right after she got here."

"So there wasn't one of the considered courtships you were telling me I needed to pursue."

Brett chose to ignore Kendrick's question. "It took some time to get her to come around to trust me, to see I really cared for her."

"It wasn't all that different when I first saw Mandy. I had been thinking about that Black Bette and Brett, you have to admit, there *is* a resemblance. I saw her and it was like a kick in the gut." He looked around, making sure no one heard him. "This isn't easy for me to say."

"I understand."

"You do? Yeah, I guess you might. I saw her and I couldn't stay away. I was so sure she was Bette, but I think I knew all along she wasn't. There was just something . . . I don't know."

"I do know what you mean. It's a feeling, one you can't

shake. You just know that you need to be with her."

"That's it. That's exactly it. So you and Jenna, she agreed to the marriage easy enough?"

"Yup. Once she did, things were good, really good and then one day this fella, Julian Carlman, showed up. He claimed all kinds of rash things about Jenna: that she stole from him, that she tried to kill him, and she promised to marry him. He was all set to take her back east. Rick put her up in the jail, for her own protection. That's where the business about him putting innocent women in jail comes from. There was something about Carlman . . . which you found out . . . that wasn't right."

The waitress brought their meals and refilled their coffees.

"When I heard you had him in custody it made my day. Heck, it made my year. Marshal's service had been after him for years. We'd get close and then he'd slip the noose, or it would seem someone else was the guilty party. He was a slippery one."

Brett nodded in agreement and watched as Kendrick took a big bite out of his roast beef sandwich and savored the home cooking before continuing, "We got your telegram and Jenna was released, Carlman arrested and then he broke out and kidnapped Jenna. When we caught up with them, he was set to . . . hurt her. Fool had this no-good jackal with him and when Carlman came after me he tripped and fell on the other man's knife. Killed him. You'd already left New York by the time I sent the telegram letting you know you didn't need to come. I sent another to Washington, and same answer. I wasn't sure where you'd turn up next."

"Seems like I've been missing a lot of important telegrams."

"Yeah?"

"Yeah. Yours, the one from the 'Frisco office that they had Black Bette and to leave Amanda be."

"Wolf would say maybe you were supposed to miss them."

"How do you mean?"

"Well, if you had gotten any of them, you wouldn't have met Mandy and you did say you love her?"

"You saying it was fated?"

"Could be."

"You think you and Jenna were?"

"Maybe. I'll tell you big brother, things didn't start out too well for us and I was an ass about some things. My marriage is good now and I will do everything and anything I can to keep it that way. I love that woman more than life itself."

Kendrick sighed. "I'd like a marriage like that someday."

"With Mandy?"

"If she'll have me. If I can find a way to turn her around about me. Say, you think we could get the preacher to marry us — like get her to marry me and then explain . . ."

"No."

"Hear me out."

"Kendrick, I am not going to help you trick that woman into marrying you. I can't believe you'd even think along those lines."

"I know, I know. Brett, since I've met her, I've done more stupid things, thought more stupid things. It's like I've lost all sense."

"Love'll do that. Trust me. I know. I almost lost Jenna with a few of those stupid things. Just be honest, listen to what she wants and try your damndest to give it to her."

"I hope I can turn her thinking about me around. And, for starters, she's gotta be hungry. I think I'll take her one of these sandwiches and a slice of that peach pie I saw when we came in."

They returned to the jail just as Rick was updating Tom

McKendrick, the other deputy, on what had transpired the last twenty-four hours. That was, except for the part about Kendrick putting Amanda in jail. The other man acted as if he didn't notice Amanda's state of dress and demeanor.

In a perverse way, Rick was pleased to see Kendrick looking so sheepish when he followed Brett back into the jail. Except for Brett's black and Kendrick's blond hair the men looked practically identical, like two sides of the same coin.

Kendrick cautiously approached her. "Uh, Mandy, I, uh, well I thought you might be hungry. That you might want a little something before . . . well before you go wherever you are going tonight." He quickly handed her the sack with the sandwich. "There's pie too."

"Thank you." She turned and primly walked over to Rick's desk, sat on the visitor's side, and took out the sandwich, ignoring the men.

"So," Brett began. "Miss Davis decide where she'd like to stay?"

"Said she'd go on out to your place, as long as you understand she doesn't want to have Kendrick speak to her."

"Awww, Rick, come on." Kendrick blurted out.

"She doesn't want anything to do with you. So for now, if you really want to have her in your life, honor that." Rick spoke low.

"Not a problem, Rick," Brett assured him. "I'll get her home and into Jenna's care and keeping."

"You do that." Rick told him with a nod.

"And where does *she* expect me to stay?" Kendrick put in, pointedly ignoring Amanda.

"As far away from me as possible." Amanda didn't hesitate to tell him before primly taking another small bite of the sandwich.

CHAPTER TWENTY-ONE

For the first time since meeting Kendrick Parker, Amanda felt somewhat relaxed. Settling on the seat of the wagon she and Kendrick traveled in she sat almost eye to eye where he stood. Yes, she felt a bit at ease, but not much, just somewhat, given their past history, which wasn't long at all. At least he now knew he'd made a mistake. The problem was, how was he going to undo the damage he'd done? Her reputation was in shreds. Everyone in St. Louis would know she'd been accused of a crime. Well, not everyone, but enough people and most especially the school. That Billy McCaffrey would have blabbed the whole story, or at least his version of it to all and sundry. What did they think when the teacher they might be hiring to come teach didn't show? Worse, what if she were expecting?

Her "Oh no!" startled him.

"Something wrong, Miss Davis?" Rick asked her in that same mild tone Kendrick noted he used when speaking to her.

"Yes. Oh dear. This is awful."

"What's wrong?" Kendrick asked.

"Obviously you are not a man of your word." Amanda rebuffed him.

"I am so!"

"Uh huh. If you are, why did you break it by speaking to me?"

"You have a problem. It's probably my fault. I'd like to help you fix it."

"Fine. Send your heartfelt apology to the school in St. Louis *for kidnapping me*. Better yet, why don't you leave for St. Louis now and don't bother coming back?"

"So you planning on staying here, Mandy?" He gave her his best smile, the one the simpering misses seemed to fall for every time. Problem was, Mandy was never a simpering miss.

"Not that it is any concern of yours, I haven't quite decided yet where I will reside. Wherever it is, it will not be within a hundred miles of you." She turned in the wagon seat and pointedly looked away from him.

"I'll wire a message tomorrow with an explanation of what a . . . reprobate I am."

"Guess she told you." Brett muttered loud enough for everyone to hear.

With silence prevailing as Brett climbed up on the seat beside her — it being clear to everyone what a huge mistake it would be for Kendrick to ride beside her — and clucked the horses into moving. Relaxing ever so slight, Mandy took the time to look around her and take in the breathtaking view. For miles around her there was nothing but open space. Not unlike the trail, but in its own way different. There was more grass and sage. The first signs of spring were peeking out in bits of green, against a crystalline blue sky. The temperature was near perfect for taking a long walk. Maybe living here wouldn't be bad . . . as long as Kendrick Parker wasn't around.

On the trail he'd talked about the war starting in the east. Maybe he'd go back to fight. Maybe he'd die!

She held back the gasp as she realized she didn't want that. Not really. Amanda didn't wish him ill, she just wished she'd never met him.

Even more, she wished she had found another way to keep him warm that night. The cad never said a word to her after. He took his pleasure and never said another word. It was as if it didn't happen to him. Well, it happened to her and it was unlike anything she'd ever felt before in her life. Undoubtedly it would never happen again, because she'd never let Kendrick Parker get that close again. There was no way she could allow it to happen, simply because she hated him. She really did. She hated that blond hair of his and hated his blue eyes and hated his smile and mostly she hated how she felt around him.

A short while after riding out from town they pulled up to a house that was larger and more elegant than the Haynes'. The house was everything Amanda would have wanted for herself with its whitewashed wraparound porch, two stories tall with window boxes dotting the first-floor windows it was perhaps the most charming home she'd ever seen. There was a porch swing, just like the house she'd imagined for herself, near the front door along with two rocking chairs where a body could sit and enjoy the sunset or just admire the lush land for miles around made her long for a home just like this one. Immediately Amanda conjured up thoughts of sitting in one of those rockers reading a book, only to have the image replaced with one of her and Kendrick sitting on the porch swing kissing, and not one of those sweet innocent kisses. No. One like they'd had when he'd made love to her.

No. He didn't make love to me. It was sex and he's long forgotten it. Sudden humiliation brought a rosy color to her cheeks. She knew it. The warmth she felt creeping up her neck to her cheeks told her she was blushing. In that instant Amanda knew the reason Kendrick either forgot or didn't mention even kissing her was because she was so pitiful, so miserable in bed the thought of touching her again disgusted him to no end. *No. That's not right. If I disgusted him, he wouldn't talk to me the way he does. He'd be glad to be rid of me. So why?*

Before she could ruminate further, a dark-haired woman, just showing the first bit of her pregnancy stepped out on the porch. "Brett, honey? Is everything all right?"

"Sure is darlin'," he assured her as he jumped off his horse and in two steps was on the porch with his arms going around her.

"Then why are you home? Why is Rick here?"

"We have some company! The ugly blond there is my big brother, Kendrick. The pretty little blond is Miss Amanda Davis of . . . from the east coast."

"Oh my goodness! Kendrick! You've come!" The brunette that Amanda now deduced was Jenna, stepped off the porch and rushed up to Kendrick. "Climb down here this instant and give your sister-in-law a big hug!"

Kendrick didn't need to be told twice. He jumped off his horse and picked Jenna up, whooped and swung her around in a quick circle before Brett grabbed hold of his wife. "You'll have plenty of time to swing your nephew around in a few years. Don't be upsetting my wife now."

"Honey, we could be having a girl and he hasn't upset me."

Brett gave her a quick kiss. "Trust me, it's a boy and Kendrick's nothing but bad news."

"If I'm such bad news why did you ask me to look into . . . she knows doesn't she?"

"Yes, Kendrick, I do. There is no way I can repay you for what you've done for me." Jenna assured him.

Amanda watched as Jenna walked back over to him and wrapping her arms around his waist, with one hand on his cheek, pulled him down to give him a sisterly kiss. Amanda couldn't believe the green-eyed monster that rose up in her at the simple innocent action.

"Oh my." Jenna turned toward Amanda. "I am so sorry. Please forgive my rudeness! Miss Davis, I am pleased to meet you. Please, please come inside."

Kendrick stepped over to help Amanda off the wagon, prompting her to slide to the other side and jump down on her own. Glaring at Kendrick, she calmly told Jenna, "I am most pleased to meet you as well and there is no need to apologize. I've shown up on your doorstep unannounced and disrupted your entire day."

"Nonsense. It's a pleasure to have a guest. Are you and Kendrick staying long?"

"We're not . . . that is . . ."

"I arrested her."

"You?" A puzzled Jenna looked from Kendrick to Rick to Brett and finally to Amanda. "Brett, is this some sort of joke?"

"No, it's not. The marshal there," Amanda made the word *Marshal* sound like a dirty word, "refused to listen to me when I told him I was not the woman he thought I was, did not bother to ascertain whether or not he had the right person and bodily dragged me from what was to be my new home in St. Louis here to your doorstep. It was his intent to send me to San Francisco to stand trial. It was his fondest wish I be hung by the neck until death."

"Well that about sums it up." Brett dryly commented.

Jenna smiled. "Now doesn't that sound familiar? Well, come inside you two. Let's get you settled in."

Behind them, Kendrick only muttered, "Uppity."

Chapter Twenty-two

Showing Amanda upstairs to one of the bedrooms, Jenna commented, "Seems you and Kendrick aren't on the best of terms."

"That would be an understatement."

"Well sometimes rough starts end up in the best marriages."

"Marriage? To Kendrick Parker? I assure you, that is *not* something that will happen in this lifetime. That man is the most overbearing, opinionated, obnoxious, rude miscreant to be born. The simple concept of listening to what another person has to say does not enter into his comprehension. It is what he wants, when he wants, how he wants without consideration for anyone else."

Jenna smiled to herself. Kendrick and Brett were definitely cut from the same cloth.

"It appears that's a family trait. At least with the older brothers. We'll talk more when you've had a nice hot bath and rested. Marta, our housekeeper, will be bringing up some hot water shortly and I'll have Brett bring up your trunks."

"Mrs. Parker . . ."

"Jenna. Please call me Jenna."

"Jenna. And please call me Amanda."

"Amanda it is."

"Jenna, please accept my apologies for that outburst. I was rude and that was inappropriate."

"Oh, Amanda, I understand completely. I made that trip myself just in the past year and know what it's like to wish for a hot bath and a soft bed. Traveling with strangers to a place you never intended to go to makes it much more difficult. Marrying Brett was the last thing I expected before I met him. And as to the overbearing, opinionated and obnoxious — that is a Parker trait from the men's father. It definitely comes from the male side of the family because Wolf is actually kind, considerate and one of the sweetest men you could ever meet."

"So this Wolf isn't Kendrick's brother?"

"Not by blood. Whitney and Clarissa were Kendrick's parents. Clarissa died when Kendrick was a baby. Brett said he was two or three when it happened. Whitney married Fallen Leaf and they had Brett when Kendrick was, oh maybe four. It was right after that Kendrick's grandparents sent for him and brought him back east. Whitney died when Brett was nine or ten and a year or so later Fallen Leaf married another man and they had Wolf. Wolf is about eleven years younger than Brett. I'll tell you, Wolf's personality is so different from Brett's and from what you just said about Kendrick it has to come from the Parker line."

"You completely lost me!"

"It does sound confusing when you first hear it. After you've had some rest, I'm sure it will make much more sense. Ah, here comes Marta now. We'll talk later. I'm looking forward to hearing what's been happening back east and even though the Emporium does its best carrying patterns, they are usually slow in coming so of course I want to hear about the latest styles."

The Parkers' housekeeper came down the hallway, telling the man with her to hurry along with the hot water. "Franco, *por favor*, while the *agua esta caliente!*"

Seeing Amanda's puzzled expression Jenna explained, "Marta and Franco speak Spanish and sometimes they speak in half Spanish, half English sentences. You get used to it pretty quickly and it makes much more sense than you'd think."

Amanda nodded just as Marta came up to them.

"Marta, this is Amanda, a friend of Brett's brother. Amanda, Marta and Franco."

"Hello, Marta, Franco. I am pleased to meet you."

Marta smiled, her grin showing she was pleased to have Amanda there. "I am pleased to meet you too. You gonna make Mr. Kendrick an honest man, huh?"

"Mr. Ken . . . ah, no. I'll be leaving soon. Maybe even in a day or so."

"I no think so. It very easy to see a couple that belong together, just like me and Franco."

Jenna winked at Amanda, giving her the heads up that this was not the time to debate the issue with Marta because the other woman would surely win, especially with how tired Amanda was.

Leaving Amanda to settle in, Jenna headed back downstairs to see what her husband was about. Finding him stepping out of the room they'd given Kendrick, she stood on tiptoe to give him a quick kiss on the cheek.

"What was that for?"

She sighed, trying to sound completely put upon. "My husband comes home in the middle of the day and rather than just coming home for a romantic interlude with me, he brings his best friend, his brother and a woman that brother can't keep his eyes off of and he wants to know why I kissed him."

"That so?"

"Yes. You start my heart pounding and my tummy swirling and with all these people I can't have my wicked way with you! So! I expect you to make it up to me tonight the very minute we are alone."

"We're alone now." Brett put one arm around her shoulder, the other hand resting on the slight swell of her belly and gave her a quick kiss.

"Much as I'd like to show you how much I missed you this morning and despite the fact your brother and his lady are occupied, Rick is still downstairs, isn't he?"

"Ah. Yeah. Rick. Forgot about him."

"Poor Rick. Besides, I need to check with Marta about dinner."

Brett started back down the stairs with her, the two heading towards the kitchen where Rick was already sitting with a cup of coffee chatting with Marta.

"Everybody settling in?" The blond-haired sheriff asked.

"I think so. Amanda looked pretty tired, so I suspect she'll be taking a nap before she comes back downstairs."

"From what Kendrick said, she's had a tough few weeks," Rick told them.

Jenna handed Brett a cup of coffee and poured a glass of milk for herself. "So what is their story?" she asked, sitting beside her husband.

"I tell you their story." Marta broke in. "Those two are in love. Just like you and Mr. Brett and just like you and Mr. Brett they don't know it. Not yet. Someone got to tell them before they waste time like you and Mr. Brett did." With her hands on her hips, she stood there defying Brett and Jenna to dispute her claim.

"Why, Marta Fuentes. I think you must be mistaken. From what Brett told me before Jenna arrived, they'd been corresponding and just about totally in love before she even arrived. Match made in heaven." Rick teased.

"Come and sit with us," Jenna asked the older woman. She adored Marta and Franco. While they might be the family's housekeeper and ranch manager, they were like family to her. It took some doing when Jenna first arrived for Marta to accept that Jenna expected her to join her and Brett for some meals. Once the older woman learned Jenna genuinely meant what she said, she often did join them.

"Least I got a wife, Rick." Brett shot at him, speaking low.

"When the time's right and the right one appears, I'll know it and sweep her right off her feet."

"I think Marta is right. Amanda says she's not at all fond of Kendrick. Any fool can see something in her eyes. And Kendrick . . . he doesn't even try to hide the fact he's following her with his eyes. I may not know much about many men, but he's definitely smitten. The way he kept putting himself between Amanda and Rick was quite a show," Jenna observed.

"I enjoyed that myself." Brett laughed.

"Kendrick's welcome to her. He'd got one thing right. When she talks, she does sound pretty uppity."

"She does that only to rile me." Kendrick walked in, hair still damp from washing, freshly shaved and in a clean flannel shirt and pants.

Marta stood, "You hungry Mr. Kendrick?"

"You sit right back down Marta. I can see the coffee pot from here and think I remember where you keep bread and meat."

While Kendrick pulled out sandwich makings Brett asked, "So does it rile you?"

"How she talks? Nope. She can be downright entertaining." He brought his sandwich and coffee to the table. "So Mandy taking a bath?"

"She is. I'll be surprised if she doesn't take a nice long nap after. And, to be honest, I'm kind of tired myself so if you gentlemen and lady will excuse me, I am going to catch a few winks before dinner."

CHAPTER TWENTY-THREE

As darkness fell Jenna tiptoed upstairs to check on Amanda. When there was no answer at her soft knock, she cracked the door open and peered inside.

Amanda lay curled up in the bed, sound asleep. Deciding to let her guest sleep and bring up a tray later, Jenna turned back around to leave.

"Mrs. Parker? Jenna?"

"Amanda! I'm sorry I woke you. How do you feel?"

Stretching and yawning wide Amanda assured her, "No problem at all. If you hadn't come in, I would have woken later and been unable to sleep the rest of the night. I'm sorry I slept so long."

"Nonsense. Like I said, I know firsthand how tiring the trip across country can be. Would you like a tray up here or are you up to joining us downstairs?"

"Is Marshal Parker there?"

"Yes. I'm so sorry, Amanda. It's his house as much as Brett's. And I do know firsthand how distressing it can be to have to spend time around someone you aren't fond of."

"Do you really?"

"Oh yes. Believe me, when Brett and I first met, we were like oil and water. I didn't want to be married — to anyone and he was dead set we were going to marry."

"That must have been so difficult. At least Kendrick doesn't want to marry me anymore than I'd consider being tied to him the rest of my life."

Not that you know of. At least not yet. If there was one thing

Jenna knew, just as Marta said, from the way Kendrick looked at Amanda—which wasn't all that different from how Brett looked at her—Amanda would be Mrs. Kendrick Parker before the year was out. She was, however, not one to pour more fuel on a flame and once the match was lit between those two, it would be an inferno.

Amanda stood and stretched with a long yawn. "If you'll give me a minute, I'll walk downstairs with you."

"Of course. Is there anything you need?"

Walking over to the trunk which someone kindly had brought up to the room, she told Jenna, "No. Surprising as it is, Marshal Parker did bring my trunks along and I have most everything I need."

"Well, if it turns out you need anything, just let me know." Jenna stepped from the room to give Amanda a few minutes to ready herself. Pulling open the one trunk Amanda spied the linens she had so carefully packed with thoughts of a new life. A life where she'd be teaching and meet a wonderful man, be courted, marry, and have a passel of children. A life that thanks to Kendrick Parker was now out of her reach. Shaking her head at her thoughts about something that mattered little she stood and straightened her skirt. Her face washed, hair brushed out, still too tired to pin it up, Amanda opted simply to tie her hair back in a bow.

When they walked into the dining room, the men immediately stood with Kendrick taking a step towards Amanda who promptly moved behind Jenna. "Sheriff, kindly keep *that* man away from me."

Brett chuckled, which earned him a glare from Jenna, making her hiss, "Do not encourage him. I'd hate to find myself asking you to remove your brother from our home because he is annoying a guest."

"Ah, Kendrick. Why don't you have a seat at the end of the table there?"

"Or in the barn with the rest of the mules," Amanda muttered under her breath but not so low everyone else didn't hear it.

"Just trying to be a gentleman," he quietly told her.

"You should have thought about that before . . ."

"Yeah, yeah. I know, before I *kidnapped* you." He cut her off, unable to help himself.

With barely a word being spoken through the meal, not even a terse "pass the potatoes" Jenna tried to find a safe subject to discuss. "Well, Amanda, Kendrick mentioned you're from Massachusetts, yes?"

"Yes. I am. A small town not far from Boston. A lovely city with a wide variety of cultural events. I've often wondered why Boston did not become our nation's capital."

"Before he died, my papa had some business dealings there and often promised to take mamma and me. Sadly, the time was never quite right to go. Someday I hope Brett and I will be able to go back east and see the sights. Maybe after we've had a few children and they are of an age to enjoy the trip."

"And after things settle down back there," Kendrick quietly stated.

"That's true." Brett acknowledged. "I doubt we'll see any of the fighting out this way if it comes to that. Being in the middle of it isn't appealing at all."

Turning to Rick Amanda asked, "Rick, have you been to Massachusetts or the east?"

Turning his deep green gaze on her Rick seemed to be studying Amanda, as if he could find the key to what made her tick. "No. I was born and raised here in Adler Creek. Haven't been out of Wyoming in my entire life."

Jenna almost spit out her soup when Amanda asked Rick, "Maybe I could persuade you to escort me back there? I'd love to show you the sites and have no doubt you'd be warmly welcomed."

"*Absolutely not!*" Kendrick burst out as he stood. Hands braced on the table, leaning over his setting, and glaring at Rick. The action left Jenna with no doubt Kendrick's fuse ran a tad shorter than her husband's and Brett's wasn't long at all. Then again, no one had challenged Brett for her attention. For some reason Amanda was openly inviting Rick to become a part of her life.

"And what is it to you, *Marshal*?" Amanda baited him.

"It's . . . I . . . well it's not his business. This is between you and me and if anyone is going to take you anywhere, it's going to be me."

"Over my dead body you thick-headed donkey's backside." Amanda stood and tossed her napkin down on the table.

"Well who better than me to take you?" he demanded.

"Anyone but you would be better," she primly informed him.

"But I'm the one who has to make amends to you. Mandy, listen to me, just for a minute."

"Would that be in the same manner you listened to me?"

She stood and looked at Jenna, "I'm sorry to ruin this lovely dinner, Jenna. I cannot tolerate another minute near *that* Neanderthal."

When Amanda turned to leave the table, Kendrick strode from his place towards her while at the same time Rick stood and took a step in her direction. It was Brett who got to her first and stood between Amanda and the other two men. At his glance Jenna came forward and putting her arm around Amanda's shoulders led her from the room. "I'm so sorry, Amanda, I know you were trying to be hospitable when you invited . . . ."

"Gotta admit she's right about one thing, Kendrick," Brett drawled.

Kendrick kept his eye on the doorway, watching the two

women walk down the hallway towards the front of the house. "What's that little brother?"

"You're a jackass."

"She didn't call him a Jackass, Brett. She called him an ass's ass. I think that's worse," Rick said through his laughter.

"It's not a laughing matter, Rick." Brett told him. "She had tears in her eyes when she left. And Kendrick, if there's any problems in my marriage bed I'm not going to be too pleased with you either. That poor woman. I can't imagine what she's been through. First moving away from her home to a city where she doesn't know a soul for a job and then to be dragged halfway across the country before she ends up in a house with a group of men who act no better than little boys."

"It's his fault. If Rick hadn't been so . . . so . . . friendly we'd be fine. I saw her first. I told you I intend to marry her, so stay away and we'll be fine. Just fine."

"I don't think so. If I remember correctly, you promised Rick you'd honor Amanda's wishes and you wouldn't speak to her."

"I didn't. I just told *him* to . . ."

Jenna returned to the dining room, hands on hips. She glared at the three men. "You are worse than schoolboys. All of you. Kendrick Parker, I may have only met you today and owe you for helping me to clear my name and for that I will always be grateful. However, I will not allow discord in my home, even if it is half yours.

"Rick Hansen, you are worse than the class clown. You baited Kendrick, making him upset Amanda.

"And Brett Parker, don't you dare sit there gloating that I'm angry at those two and I think you are innocent. You are just as bad as Rick."

"Sorry, Jenna." Rick mumbled low.

"Sorry, Jenna." Kendrick managed as he lowered himself back into his chair.

"Me most of all, Jenna. Sweetheart you know I'd never do anything to upset you." Brett told her while he pulled her into his arms. "What can we do to make it better?"

"I'd suggest Kendrick stay away from her for a few days at least. Give her chance to adjust to things and make decisions about where she wants to go and what she wants to do."

"You're right, sweetheart."

Kendrick stood, clearly abashed. "I'll stay in town for a few days . . . if Rick will promise he won't set foot out here until Amanda and I work things out."

"Kendrick, she doesn't want to work things out with you," Rick told him.

"You don't know that. In fact I'm sure she feels the same way about me that I do about her," Kendrick responded.

"That's enough." Jenna cut in. "The three of you are like children on a playground."

"I didn't get involved . . ." Brett started to assure her.

"You are trying hard not to, husband dear."

Jenna accompanied Amanda upstairs. Gaining the room she'd been given Amanda turned to Jenna. "I'm so sorry about that outburst. I don't know why, but that man brings out the absolute worst in me. He riles me more than anyone I have ever met before."

"That's about how it was with Brett when we first met. We were both pretty stubborn."

"I know he's your brother-in-law and therefore family, and it's wrong of me to make a scene in your home."

"Not to worry. Really, I do understand."

"Well, thank you. Jenna, you do have a beautiful home."

"A bit surprising, isn't it?"

Amanda sat and patted the bed beside her, inviting Jenna to sit and visit with her. "Why do you say that?"

"Well, I don't know if you noticed with the wagon train you were on, but those wagons aren't all that big. There's not a lot of room for much and until the trains come out this way, it's not all that easy to bring furniture and supplies out this way."

Amanda considered that. "You know, you're right. I hadn't thought about that. Yet your home has really all of the amenities."

"It does. We owe it all to Kendrick and Brett's dad. He wanted his wife to be happy and from what Brett has said . . . now you don't repeat this to Kendrick because it is about his mother."

"Not a word."

"She liked her material comforts and apparently the only way Whitney could get her to consider moving out here was to promise her a house to rival those of Georgetown."

"Ah, I thought I recognized some of the layout. It is very much like what I've read of the houses there."

"Yes. From what Brett has said his father had brought two whole other wagons with them just to be sure his wife had all the amenities she wanted. I have to admit, I'm glad he was that much in love with her to do that. It's certainly made my life easier. Not that I need all this," Jenna gestured around the room, "all I need is Brett to be happy. We could live in a cave and it would be just fine with me."

"I know we just met, Jenna, but it's easy to see how much in love you two are. I truly hope one day I'll meet a man who loves me as much."

"You will. Believe me when I say, you will. Well! You do look a bit peaked so I'm going to leave you to settle in for the night. Can I bring you up a tray?"

"No. Thank you. No. I'm fine. You're right, I am tired and am looking forward to a good night's sleep in a soft bed. I'm not complaining, it was my choice, but at the Haynes' I slept in a chair so I could keep an eye on Kendrick while he was sick. When he was on the mend I continued to do so, so that the family wouldn't know we weren't married."

"That was smart of you to do."

"I didn't do it for Kendrick as much as for me so that I wouldn't be in the position of answering questions that were better left unasked."

"Well you have a good night and I'll see you in the morning."

"Thank you, Jenna. I truly do appreciate your hospitality and I promise tomorrow I won't let my personal feelings about your brother-in-law ruin your day."

"You didn't ruin my day today at all. I have to admit it was pretty amusing to hear you two bicker. Good night Amanda."

With Amanda upstairs resting, the others retired to the parlor to talk and give Jenna a chance to get to know her brother-in-law. With everyone settled, coffee poured, Kendrick spoke up. "There's no easy way to say any of this, Jenna. No doubt you figured out quite a bit on your own about your Uncle Julian."

"Some. I know I never cared for him and when he showed up here, I'll admit I was terrified. Thankfully Brett and Rick kept me safe until . . . well until the matter was settled once and for all with his death."

"I suppose Brett told you some of what I found out?"

"You mean that you found out Uncle Julian killed both my mother and father?"

Kendrick released a sigh of relief. "Yes. Exactly. Given your state, with the baby and all and seeing how protective my little brother is, I wasn't sure what you knew."

"Brett and I have no secrets. I have to admit, it was devastating and at the same time a comfort to hear that."

"How so a comfort?" Kendrick asked.

"Well, I grew up never doubting my parents' love for me.

I'll admit my papa indulged me in many ways, including making sure I had an excellent education. And my papa doted on my mother. There was nothing he'd deny her. Nothing at all. The coach she was in he bought just for her and it had many additional safety features. He had that coach checked out weekly. I knew, I just knew, that the axel breaking was no accident."

"No, it wasn't. From what I learned your uncle had it tampered with."

"I still cannot imagine how someone could harm their own family like that. More than the loss of my mother though I am at peace about my papa's passing. When I was told he took his own life I couldn't believe it. He missed my mother and felt guilty about the coach's axel breaking, but he cared for me. He would have never left me alone. It may make me a bad person, but I have no sadness that my uncle Julian is dead. He was evil and from what you have told us, he was worse than we thought."

"He was. I would have liked to have arrested him and brought him to justice," Kendrick told them, "but he would have ended up dead the same. I'm just sorry you had to go through all that."

"Well, if I hadn't, I wouldn't have met Brett and I cannot imagine my life without him in it." Jenna leaned into her husband and gave him a quick kiss on the cheek.

"Good. We should all have a marriage like that."

"What else did you find out, Kendrick?" Brett asked while at the same time looping his arm around Jenna. A protective gesture that let the world know no one would hurt his wife but assuring that he'd be there when Jenna heard the news.

"Seems your uncle was involved in a number of unsavory activities."

"Such as?" Jenna softly questioned.

"Human trafficking, stealing cargo. He was a southern

sympathizer and adamantly against Mr. Lincoln. I can only imagine what he would have done or been party to with all the talk of secession and war. I did hear at one point some southerners Carlman had dealings with had a plot to assassinate Lincoln."

"I see." She shook her head in disgust. "It seems what he planned for me he'd done before and I got off better than most. And to think he could have been part of what could destroy the union"

"You did indeed. The world is a better place without him in it."

CHAPTER TWENTY-FOUR

Used to waking with the first shards of sunlight edging through an opening after her time on the wagon train, Amanda woke early the next morning, her stomach roiling worse than it ever had before. Telling herself it was just that there'd been more excitement the past day or so than before and not wanting to disturb her hosts, she gave herself a quick sponge bath, dressed in a plain gray skirt with pale blue blouse with the slightly puffed out upper sleeve she liked best and headed downstairs. Hoping to find some coffee left over from the evening before, she was surprised to find Marta already up and preparing breakfast.

Entering the cheerfully arranged kitchen Amanda instantly felt at home. Like the Haynes' there was a big black stove, its bent legs giving it the appearance of weighing more than the wooden floor could handle. Cream colored eyelet curtains covered the windows, now pulled back to let in the morning sun. In the center of the room sat a large, what appeared to be oak table.

"Ah, Miss Mandy!" The older woman greeted her. "You up early, but not too early. Come. Sit. You gotta be hungry after no eating dinner last night."

"Oh, Marta! I ate. Just not very much. It was . . . it was a long day and I was just tired."

"Tired of Mr. Kendrick." She told her with a smile. "Mr. Brett, he the wild one. Mr. Kendrick, always so serious."

Sitting in the chair Marta motioned her to she shook her head. "Serious isn't the word for him. Stubborn, obdurate, intractable, . . ."

"Mule-headed probably sums it up just fine for Marta."

Amanda gasped at Kendrick's entrance. His buckskin breeches seemed to fit him like a second skin. The play of his muscles beneath the heavy fabric left nothing to her imagination which, since she had met him, had become quite fertile, especially since that night she'd shared his bed. She momentarily considered why, with how form fitting they were, the seams didn't simply fall apart when he bent over. Feeling the heat of the blush she seemed to have whenever she was near him Amanda blurted out, "I thought you left."

"Nope. That coffee ready, Marta?"

"Yes, sir, Mr. Kendrick. Hot and strong, just like I remember you like."

"You havin a cup, Mandy?" He asked while pouring his own and not bothering to turn to look at her.

"I was until you showed up. I believe I'll take a walk in the morning air and await Mrs. Parker outside."

"Believe I'll join you."

"That won't be necessary, Marshal."

"No problem."

"It will be if you foist your presence on me. What about your promise to leave me be? Do you not understand I find your company the most distasteful I have ever had the misfortune to endure?"

"Don't like my company, Mandy? Besides, I said I wouldn't speak to you, not that I wouldn't be in your company." His smile went right to her heart and sent a shiver down to her private parts, making her tingle.

"I detest your company, you, you . . ."

"Miscreant?"

"Ohhh." She quickly stood and made for the door only to run head long into Brett, nearly toppling him with the speed she tried to make."

"Omphphph! Where's the fire?"

Amanda pushed past him, Kendrick a step behind her. "Mandy! Wait! I just want to talk to you."

"Try please," Brett told his older brother as he pushed by.

Kendrick stopped short. "Please?"

"Yeah. Please. Try, please let me talk to you Mandy."

"Not uppity enough for her. Mandy!"

She practically ran for the front door, pulling up short when her stomach lurched. Hand to her mouth she stopped long enough to gag before running faster for the door. Outside she barely made it behind a bush before her nausea had her retching.

"Mandy? Mandy, what's wrong?" Kendrick came up behind her, his large form practically enveloping her.

Wiping her mouth she managed, "You. You are what is wrong. Can't you stay away from me?"

"No."

"You make me sick. Just go away."

"I'll get Jenna."

"Don't do me any favors." Covering her mouth she pushed past him, muttering that because of him she couldn't even enjoy the fresh morning air.

Starting once again to follow her, Brett stopped Kendrick. "I'd let her be, big brother. Seriously. I'd let her be."

"Would you let Jenna be?"

"Jenna's my wife. Not a woman I took against her will."

A short while later Jenna brought a tray up to Amanda. Knocking lightly she poked her head in the door when Amanda asked who it was.

"Mrs. Parker, I'm so sorry. I've created such a ruckus in your home."

"Nonsense. Men can be pigheaded and Parker men, I've learned, can be the worst of them. I spoke with Brett and he promised he'd make sure Kendrick didn't bother you

222

anymore. Now, can you eat a bit?"

"I suppose Mr. "Can't-mind-my-own-business" told you I had a slight upset stomach this morning."

"He did. He is a bit worried about you."

"I don't see why I should be of any concern to him. But if he continues to pester you about me you could just tell him it's because of all the upheaval he's caused in my life."

"Makes you nervous, does he?"

"Irritates me beyond words."

"Do you think he would bother you so much if you had met him under other circumstances?"

Amanda considered that while she took a bite of the toast Jenna had brought her. If she said yes, she'd be seen as perverse. If she said no, Jenna would tell Brett who would tell Kendrick who would redouble his efforts pestering her. There was no way she could win on that score. "I'm not sure. His actions have colored my entire perception of him black."

"I see. Well, hmmm I'll see what I can do about having him leave you be."

A few hours later, feeling better, Amanda once again ventured downstairs, relieved to find Kendrick seemed to have left.

Sitting with Jenna while she sewed on what appeared to be some baby garments, sat a man, his long, dark hair worn loose and trailing down his back. His buckskins were reminiscent of Kendrick's except for the woven patterns on the shirt. The moment Jenna saw Amanda, she invited her in to sit.

"Oh, I don't want to intrude!" Amanda told her with a quick look in the man's direction.

"Nonsense!" Jenna assured her. "This is Kendrick and Brett's younger brother, Wolf and he'd be most put out if he didn't have the chance to chat with Kendrick's lady."

"I'm not Kendrick's anything, Mrs. Parker; I am most assuredly not Kendrick Parker's lady." Amanda could barely keep the tension out of her voice.

"It seems both of my older brothers have the same way with women, a way that ruffles their feathers rather than welcomes them to their hearts. I would do it different."

Amanda couldn't help but chuckle, "You mean you wouldn't kidnap them? Seriously, I'm not Kendrick's woman. We don't even like each other and as soon as possible I'll be heading back to St. Louis. Hopefully he hasn't completely ruined my chances for a job there."

"Maybe not. Jenna says you are a teacher."

"Yes, I am."

"There will always been the need for those that can teach."

Amanda considered his words, suddenly smiling, hopeful. "Mr. Wolf. You know the trails to the east, don't you?"

"I have never been."

"But you could. You know how to follow a trail, right?"

He considered the question. "Yes. It is not hard to do."

"Then *you* could bring me back east! I wouldn't have to wait for the Sheriff to find someone to bring me. You could bring me."

"Oh, Amanda. Oh no. I don't think so," Jenna hurried to say before Wolf could answer.

"Why? Mr. Wolf, wouldn't you like to see the east?"

"No."

"No?"

"No. My life and family are here. It is best you wait for Rick to help you."

"I . . . oh . . . please, excuse my behavior. That was inappropriate of me."

"It is no matter, Amanda. I am flattered you would ask."

Relaxing into everyday conversation the afternoon passed quite pleasantly. Jenna's descriptions of Adler Creek left Amanda feeling as though it was the kind of town she'd enjoy living in, if it didn't include Kendrick Parker. To her dismay,

Kendrick arrived in time for supper. Rather than give the appearance of being uncivilized or just plain rude, Amanda said nothing about Kendrick's presence, although she ignored him from the moment he walked in with Brett. Over dinner, with gentle questions, Jenna and Wolf drew Amanda out somewhat by asking about her life in Massachusetts.

"It's really quite boring," Amanda told her.

She missed Jenna's quick look at Kendrick as well as Kendrick's look of utter interest in what Amanda had to say. "I thought my life back east fairly dull myself. Did you have brothers or sisters?" Jenna asked.

"No. I was an only child. Fortunately, my parents believed in educating women and they arranged for an extensive formal education for me. They weren't rich . . . my father was a shop keeper, but they were prudent with their money. I felt teaching afforded me the best options for my future and pursued that as a career. When my parents died, I tried to obtain a teaching position in Peabody, but was unable to procure one, so looked elsewhere for a position."

"That's Amanda talk for she got herself an education, couldn't find a job and went to St. Louis where she had the good fortune to meet me." Kendrick broke in, earning himself a kick under the table from both Brett and Jenna. "Ouch! What did you kick me for?"

"Keep you from making a bigger fool of yourself than you already have," Brett muttered.

"While your sentiments are appreciated, Mr. Parker, I am sorry to tell you your older brother is incapable of any sense at all."

"Kendrick." Jenna's soft voice caught their attention. "It probably would be best if you didn't rile Amanda."

"I'm not! I'm just interpreting what she was saying."

"I think they understood just fine. I'll tell you this, Marshal, for a man who says he is sorry for what he has done and regrets his actions, you seem to spend a considerable amount of time making the situation worse."

Kendrick hung his head, poking at his meal with his fork. "My apologizes, Mandy. I guess I can't help but make a fool of myself around you."

When no one spoke for several minutes Jenna ventured a question to once again draw Amanda out.

"So, how did you find the position in St. Louis?"

"Well, when my prospects in Peabody didn't turn out as I had hoped, I saw an advertisement in the local paper for a schoolteacher in St. Louis. It was quite simple really. I responded and a few weeks later received what I felt was an offer of employment. I immediately packed my belongings and traveled to St. Louis. It was there I had the misfortune to encounter Marshal Parker. The rest, as they say, is history. A sorry one at that."

"Come on, Mandy, I'm not that awful, am I?"

"You are the most horrid creative I've ever had the misfortune to meet." She snapped.

"Dang, big brother, she really doesn't like you much at all, does she?" Brett managed around a solid belly laugh.

"It's not funny, Brett." Kendrick pointed his fork at his younger brother. "How would you feel if Jenna thought you were rotten to the core?"

Amanda gasped. "Marshal, you cannot begin to compare your crude manhandling of an unsuspecting victim with the love and devotion Mr. Parker shares with his bride!"

Brett looked at Kendrick, trying almost in vain to control his laughter. "She means that she wouldn't marry you if you were the last man on earth."

"Marry!" Jenna, Mandy and Kendrick all blurted out at once.

"Brett, I don't think it's for us to say," Jenna told him while placing her napkin beside her plate.

"You most certainly understand my sentiments, Mr. Parker," Amanda said.

"Why thank you, little brother. I believe you just made the situation even worse." Kendrick growled.

CHAPTER TWENTY-FIVE

"He's gone to town," Jenna told Amanda when she saw her creeping down the stairs, surreptitiously checking out the lower level for any signs of Kendrick the next day.

"Thank you. I know I must seem the most ungrateful and cold-hearted woman you have ever encountered, but that man . . ."

"No, you don't. Not at all. I know how I felt when I first met Brett. He was so determined to marry me and refused to listen to anything I had to say. He was bound and determined that he was going to make our marriage work, no matter how hard I tried to the contrary. Anytime I tried to speak up, he would refuse to listen. Our first few months of marriage were pretty difficult."

"That is exactly how Kendrick is! Every time I tried to tell him he had the wrong woman or that I had never been to California, he refused to listen. There were even a number of times he bullied me into being quiet. Of course I now realize that he knew what he was doing was wrong and that he had every opportunity to make things right. He refused to do that. That man is the most stubborn creature I have ever met."

"It does seem like a Parker trait." Jenna laughed lightly. "Mandy, I have to tell you though, for all our early struggles, Brett and I have one of the strongest marriages I have ever seen."

"I can't imagine someone wanting or loving me that much."

Jenna studied her houseguest a few moments, debating on

whether or not to tell her what she felt when she saw Amanda and Kendrick together or how Kendrick spoke about her when she wasn't around. Deciding that Amanda wasn't quite ready to hear her impressions and that it was Kendrick's place to declare himself, she merely said, "I'm sure somewhere out there is exactly the right man for you and when you're ready, he will sweep you off your feet."

"Ah, Jenna, that's the stuff of fairy tales and penny novels. Not what happens to a schoolteacher."

"You never know. You never know. The man of your dreams could turn up when you least expect it."

Later that afternoon Rick arrived. Opening the door Jenna greeted him, "Rick! Is something wrong? Is Brett . . ." spying the bouquet of wildflowers in hand she continued with a smile, "I see. Come in. I'll tell Amanda you're here."

"Thanks, Jenna."

When Amanda rounded the corner a few minutes later, smoothing back a few loose strands of hair, despite the fact that Jenna had told her Rick had come by, he still surprised her. "Miss Amanda, I thought you might enjoy these." He thrust the flowers at her, a blush crossing his cheeks.

"Oh! Yes. Oh my. They are lovely. Thank you, Sheriff. Um, ah, let me, ah . . ."

"Why don't I fetch a vase." Jenna came up behind her. "And you two go on and have a seat in the parlor."

"Actually, Jenna, I was hoping Miz Davis might want to accompany me on a ride. I brought a wagon from town and thought I'd show your guest around the area. Would you enjoy that Miz Davis?"

"Amanda, please call me Amanda and yes, I'd enjoy that very much."

Jenna stared at Rick, hard, before telling them, "Well that sounds dandy. Just dandy. Would you like me to put these in a vase and up in your room, Amanda?"

"Would you mind?"

"No, not at all. You two have a lovely time."

Rick dipped his head in thanks to Jenna. Taking Amanda by the elbow he mentioned, a bit too casually for it to truly be causal, "By the way, I brought us a picnic from Milly's in case Amanda would like some supper while we're out."

Before Jenna could respond he had Amanda out the door and headed towards the wagon.

Watching them drive off Jenna wasn't surprised to find Marta standing beside her. "What you think Mr. Rick is doing?"

"I don't know, Marta. I don't know. He knows Kendrick is courting her, or at least he would like to. It's not like him to step in another man's shoes like that."

"She a pretty girl."

"Yes, she is. Maybe Rick is so attracted to her he won't mind having to fight Kendrick for her hand."

Marta didn't sound quite as horrified as Jenna might have expected when she asked, "You think it gonna be a fight?" It seemed a love triangle was a bit of drama Marta just might enjoy. Truth be told, Jenna wouldn't have minded either — like something out of penny novel.

"Not a physical one, but if he doesn't watch his step, there will be words. Trust me, there will be words. I don't know Kendrick except for what he's said about his intentions towards Amanda. He's not going to be very happy if another man pursues the woman he's set his sights on."

When Brett and Kendrick returned home a bit later, despite the men making themselves comfortable in the parlor, Jenna couldn't miss Kendrick constantly looking towards the stairs. When he got up and paced to the door for the third time, she decided to put his curiosity to rest. "Amanda's gone out for a bit."

Kendrick spun back around to look at her, "What? Where

did she go? Where could she go? She doesn't know anyone in these parts."

"For a ride."

"A ride? She doesn't ride that well. She doesn't know the area. Woman could be out there, hurt or worse." He reached for his hat and started for the door.

Jenna rose and hurried towards him, laying a hand on his arm, "She's fine. She has an escort and they may have supper on the range."

"An escort? Who? Where'd she . . . Rick! Shit! Excuse my language, Jenna. Rick took her?"

He stormed out the door before Jenna or Brett could react.

"Brett, go after him."

"Why?"

"Why? Because he's going to make it worse."

"How?"

"How? He's going to get into a fight with Rick, one of them might get hurt and it will make Amanda mighty angry."

"Well then they'll have it out."

She lightly punched his arm. "Brett Parker! She's already mighty angry. If either one of those men gets hurt, it's not going to make her happy. She'll not only be angry, but she'll feel responsible."

"But Jenna, it took you getting mighty riled at me for us to find our way to each other."

"Yes, it did. But Brett, think about it. It was between you and me. There wasn't another man involved now, was there?"

He rubbed his jaw, considering. "No. I'm the only man in your life. Only one ever been there and the only one you'll ever have."

"If I didn't love you so much, I'd be miffed at you for that. Now, will you go after them?"

"All right. All right. I'm going. Brother shows up and brings more trouble with him than . . ." he continued muttering to himself while walking out the door and looking towards the cloud of dust in the distance, wondering if Kendrick was traveling in the right direction or if he'd just get himself lost.

As luck would have it Kendrick had gone in the right direction and Brett came upon Kendrick, Rick, and Amanda just as Kendrick was about to introduce Rick's jaw to his fist. "Whoa! Hold it!" Brett yelled as he jumped off his horse.

"Mr. Parker! Thank goodness you are here!" Amanda ran up to him and grabbed his arm, "You have to stop them."

"That's what I'm here for." Dismounted, he stepped between his brother and best friend.

CHAPTER TWENTY-SIX

"I don't need your help, little brother," Kendrick growled as he pulled off his jacket, tossed it along with his hat to the ground just before he began to circle Rick with his fists up.

"Kendrick, don't do this," Rick told him, palms up and facing outward, signing he didn't want to fight. Shuffling backwards while facing his erstwhile attacker, dust kicked up from the ground.

"Don't do this? I found her! I saw her first! She's mine. You want a woman, go find your own. Who the hell do you think you are butting in on my . . ." He caught sight of Amanda standing to the side, hands on her hips, lips in a tight line, a sure sign she was more than irritated and he'd be in for more than a tongue lashing by time she was done with him. At least then though, she'd talk to him. Kendrick watched as she glanced at Brett and from the expression on Amanda's face, she was even less pleased with him than she had been before.

"Your what, Marshal Parker?" Amanda demanded.

Oh she was really mad this time. He'd really set her off now. "My . . . my . . . my suspect!"

"Your *suspect*?" She strode over towards Kendrick and Rick before Brett could stop her. From the way she shoved Brett aside when he approached her, Kendrick had no doubt about just how angry she was. "*Your* suspect?"

He stepped towards her, Rick completely forgotten. "Well yeah. Yeah, you were my suspect and now, well now your, ahhhh, well don't you see? You belong with me. I mean . . . I'm the one who you need, who should be . . ."

"What? Mr.-I'm-going-to-tell-you-what-to-do-every-mi-nute-of-your-life, can't form a coherent sentence? My, my." She'd advanced to stand right before him, completely un-afraid, he noted. Hands on her hips she was a sight to see and what Kendrick wanted to do more than anything in the world was give her one great big, wet kiss. When she took her hands off her hips and he saw one of them raised in his direction for a fleeting second, he thought she was going to reach around his neck and pull him into that very kiss he wanted.

He leaned towards her. Bringing his face closer.

He lowered his lids, oblivious to the two other men stand-ing nearby.

He whispered her name, "Mandy."

The crack of her hand against his cheek sent him reeling. The woman sure could pack a wallop!

"What did you do *that* for?" Kendrick rubbed his jaw.

"What do you think, you asinine piece of cow manure?" She turned towards Rick and Brett. "And the two of you are no better. Laughing at . . . at . . . standing there laughing. Can't the three of you ever be in each other's presence without instigating the worse sort of juvenile antics?"

"Dang, that's gotta be the first time she's been at a loss for words and uppity ones at that. Keep on laughing, this is an all-time first." Kendrick managed, while fingering his jaw.

She whirled on him, arm up in the air.

"Go on, sweetheart. Being hit by you again is worth the price of you without words."

"I'm not your sweetheart. I'm the woman who hates you and everything about you. I'm the woman who wants noth-ing to do with you. It is beyond comprehension how you came to be a Deputy United States Marshal because, at the very least, you are incapable of keeping your word. *About an-ything!*"

"Oh, Mandy, darlin' . . ."

"Ohhhhhh, I am not your darling . . . with a *g* on the end . . . either." She advanced towards Rick and Brett, now acting at least suitably subdued. Despite the lack of laughter spilling from their lips, they couldn't keep the twinkles out of their eyes. "Sheriff, I'm sorry that man ruined our picnic. I sincerely hope, when you have gotten your own sense of frivolity over this situation under control, you will again call on me."

"Friv . . . Miz Davis. I apologize. Truly I do. Please, let me help you into our wagon and we'll picnic elsewhere."

"Absolutely not. No. Not after you encouraged him to behave like such a barbarian."

Rick looked over her head at Kendrick. "I'm seeing more and more what you mean about how she talks. Definitely enter . . ."

Amanda stomped on his foot and marched away from the men.

"Well there you go," Kendrick told him.

"What?" Rick's green eyes showed the pain he felt from the stomping Amanda'd given him.

Amanda turned towards Brett, "Mr. Parker, will you kindly return me to your home? It appears these two are peas of the same pod and can beat each other to death for all I care."

"Uh, sure." With a smile at his brother and best friend, he informed them, "You two boys play nice now, ya hear? Kendrick, can you bring my horse?"

"I'll take you home, Mandy." A clearly chastised Kendrick muttered.

"You thick-headed clod. Don't you understand I want nothing, absolutely *nothing* to do with you?"

"I kinda get that, Mandy. And because I do understand I'm hoping to change your opinion of me."

"Kendrick." Brett took his arm. "Just bring my horse, okay?"

"Yeah. Sure. Be glad to. Least I know you won't try to court my woman."

"I'm not your . . ."

"Leave it be, Amanda. He's trying to leave you be."

"I am not."

"Yes. You are." Brett's tone brooked no defiance. Kendrick's shoulders slumped in defeat.

Watching Brett and Mandy leave the area, Kendrick mumbled to Rick, "Wonder why she isn't miffed at him for what he said."

"She's probably tuckered out from all the . . ." he started to laugh, "fisticuffs she engaged in."

Kendrick joined Rick in his laughter, the two of them doubling over. "Yeah, that's exactly what she'd say. Fisticuffs. I'd like to know why, though, you are courting my woman."

"She's not *your* woman, Kendrick."

"Yes she is. I told you. I found her. I brought her here. And . . . it's on me to make it right for her. You and I haven't seen each other for years but I can't believe you'd stoop to go after another man's woman."

"Did it ever occur to you I only meant to make her feel welcome and maybe tell her you really are a decent man?"

"You, you were going to do that?"

"Thought about it."

"And?"

"I'm still thinking about it. What I think or do isn't important though. It's what you do, especially in front of her, if you want to win her over."

Chapter Twenty-seven

Giving Amanda a few minutes to compose herself Brett drove the wagon in silence. When it seemed Amanda might be ready to listen a bit, speaking low, he told her, "Kendrick's not really a bad sort."

"Not a bad sort? He's despicable."

"In a way I can see your point. Still, I'm thinking if you knew a bit about him some of what he does might make some sense."

"I doubt it. Besides, he's your brother. It is incumbent on your familial relationship to defend him."

"I guess you would doubt his intentions after your relationship so far."

After riding a few more minutes Brett was a bit surprised when Amanda spoke, "If I was amenable to hearing about him, what would you say?"

He paused a breath before speaking. "Well, he grew up without a mother."

"He told me that."

"It wasn't just that he didn't have a momma. He never knew what it was like to have her. Our pa — Kendrick and I have the same pa you know." At her nod he continued. "Pa wanted to raise him after his ma died. His grandparents though, they never wanted our folks, his folks to come west."

"I can see their point."

"I suppose. They did and Clarissa, his ma, died. His grandparents insisted he go back east. I didn't even know I had a brother for a lot of years. Pa finally convinced the grandfolks to let him come and visit. It was after my pa remarried and I was born. I was pretty excited to find out I had a big brother."

"Was he happy to know he had a younger brother?"

"To be honest, I don't know. I never asked him. Being a teacher, you know how kids are. I can tell you he sure didn't act like it!" Brett chuckled and tilted his hat back a bit on his head. Letting the horse take her own lead back to the ranch, he relaxed his hands on the reins.

"How did he act?"

"Quiet. Surly. Every time he came out this way, he kept to himself the first few weeks. Wouldn't talk to anyone. Wouldn't eat for days. It took some doing, but my ma coaxed him out of his shyness, I guess. He still didn't talk much, but he seemed a bit happier. The first trip out he even said that he'd been wanting to come. Maybe it was being with a family, his family and how we were made him feel left out. By the end of each visit though he was running and playing with Rick and me. When he went home, he wrote a bit. One time when he came to visit again, a few years later, he said he wrote more but his grandparents didn't send the letters."

"Did they tell him that?"

"No. That was the part that I think hurt him the most. If they had said they weren't going to send 'em it would have been one thing. Instead, he found a few, over time, in the fireplace half burned."

Amanda shifted so she partly faced Brett. Her hand gently on his arm she blurted out, "That's awful! How could someone do something like that to someone they say they love?"

"Love can make you do some pretty stupid things. Especially when you love someone, and you don't realize you've fallen in love or think you shouldn't be."

"But that's between a man and a woman, not family. How could parents or grandparents do such a thing?"

"Don't rightly know. I guess they thought they were doing

the best thing. When Kendrick had a bunch of the letters, he showed them to his grandpa and said he wanted to come visit again. They got better about letting him come after that. Every time though it would be the same. He'd get here and be quiet, keep to himself for a time. Then he'd be more sociable."

"Did anyone ever talk to him about it?"

"Yeah. Actually it was Wolf."

"What about Wolf? Why doesn't he live here with you?"

"He's busy with his people. He's got this way about him, studying people and things. How they work. He makes a lot of sense. When Kendrick left and my pa died, my ma married Wolf's dad. Kendrick managed to come out to visit and Wolf asked him why he was so awful when he'd get here."

"What did he say?"

"That his grandparents weren't very affectionate. That and, well—" Brett gazed out on the plain, debating breaking the confidence Kendrick had shared with his brothers. "Amanda, I tell you this, it's not something to tell Kendrick you know. If he tells you, you got to act like you don't know. All right?"

"Yes. Of course. What did he say?"

"That they told him he was the reason his ma died."

"Oh no! How awful. How could a grandparent say such a horrid thing? No wonder he's such a solitary man. It's good he has you."

"So you understand?"

"I understand a bit about him now that you've told me. Still, Mr. Parker, it does not excuse his continuing his journey out here with me when he knew I was not that woman, Black Bette."

To say the next few days were tense would have been an understatement. Amanda wondered if perhaps she picked up the influenza Kendrick'd had on the trail. Not a day went by where she didn't wake up with her stomach feeling like she would lose everything she'd eaten the day before. More than once through the day she'd felt quite light-headed.

Rather than keep his promise to stay in town, Kendrick moped and skulked around the house making sure Amanda didn't see him so he wouldn't upset her while at the same time keeping an eye on her, waiting for his chance to make amends.

Brett tried to keep his brother from making any more stupid mistakes where Amanda was concerned.

Jenna was torn between wanting to do what she could to help Amanda feel comfortable in her home and make her decision and wanting to do what she could to give Kendrick what she knew in her heart he wanted most. She watched Amanda closely for any sign that she cared for Kendrick.

Rick rode out to the ranch more frequently than he had in the past. Jenna wasn't sure if he was coming out so often because he wanted to keep an eye on Kendrick, was romantically interested in Amanda, wanted to taunt Kendrick, or just enjoyed the Parker hospitality. Then again, they'd all known each other since they were children and Brett often said Rick was more like a brother than friend. If that was the case, then he was there only to see a friend.

At the end of the week Amanda came downstairs with several letters. Finding Jenna in the parlor she asked how she could go about posting them.

"I'll have Brett take them to town. The Express rider should be coming through any day now."

"Express rider?"

"Yes! The Pony Express riders come through Adler Creek weekly. It used to take weeks for mail to go through, depending on a wagon scout heading back or bringing a wagon through. Now we get our mail within a week or two."

"That would be ideal. I would appreciate him delivering these for me."

"We'll give them to Brett tonight unless . . . unless you'd like to join Marta and me when we go into town later today."

"I don't know . . ."

"Are you feeling ill?"

"No. I'm fine. Really. I've just been tired the past few days, I suspect from the trip here and worrying what was going to happen. Now I just need to decide what to do with my future. These letters are to a few schools in Massachusetts, the one that I was supposed to teach at in St. Louis and to the Haynes' in Lancaster to see if they have a position there. If I can't find one, I don't know what I'll do. I don't like to speak ill of someone's family, but your brother-in-law has near ruined my life."

"Amanda, I completely understand how you feel. Believe me. When I thought I killed my uncle not a day went by I wasn't worried Brett would be the one to arrest me."

Amanda sat up, releasing a long sigh. "You thought you killed your uncle? Oh my goodness, Jenna. I must apologize, in my self-absorption I never asked what brought you to Adler Creek. What happened?"

"It's not the best story. At least not until I met Brett."

"Tell me?"

The women settled on the settee and Jenna began her tale, "Well, I grew up in New York City. I was an only child and I have to admit I was pretty spoiled. There was nothing my mama and papa wouldn't do for me. A few years ago my mother died in a tragic accident. Then, a little over a year ago I came home I'd . . . well Brett doesn't know this part, but I had just accepted a marriage proposal from a gentleman I knew there. I know now it wasn't a love match. He was a proper young man. Exactly what my parents would have wanted for me, but there wasn't the . . ." she glanced around

241

the room before whispering, "passion I feel with Brett."

Amanda smiled, enjoying the secret smile and soft blush that crept into Jenna's cheeks. "I can see that between you two. I don't think I've ever seen a couple so much in love. So how did you end up here? Did you come west with that gentleman or did you answer that ad for a mail order bride that I heard the one gentleman posted?"

"Ah, that was Henry Bascom. No, I didn't answer the ad. In fact, I never even had a chance to tell my papa that I'd received a proposal. I came home from an outing with my young man and found my papa . . ." tears formed in Jenna's eyes.

"Oh, Jenna, I'm sorry to have asked. Please forgive me?"

Patting Mandy's hand Jenna assured her, "there's nothing to forgive. Tears aren't always a bad thing and it's good to be able to remember and talk about my papa."

"If you're sure."

"I am. He was such a special man. I came home, all excited to tell him and, well I found he'd been shot. At first, we thought he'd shot himself but, as Kendrick found out, it was murder. My Uncle Julian happened to be in New York. I thought at the time that it was a remarkable coincidence. As it turned out, he killed my papa. But then, at first, before I knew since he was my appointed guardian, he brought me to his home in Maryland. My first night there, he crept into my room and tried . . . he tried to force himself on me."

"Oh, Jenna! I'm so sorry! How horrible. I can't . . . I can't imag . . ." Amanda dipped her head down, feeling her own cheeks heating at the memory of what she'd done with Kendrick. Worse, how she lay awake night after night reliving those moments with him. Wanting just one more night to store up memories of the man she was . . . no she couldn't be . . . falling in love with?

"It's fine now, Mandy. When he came after me, I picked up

242

a lamp and hit him on the head. There was so much blood I thought I'd killed him. I was so surprised by my actions that I grabbed a few items and ran from the house in the middle of the night. I found my way to the train station, climbed into a box car and the next morning found myself in Virginia and at an inn with a group of women who were coming west to be brides. Henry Bascom, the banker here in Adler Creek, had posted an advertisement looking for mail order brides and this group of ladies were coming west to marry. At first, I thought I could hide from the law by being with them. I'd planned to create a whole new identity and then just leave them in St. Louis and start a new life for myself."

Amanda leaned towards her new friend, "And did you?"

"In a manner of speaking I did. My given name is Jennifer . . . I changed it to Jenna. In St. Louis I tried to leave but the wagon master, Dusty Hendricks . . ."

"He's the one we had coming west as well. I can't say I liked him very much. However, that was all Kendrick's doing, making me out to be a criminal."

"Dusty can be bull-headed, or so I learned. He was determined I come to Adler Creek and marry. We were a few days away from Adler Creek and Brett came out to meet the wagon train with a few of the other men. He came right up to me and now, looking back, what he did was so romantic."

"What?"

"He came up to me at the river and told me that we'd marry. He said he'd protect and care for me, that he'd provide for me and wouldn't force himself on me. He was sure enough of himself to say I'd share his bed." The blush that had finally subsided rose once again on her cheeks.

"Before you married?"

"Oh no! Brett is one of the most honorable men you could ever meet. No. He insisted we marry, and right away, but that he would wait until I was ready to share his bed. When I realized I loved him and that he was the only man I would ever want to spend my life with, our coming together was more than wonderful."

"Your story sounds almost like one of the penny novels, only better."

Jenna giggled. "I suppose it does sound like that. It will be like that for you too, Mandy. Honest. When you are with the man you love there is nothing to compare. He becomes your whole world and all you want to do is be with him."

Amanda considered that. Kendrick wasn't honorable. Not because he'd bedded her. That was all her own fault. The whole time on the trail he'd held her at night, kept her warm, but made no move to be intimate with her. She'd done that all on her own. No, he was dishonorable, because he'd taken her away from the life she'd intended to live. A life that would have been safe and secure and where she wouldn't feel daily that her heart was breaking.

"I can see how alike we are," Amanda finally told Jenna, "and yet so different. In your case Brett had no idea what had happened to bring you west. In mine, Kendrick believed I was that other woman. I could forgive that. What I can't forgive is not only that he refused to listen to what I had to say. It is that even when he began to realize he had the wrong woman, he continued on our journey. When Billy McCaffrey brought that telegram to him, he should have turned right around and returned me to St. Louis. He could have explained to the school then and there and my life would be exactly the way I wanted it."

"I wish I had some way to make it better right now, Amanda. That somehow I could undo what has happened. Since I can't do that, I can try to help you find what you want."

"I appreciate that more than I can say. Not many people would invite a total stranger into their home and have them stay."

"You aren't a total stranger, Amanda. You're Kendrick's . . . well Kendrick knows who you are, so in a way you are like fa . . . well, a good . . . a friend."

"If it weren't for *that* man I wouldn't be here."

"Well, you're welcome to stay here as long as you like or need to. Since no one knows what happened, no one here, except for Brett, Rick, Marta and Franco know what happened with Kendrick, you could come into town and not get too many odd looks. You wouldn't be scrutinized by anyone if that is what you are concerned about."

Amanda rubbed her stomach, considering Jenna's words. "You know, yes, I'd like to join you this afternoon. It sounds like fun."

"Good. And you know, I thought I heard at church a few weeks ago that we're looking for a teacher. You might even consider staying here and teaching in town."

"I don't think so."

"Adler Creek's a nice town."

"I'm sure it is. It is, however, a town to which Kendrick Parker may well return and I have no desire to see him under any circumstances ever again.

CHAPTER TWENTY-EIGHT

When the women arrived in town a few hours later, while Marta headed off to the Emporium and general store in search of the food stuffs she needed to replenish the pantry, Jenna took Amanda to the sheriff's office so she could let Brett know they were in town. "He's always been a bit protective. Since I've been pregnant, or at least since he's known, he's even more so. If I didn't let him know right away I was here I'd be hearing about it for the next month!"

As they walked in, Brett's smile was instantaneous. From his broad grin to the crinkling skin around his eyes he was clearly happy to see his wife.

Kendrick had been sitting beside the desk. He stood, slowly, warily, hungrily watching Amanda as if waiting for her to pass some sort of sentence on him while at the same time wanting to take her into his arms and kiss her senseless. "Jenna. Amanda." He quietly greeted them.

Jenna in turn greeted him warmly. Amanda turned to look out the window, hugging her arms around her waist, her shoulders climbing upward towards her ears. It didn't go unnoticed that he'd called her Amanda.

"Ah, guess I'll go check on . . . take a walk . . . see you later, Brett." Kendrick ambled towards the door, shooting a look at Amanda standing there looking as if she might shatter if anyone touched her.

When the door closed behind him Brett asked his wife "What brings my lovely wife to town? Just missing me maybe?"

"I always miss you. Today though, Marta needed some supplies, Amanda has some letters to post and most important, I wanted to see my husband!"

"Now that's what I like to hear. You sure that's all. You just wanted to see me?" His hand caressed her belly, as if soothing the child within.

"I'm fine. Expecting is what we women do! There were a few things I wanted to look into, see if Belle is around and thought maybe you could take supper with us?"

"That sounds like an excellent plan." He nodded towards Amanda who still stood looking out the window. "Should I invite Rick?"

Jenna looked from her husband to Amanda, considering. "Amanda? Would you mind if Rick joined us for supper?"

As if waking from a daze Amanda turned, "What? Oh. Yes. That would be fine."

"Well good. I'll let him know."

At Brett's raised brow, in that silent communication a couple in love can share, Jenna shrugged her shoulders. She knew he wanted to know if Kendrick was invited. Amanda clearly didn't want anything to do with him, even though it was becoming increasingly clear Kendrick wanted plenty to do with her.

"Good. We'll be off then. Do you need me to pick anything up?"

"Nope. See you about five."

At the door, Amanda turned back towards Brett. "Mr. Parker. Brett, I know you haven't seen your brother in some time. I'd hate to keep you from him. If he will promise to mind his manners, I think you should invite him to join us. Just please ask him to refrain from speaking to me."

Brett nodded, "I will do that. I'm sure he'll enjoy the company."

They dropped off Amanda's letters, did some shopping,

had some coffee, which upset Amanda's stomach, and stopped by the church to inquire about whether or not the teaching position was still open. Jenna was thrilled that it still was. Amanda was unsure. "Why don't we both consider it and chat next week?" The reverend agreed that was an excellent idea "Beings as you are friends with the Parkers, I can tell you we'd love to have you here to teach."

"Thank you reverend. I am still hopeful that the position I was offered in St. Louis will still be open to me."

"St. Louis? If it's money I'm sure we can match their offer. Perhaps even better it."

"I appreciate that. It's not money . . . it's . . ."

"And St. Louis, Miss Davis, from what the Express rider said the other day, the war is likely to find itself there."

"I see. Still. I need to be certain."

Entering the restaurant for dinner, Amanda noticed Kendrick's hair was slightly damp, his chin freshly shaved, and the scent of bay rum ever so slightly surrounded him. His shirt was a crisp white cotton, with the two top buttons undone, showing a hint of his chest. Heat rushed to Amanda's cheeks as she remembered caressing that chest, what it felt like when he lowered himself on top of her, the soft hair covering him tickling her breasts just before he entered her that night not so long ago. The pooling of moisture between her legs surprised her as did the fluttering in her belly just from looking at him. Much as she hated to admit it, the man was more potently attractive than he had a right to be. She dared not look at how his buckskins molded to his thighs.

Seeking to stay as far away from him as possible, she moved to sit on the opposite side of the table from him. She soon realized *that* was a mistake, because she then had a direct view of his chest and face. That smile, those white teeth, the wounded look in his beautiful blue eyes. Yes, she decided, he looked wounded, hurt, like he'd lost something dear to him.

"Millie's is the first restaurant here in Adler Creek and she makes *the* best fried chicken and mashed potatoes," Rick told her.

"I'm kinda partial to the steak." Brett said.

Kendrick, she noticed, said nothing. He just sat and looked at her with that wounded expression in his eyes. It seemed as if he'd lost his best friend.

Their meals ordered, there were a few moments of awkward silence before Brett asked, "So, Amanda, you get those letters posted okay?"

"I did. Thank you for asking."

"What letters?" Kendrick leaned forward as he spoke for the first time that evening, except for ordering his meal.

"Not that it is any of your business, I wrote the school in St. Louis to see if the position was still open."

"Didn't need to do that. I told you I'd send a letter." Though spoken low, Kendrick's disapproval of her writing her own letter was obvious.

"Yes I did. Just because you wrote something, probably some illiterate gibberish, doesn't mean I shouldn't express my own desires regarding the position."

"It wasn't gibberish. I sent telegrams, three of them, explaining what happened."

"Anything coming from you would be unintelligible."

"I'll have you know I was educated in some of the best schools in the east."

"Just because you were physically at those schools does not mean you learned anything. A buffoon with your limited intellect . . ."

"Ah, you two want to take it outside? The rest of us would like to enjoy our meal." Rick quietly interjected.

"I apologize, Sheriff . . . Rick. It seems despite my best

attentions Marshal Parker continues to provoke me without even trying."

"Well you're the one who wanted me here tonight."

"I didn't *want* you here. I simply felt it would have been unkind to your brother to take a meal here in town with he and his wife and not include you."

"Well now *ain't* that a surprise."

"Excuse me?"

"No uppity words to spout about what *you* wanted for tonight?"

"My language only sounds uppity to you because you are little more than an ignorant ape yourself."

With his knife in one hand, fork in the other, he rested his hands, the utensils straight up, on the table, "Does that mean I've moved up in the world? The other day I was an ass."

She felt her color heightening. "That was a jackass you Neanderthal."

"Like I said," Rick broke in. "You two want to carry that outside?"

"Again, I apologize." Amanda quietly assured him.

"Sorry, Rick. She riles me, that's all."

"*I* rile *you*?" Amanda stood and slammed her hands on the table. "*I* rile *you*? I'll have you know just the sight of you . . ."

Suddenly the room was spinning. Amanda felt like she was in a vortex with nothing stable to hang on to. From a distance she heard his voice. "Mandy? Mandy? Are you all right?"

Unable to focus she felt hands, strong hands, on her shoulders, guiding her ever so slightly backwards, helping her into a chair. "Here, sweetheart, bend over. Put your head down. That's it. That's my girl. Hand me that water, would you?"

His girl? Water? Who was handing him water? Sweetheart?

"Here you go. Can you drink this? Just a little? Take a breath. That's it."

The feeling of something on the side of her head near her forehead. A sensation of something warm. The brush of something familiar. The feather light touch she'd felt on her lips the first time Kendrick kissed her.

The feeling of a fog surrounding her cleared. The first thing she saw was a pair of stormy blue eyes. The concern in them tugged at her heart. "Goodness. I am so sorry. I . . . that has never happened to me before. I just felt so . . . weak."

Jenna patted her hand. "You came close to fainting. How do you feel now? Do you want to go home?"

"No. No. I'm fine. I think maybe I was just a little hungry. I'm so sorry I ruined the evening."

"Amanda, you certainly didn't ruin the evening." Brett assured her. "Big brother here even got to save you from falling on the floor, he took charge right off and made sure you were safe "

Amanda tried not to make a face or appear ungrateful. "Thank you. I'm glad you were here to catch me."

"Me too. You sure you're all right? I'll take you home if you want to go. We can leave right now and I'll . . ."

"Really. I'm fine. I'm just a little hungry."

The rest seemed to believe she was fine, and the meal proceeded. All mention of her letters was dropped, and conversation centered around the Parkers and Rick as children. Through almost the entire meal Amanda could feel Kendrick's eyes on her. Watching her. It was as if he suspected something she herself did not want to acknowledge.

After dinner Brett, Jenna and Amanda met up with Marta and they started home. Before they were very far from town Kendrick rode up. "Just wanted to be sure Mandy got home all right. That there are no more episodes."

Amanda had no answer to that.

The next morning, as usual, her stomach roiled. Even eating the crackers she'd brought up to her room her stomach wouldn't settle. Her breasts felt ever so tender when she pulled on her chemise and the waist on her skirt was a tad tight. Letting her mind drift back over the past few weeks she forced herself to look at the thought she'd been avoiding. *When was my last monthly?* She counted back the days, weeks and it had been almost four weeks before they arrived in Lancaster.

"But that's not possible? The latest medical pamphlets say it can't happen but for a few days. How can that be?"

She knew well enough from friends and things she'd read it was possible to conceive the first time a wife was with her husband . . . or a woman with a man. "Oh dear lord, no!"

Curling into a ball as much because of the nausea as well as for the realization of her fears, Amanda spent the next hour or so crying. She had to leave. Soon. Today. Before Kendrick Parker knew she was carrying his child.

CHAPTER TWENTY-NINE

When Amanda went downstairs the next day the entire Parker family turned with expectant looks in her direction. Kendrick stood and stepped over towards her, his movements tentative. She fought the urge to cringe. It wasn't her fault she was pregnant. It was her choice to remove her clothes that night.

Her choice to climb into bed with him.

Her choice to allow his kisses and touch.

Her choice to fall in love with him.

Choice? Can anyone choose to fall in love, she wondered.

At any point she could have stopped him, moved away. Now, weeks later, looking up into his big blue eyes, she acknowledged to herself that she had wanted to be with Kendrick Parker the way a man and a woman are together for longer than that night in Lancaster. Even knowing she was innocent of the crimes he accused her of committing, for once in her life she wanted to feel desired by a man. That this man was devastatingly handsome only fueled that desire. From what she'd seen since the truth was known was that he was an honorable man. If he knew, he would do the right thing. Of that Amanda had no doubt. The last thing she wanted was to have a man feel like he'd been trapped in a marriage to her.

"How you feeling this afternoon, Mandy?"

"Fine. I'm just fine. Thank you for asking. I'm sorry I missed breakfast. It seems last night was more tiring than I thought."

"I'm guilty of sleeping in as well," Jenna smiled at her.

"Our little one here was pretty active last night." Jenna patted her stomach, seeming oblivious to what was really going on with Amanda.

"I was thinking this morning. Well, I've considered it and believe it is time for me to leave." Amanda quietly told the assembled group.

A chorus of "What?" resounded from Brett, Jenna, and Kendrick.

"I think it's time for me to leave and head back east. I'm sure Kendrick's telegrams were just the thing for the school in St. Louis and they'll be more than happy to have me take the position I planned to fill. If you wouldn't mind, Brett, I'll pack this afternoon and perhaps you could give me a ride to town?"

"Owww." His eyes widened while Jenna leaned in his direction, unaware of the look of utter panic on Kendrick's face. "Uh. Well there's no one headin east for at least a month or two. We've no way to get you where you're going."

"Wouldn't the Express rider . . ."

"He's not gonna want to deal with a woman." Brett told her. "I'll check and see when Dusty's expected back and make sure you've got passage to go with him.

"Yes. That would be best." Jenna told her. "Besides, there's the town social Saturday night. You won't want to miss that! And it's the anniversary of some of our weddings. You're almost like family and if you weren't here for our anniversary it would make me sad."

"And you know how it is for pregnant women when they're sad," Brett put in.

That was the wrong thing for him to say and she had to fight the tears that threatened to form, "I don't . . ."

"It's a sad state if pregnant women are sad. It can make things very sad and complicated," Kendrick told her. "You don't want to complicate Jenna's pregnancy by making her sad, do you? Or make her unhappy. She'd be sad and devastated if you left, Mandy."

"Where did you learn about pregnant women?" Brett blurted his question to Kendrick.

"Like I said last night, I was educated at some of the best schools. Pregnant women and how, how . . ."

"Sad?" Brett helped.

"Yeah, sad. They were mentioned in some of my classes, many of them in fact. I know all about pregnant women."

Amanda didn't believe him for a second. "You, a man, knows all about pregnant women? Did you also go to medical school, Marshal?"

"Uh no. But I paid attention. I knew some day I'd need to, well, I just know it'd be really rough on Jenna if you were to leave now."

"Well, fine . . . if you'd find out when Dusty will be back. And, ah, the social. It sounds like a lot of fun. So I'll stay . . . till Sunday. Then I will find some way to return to St. Louis."

The next day Kendrick openly moved into the Parker house. By tacit agreement, he avoided talking to Amanda when no one else was around and when they spoke, he kept it to safe subjects. He wasn't sure how long he needed to keep this up before telling her how he felt about her, or, that he never sent the telegrams east and worse, he took her letters from the postal clerk. He didn't know what possessed him. He'd never done a dishonest thing in his life. At least not until he met Amanda Davis. All he knew was he had to find a way to convince her to stay. Meeting Amanda was when he started down the road of deception and doing whatever it took to get his way.

At one point he was ready to blame all that had happened on Brett. After all, if his younger brother hadn't married before him, he would have been just fine waiting to marry. Heck, he might have even stayed in St. Louis a spell and courted Amanda . . . had he met her before leaving for Wyoming. It wasn't Brett's fault though and Kendrick knew that. He saw Amanda and he wanted her and created a situation to have her. To himself he acknowledged that was why he never listened to her when she tried to get him to listen. If he had, he would have found out she wasn't Black Bette and then, well he would have lost her.

Now, it seemed pretty certain he'd lose her anyway. Once she found out he never sent the telegrams she'd be angry enough to never speak to him again.

With her bringing up leaving a few days later, he knew he'd have to do something about it and soon. Thing was, with how she made a point of telling him how much she disliked him, he'd have to find some way to change her mind and then tell her how he felt. Maybe then he wouldn't have to tell her that he'd burned her telegrams or that he'd gone to the express office and told them she'd changed her mind about sending the letters.

Over dinner Friday night Brett mentioned that no one had any idea when Dusty would be back in town, however, the reverend had stopped by the jail to see if Amanda had decided about the teaching job.

"Teaching job?" Kendrick asked, unable to keep the hopeful tone from his voice

Amanda tried not to read too much into his tone or eager look in his eyes. "It was just a general question. I'm not really interested. I've wanted to make a life for myself in St. Louis for so long I can't imagine living anywhere else."

"School's interested in you Amanda. The reverend said to tell you they'll pay you three dollars more a month than the school in St. Louis. Kendrick told him about how you were with the children on the trail and the town would sure appreciate it. Why not try it for a year and see how it goes? Especially with all the talk of war back east. Adler Creek's a nice town. A good place to start a new life."

Because in less than a year I'll have Kendrick's baby, and everyone will think I'm a loose woman. No school was going to want an unwed mother. A widow—no problem. She had to be away from here so she could use widowhood as an excuse for her illegitimate pregnancy.

"That sounds like a good plan, Amanda." Kendrick told her.

"I'll consider it." At least she was forewarned. There would be questions about her teaching in Adler Creek the following evening. And why was he suddenly calling her Amanda?

CHAPTER THIRTY

Amanda didn't want to think about why she took extra time in her bath and care dressing for the social. She called herself a wanton for just a moment when her gaze caught how the gown Jenna lent her accented her fuller breasts. Thrilled for Jenna about her baby, Amanda felt guilty not telling the other woman about her own pregnancy. Jenna Parker was the kind of woman who would enjoy being with another woman in the family way. It was like betraying a friend.

Jenna was the sort of woman who was a friend for life, unless you did something to betray her trust. She'd been more than generous lending several of her dresses to Mandy. Kendrick offered to buy her any number of them, but she vowed she would never accept anything from him.

Now, studying her reflection and the glow to her cheeks, and, well the reminder of just what that meant and how she had to get away from Kendrick soon was a sobering thought. That Jenna hadn't mentioned anything about her missing her monthly, because surely another woman would notice, was a passing thought. She quickly dismissed further thoughts of hoping she looked attractive because if her mind continued on that road, she'd have to admit her growing attraction for Kendrick and any chance for a relationship with him was doomed from the start. From his initial contact with her, to the pregnancy she knew she soon needed to find a way to hide, everything was against them. He was not the man for her. Fevered kisses and hot touches did not a solid marriage make.

When she and Jenna came downstairs it was all she could do not to betray her true feelings when she caught sight of Kendrick.

He'd discarded his western garb to present the appearance of a proper eastern gentleman. A sparkling white shirt with a high starched collar peeked from under a black bow tie, and a gold and green gilt-edged vest accented his powerful chest. A black wool frock coat set off his dark gray pants. Polished boots and a gold pocket watch completed the very handsome image he presented. Amanda was glad she'd accepted the dark blue moiré Gibson girl skirt and pale blue tie back blouse in the same fabric Jenna had lent her. It was a snug fit and probably the only time she'd be able to wear it so she planned on enjoying the snap and feel of the fabric. At least until the baby came. Kendrick's baby.

Arriving at the social, several of Jenna's friends, also rounding with their own pregnancies, hurried over to them.

"Isn't this fun?" One of the women she'd met on their trip to town she recalled was named Bea asked. "Here we were, all brides together last year and now we'll all be having our babies together. A generation of 'Bride babies'!"

Jenna introduced Amanda to several of the other women as a friend of the family who'd come from back east for a visit. When asked, Amanda answered she wasn't sure how much longer she'd be there but assured everyone she found Adler Creek to be a wonderful town. She was relieved no one mentioned her being a teacher. It seemed Kendrick was going to be on his best behavior for the evening.

Children ran and played while the adults sat at gaily decorated tables both inside the church and a few outside for those who didn't mind the slight chill that came with the evening air. Light snacks sat on the buffet tables until the main meal was served.

Despite her best intentions to ignore him, Amanda couldn't help but watch Kendrick. She half expected him to be his surly self and keep his own company as he had on the trail. At a minimum, she had suspected he'd speak with only a few of the adults. Actually, since arriving in Adler Creek he seemed almost a different man. More outgoing, at least around his brother and Rick. Tonight though, he spent most of his time with the children, showing them tricks with his gun or doing what appeared to be magic with a handkerchief shaped like a white mouse running around his shirt. He pulled coins out of the children's ears and gave a few of the little girls piggy-back rides. It surprised her how at ease he was with the children and it broke her heart because there was no way she could tell him she carried his baby. She might be falling in love with him, but to saddle him into a marriage simply because she'd left her good judgment at the door would have just been wrong. Still, his actions around the children tugged at her heartstrings, making her want that special relationship with him.

Rick joined the Parkers at their table for dinner and graciously chatted with the townsfolk that came by. It soon became apparent that many of the residents stopped by believing Amanda was there was his guest. Rumors began to fly that the big blond sheriff was courting a distant relative of Jenna Parker. While Amanda wanted to hush up the talk, Jenna pointed out that if the townsfolk thought that they wouldn't be asking her any questions her relationship with Kendrick.

The array of foods available had the tables near groaning. A pig roasted over an open fire which fortunately tantalized Amanda's taste buds rather than sending her to the privy from the smell. Three kinds of potatoes including some mashed with fresh butter and cheese, fresh corn on the cob, greens, baked breads just out of the oven and an assortment of fruit pies topped the meal. Pitchers of buttermilk and lemonade sat on each table. At Rick's suggestion each member of their party chose a different type of pie and they all sampled each other's. It was a camaraderie that Amanda always wanted, but never thought she'd have.

Dinner done, the tables were cleared for dancing and Amanda accepted turns with Rick, Brett and a few of the other, apparently single, men from town. Kendrick sat at the table, his expression unreadable. She told herself not to be hurt that he honored her wishes to leave her be and did not invite her to dance.

After the first few sets Amanda pled a break for some air. Kendrick was nowhere to be seen as she strolled toward the fence that surrounded the church yard. She told herself it was a relief because he would have only been surly. Yes, he would definitely have been surly. Amanda had no doubt that while he wouldn't ask her to dance, he'd stare down any of the other polite, kind and courteous gentlemen who approached her. Enjoying the much-needed break she inhaled the early evening springtime scents. So different from what now seemed like the crowded streets of Massachusetts or the dusty sidewalks of St. Louis. The wide-open space and fresh air were a pleasant change from what she'd known. Across the way, she spotted Kendrick talking with a few of the men. She told herself he wasn't half as handsome as she found him, that it was an illusion, brought on by the strain of all that had happened.

A few minutes later Rick stepped over to join her. "Folks are saying I'm courting you."

"I apologize, Sheriff. I told Jenna we needed to put a stop to it. She felt for this evening it would be acceptable. Even with how Kendrick behaved a few weeks ago."

"Back to your uppity talking?" He smiled letting her know he thought Kendrick's description of her speech amusing.

"Perhaps. I do feel bad folks think you and I are . . . well I think I'd rather have people think I'm tied to anyone but Kendrick Parker. I'm sure such talk interferes with your courtship of any of the women here in town."

Almost as if he'd heard her Kendrick turned and looked up. Even in the fading light Amanda could see his eyes. The look of hurt and abandonment was there, not that it ever really left. What Amanda at first thought was ice in his gaze was actually the look of a little boy who was lost; a child, now a man, who had lost his mother and desperately wanted to be loved both as a child and now as a man.

Seeing where and at whom she looked, Rick told her, "He's not a bad man, you know. I may not have seen him for a few years, but I know from Brett the important things he's done. Family's important to Kendrick. Even though he grew up with his grandparents and his brothers were out here, he has an inbred sense of family. Not from his grandparents. I only met his grandfather once when I was a boy and he was a cold man. No emotion. I think Kendrick learned to hide how he really felt about most things because of how his grandparents treated him."

"Brett told me a bit about that. It's sad to think of a little boy wanting his mother's love, missing it, and his grandparents simply telling him to buck up."

"Like I said, family matters to him. When Brett asked him for help, he dropped everything to clear Jenna's name. If there is nothing else I'm sure of, it's that Kendrick Parker's a good man. A woman could do a lot worse than marry a man like that. Man like that won't break your heart. It's a shame you won't give him a chance."

Across the way Kendrick didn't move, didn't seem to hear the men next to him speaking. From the lonely look in his gaze, all that seemed to exist for him was the woman who had another man beside her as she watched him.

CHAPTER THIRTY-ONE

The rest of the evening flew by. Amanda managed two more dances before pleading she was too fatigued to dance anymore. She was relieved when Jenna said she too was exhausted and ready to return home and sleep.

The next morning when Amanda woke, she made a decision. She would tell Jenna and Brett she was pregnant and ask their help to decide what to do. If they still thought she should stay in Adler Creek, she would. If the teaching job in town was open and they would accept a woman in the family way she would take the job teaching. And Kendrick? Rick was right. She could do much worse. She would tell him she was pregnant. Not with his child but that she was when they left St. Louis so he would believe it was with someone else's baby. If he thought there was another man in her life, maybe he'd go his own way because she would be the worst thing that happened to him. If he wanted her, even with another man's baby, well she could do a lot worse. Maybe in time he'd come to love her.

When she was sure the morning heaving was over, she started down the stairs. Hearing voices in the dining room she was surprised the day's morning spell had passed so soon.

On the second step from the top, the foggy feeling she'd felt in the restaurant returned. She reached for the banister, grabbing at air as darkness surrounded her.

The thud from the hallway startled Kendrick, Brett, and

Jenna. Before anyone else could move, Kendrick rose and heading out the door uttering only, "Amanda."

He was beside her in an instant, "Amanda? Sweetheart? Mandy, talk to me." He knelt by her side, feeling quickly for a pulse while turning her into his arms. "Brett!"

As he turned her, he glanced at her legs and saw the blood flowing from below her waist. A steady stream seemed to pour from her. "Get the doc! Now! Oh my God! Mandy! Sweetheart, talk to me. Amanda, Mandy, can you hear me?" Kendrick's panicked tone spurred the others into movement.

"Jenna, get Marta, tell her to boil some water and then stay in the kitchen," Brett ordered his wife.

"What? Brett? Oh my God! She's miscarrying!"

Both men looked at her, their "What?" echoed through the house.

"Honey, you don't need to see this." Brett tried again to get Jenna to leave.

"I've seen blood before, Brett. Kendrick, if she wakes keep her still. Brett, get Franco and have him send for Doc. I'll get Marta boiling some water."

"Amanda!" Kendrick called to her again. "Brett, what does she mean miscarriage? How could she have a miscarriage? She's not pregnant."

"Ohhh." Amanda groaned as she came to. "My stomach. Ahhhh! I hurt. Oh lord I hurt." She tried to curl up in a ball. Kendrick held on to her tight, his own world spinning around him, memories flooding back.

Mandy hanging up freshly washed sheets on that brisk morning in Lancaster.

The flash of a red spot on sheets after his fever broke.

The feeling of sexual release.

The scent of sex in the air.

He'd bedded Amanda Davis and hadn't remembered it! "No. No. Mandy, I'm so sorry." Something worse than embarrassment flooded his senses. Something darker. Something despicable and lower than he'd ever felt. He'd taken an innocent woman, a virgin judging by what he now remembered of the sheets as the fever broke. Did he force her? Did she fight him and he forced himself on her? Worse, would he lose the woman he loved because she was losing the child he fathered — and there was no doubt in his mind he'd fathered her child. "Brett, please, help me save my child. My child! Mandy, Mandy, don't leave me."

Brett strode back into the hallway with Jenna close behind.

"Marta says to get her into bed, and she'll bring water." Brett told them.

"What about the Doc?" Kendrick asked, unable to keep the wild fear from his voice.

"Franco's getting him."

"Come on Kendrick, let's get her upstairs." Jenna prodded him.

Jenna led the way and pulled down the sheets from the bed Amanda had carefully made.

Kendrick gently laid her down and seemed to fight with himself to take his hands from her.

Jenna moved to unbutton her blouse and loosen her skirt. "Get some towels, Kendrick."

"I can't leave her. She needs to know how I feel."

"Get the towels." Her tone brooked no argument.

"Jenna, I can't. What if I lose her before I tell her I love her? And our baby, what about our baby?"

"She's not going to die Kendrick. *Get. The. Towels.*" Jenna demanded, her voice pitched low but with authority.

"You don't know that." He sat heavily on the bed, holding Amanda's hand in both of his. "She needs to know I love her."

"I do know that she'll be fine. Kendrick, I was pregnant when my uncle showed up here and tried to kidnap me. If I didn't die from the way that man tossed me around Amanda won't die. Doc saved me and our baby."

"You had Brett. You didn't fall down the stairs. You knew Brett loved you. This is my fault. It's all my fault. She doesn't know. She doesn't know I love her. I should have told her, from the beginning I should have told her." He brought Amanda's hand up to his cheek, as if her touch would warm him.

Marta bustled in, bucket of hot water in tow. "Mr. Kendrick. You go get towels and more water."

"I'm not leaving her."

"You leave or I'll make you wish you weren't born. Now go."

For some reason, Marta's threat permeated his grief and Kendrick stumbled from the room in search of the towels and more hot water.

"Brett," Jenna ordered, "go with him."

He left to follow his brother without a word.

Both women worked at removing the rest of Amanda's clothes and cleaning her up, finishing just before Doc arrived. By time he was upstairs the blood had stopped flowing and Amanda was resting quietly. A single tear slipped down her cheek.

"It's okay, Amanda. It's okay."

"No. No it's not. I lost the baby. I lost Kendrick's baby. Oh God, Jenna, don't tell him! Please! You can't tell him."

"He knows, Amanda."

"No, no. He can't. Now, now he'll hate me forever."

"No. Honey, no. He could never hate you. I swear to you. Don't you know he loves you?"

"I hurt. It hurts so much. My heart, it hurts so much."

"It will for a time," Doc told her. "From what I can tell, you'll be just fine. You just need to rest a bit. That's all. Just give yourself time to rest."

Unable to fight sleep any longer Amanda closed her eyes

and fell asleep. Jenna sat with her a short while before going downstairs to find Brett and Kendrick in the library. A half full glass of whiskey was in Kendrick's hand. At Jenna's look Brett told her, "He's not drunk. He poured that glass when you sent him out of Amanda's room, and he hasn't taken a swallow since."

Kendrick looked up at Jenna, his heart in his eyes, pleading. "Have I lost her?"

"Oh Kendrick, no." Jenna walked over and sat beside him. "Amanda's going to be fine."

"What about my child? How's my child?"

Jenna looked at Brett, who cast a worried look at Kendrick. Drawing in a bracing breath, Jenna told him. "She's lost the baby. She'll be fine, soon, but she lost the baby."

He shook his head, confused at himself. "How could I not know? What kind of man am I that I didn't know I made love to her?"

"You sure you're the father?" Brett asked.

Kendrick nodded. "Of course I'm the father. The signs were all there. I was just so wrapped up in how I was going to tell her I'd made a real bad mistake and get her to fall in love with me, I didn't see what was right in front of me."

Jenna stood and went to sit at Brett's side and reached across his lap to take Kendrick's hand. "What happened?"

Kendrick sighed and leaned back. His eyes closed as if he couldn't bear to look at anyone or let anyone see into his soul. "Like I said before, I knew . . . I suspected shortly after we left St. Louis, she wasn't Black Bette. It seemed almost as if every day she'd do something that made her more and more special. By time we were a few days out, I couldn't help myself and I kissed her. A better man wouldn't have done it. A better man would have turned right around and taken her back to St. Louis and done whatever he could make it right. Once I kissed her though, I couldn't let go. I had to find some way to win her over.

"One night she got up and was heading out to the river and I followed her. She thought it was because I didn't trust her. I did it because I was afraid something would happen to her. That Mandy'd get hurt. She was fine. I fell in the river and hit my head. She got me out and called for help. The woman saved my life. A few days later, I took ill and when we couldn't go on with the wagon train Dusty found a family for us to stay with, the Haynes' that Mandy talks about—just outside Lancaster in Nebraska.

"I don't remember the first few days there. Mandy said I'd been running a high fever, high enough that she was pretty worried about me. I woke up one morning and I thought she was in bed with me . . . without her nightshift. A part of me *knew* she was there. Instead of waking full up, I fell back asleep and when I woke a bit later Mandy was gone."

"Gone? She left you?" Brett asked.

"No. She brought me some breakfast and helped me get to the privy. When I got back, she'd taken the sheets off the bed. I thought I saw something red . . . now I know for certain it was from her . . . that she'd been innocent, and I took advantage of her. I don't know which is worse—that I kidnapped her or took her against her will."

"She say that to you?" Brett raised the question.

Kendrick shook his head, slowly as if in a dream. "No. Mandy's a lady. She'd be too embarrassed to tell anyone, especially me, what I did. She was quieter after that night, didn't have much to say to me."

Kendrick stood and started to pace. "*Shit!* Excuse me, Jenna. Seems I get worse each minute."

"It's all right, Kendrick. Believe it or not I've heard the word before." Her smile wasn't mocking or implying humor. Rather it was one of compassion.

"She almost died . . . she could still die . . . because of me.

Probably the most decent woman I've ever met, excepting you of course, Jenna, and she could die because of me and how selfish I am. So now what, little brother? Do you arrest me for rape? Murder?"

"Amanda's going to be fine. She'll be sick for a bit. Doc said she'll be sore, but she'll be all right. So you haven't killed her. As to the other . . . well let's see what she says when she feels better. Maybe Jenna will be up to talking to her about it."

"Of course I will. You know Amanda and I have talked a few times about how much like Brett and I you two are. She says she sees only the differences. I'm pretty sure she also sees what is the same, although Brett will probably beg to differ on this point. In the beginning of our relationship he talked and talked and talked. He never took the time to listen to me. To hear what I had to say until it was almost too late. I had to sit him down and put a napkin in his mouth to make him listen to me."

"Yup. That is true." Brett smiled, clearly remembering the incident.

"He was so afraid that I'd say something he didn't want to hear, so he kept me from talking. When he finally listened, I think he was pleased to hear what I had to say. I think you and Amanda are a bit the same. You talk and expect her to listen. You don't ask her what she thinks or what she wants, because you don't want to hear that she doesn't feel the same. I think the two of you need to sit and listen to what each of you has to say. And, you need to forgive yourselves."

Kendrick stopped his pacing and turned to Jenna. "You know, I thought Mandy was the smartest woman I ever met until now. You're right." He headed towards the door.

"Where you going, Kendrick?"

"To Amanda. To tell her I'm sorry and I love her."

"Whoa, Big Brother! Hang on there."

"What?"

"What? Kendrick, she just suffered a miscarriage. You need to give her some time to heal, to adjust," Jenna told him.

"I understand that. Don't you think though it'll help if she knows I feel bad about what I did? That I want to make it up to her. That I plan to spend the rest of my life, if she'll have me, making it up to her."

"I agree . . . but not today."

"Can I at least look in on her?" He sounded like a little boy asking for the best gift ever coupled with the fear he wouldn't get it.

Jenna looked at Brett who only lifted a brow, indicating he was deferring to his wife. "Doc said she shouldn't be upset."

"I won't upset her. She won't even know I'm there. I promise. Jenna, Brett, I just need to see for myself she's all right. That was my child we lost today." His voice cracked.

Moonlight was bright enough to illuminate the room so Kendrick could see Amanda's face clearly without lighting a lamp. Even as pale as she was from the loss of blood, she was beautiful. Her long dark blond hair seemed ethereal in the pattern it spread out on the pillow. In repose she showed no signs of the sad loss of a few hours before.

Then again, maybe it wasn't a sad loss. Maybe she was relieved she no longer carried his child. "I love you, Mandy," he whispered. So softly he wasn't even sure the words were not his imagination.

Jenna gently tapped him on the shoulder and guided him out of the room. "I'm going to stay with her tonight. If she asks for you, I'll come get you."

"Why would she do that? She hates me."

"I don't think she hates you at all."

CHAPTER THIRTY-TWO

When Amanda woke the next day, she was at first surprised to see Jenna sitting in the large, overstuffed chair in the corner. Then what happened the day before came flooding back. "Ohhh." She couldn't hold back the sob.

Jenna instantly woke and crossed the room over to the bed. "Amanda. It's okay sweetie. Let it out, let it out."

"My baby, I lost her, didn't I?"

"Yes. I'm so sorry. Yes, she's gone."

Amanda let Jenna pull her into an embrace while she cried. Finally wiping the tears from her face she looked up at Jenna. "Maybe it's for the best, you know?"

"How?"

"Kendrick. He's the type of man who would want to do the honorable thing. I didn't know how much longer I could hide the pregnancy. If he had found out, he would have wanted to . . . demanded most likely . . . that I marry him. Now I don't have to worry about him trying to force me into a marriage I don't . . . I don't . . . I wouldn't want. One I'm sure he wouldn't want."

"Amanda, you and Kendrick need to talk. Maybe not today, but soon."

"There's nothing to say. Now we can most assuredly both go our own way and never see each other again."

"That's not what he wants."

"How can you say that?"

"Because he told me. Amanda, he's taken the loss of your child, his child, hard. This is a time for the two of you to be together. He cares for you, deeply. You need to give him the chance to talk to you."

"Maybe some other day. I can't . . . not today." Tears spilled again and sensing Amanda's need to be alone Jenna stepped from the room.

Over the next few days Kendrick repeatedly tried to see Amanda. On each occasion, she turned him away. With each rejection, he retreated more and more into himself. The loss of their child seemed to take all ambition from him.

A week after the miscarriage, waking from a nap Amanda felt strong enough to venture downstairs. Hungry, she started for the kitchen where she found Kendrick, his head laying on the table, an empty glass on its side near his hand. "Kendrick?"

He raised his head. The whites of his eyes were bloodshot, making the blue a more vivid color. "Mandy. I'm sorry. I'm so sorry." He tried to stand, his legs wobbling beneath him making the effort futile.

"Look at you! What have you done to yourself?"

"I . . ." he burped, the scent of whiskey fresh in the air. "Sorry."

His cambric shirt was wrinkled, his hair mussed, and he smelled like he hadn't bathed in a few days. Jenna had told her he was taking the miscarriage hard. Amanda didn't realize how hard until she saw him then and there.

"Are Brett and Jenna around?"

"No . . . went to town."

"What about Marta and Franco?"

"Uh uh, with her relatives."

"How long have you been here?"

Kendrick looked out the window. "I'm sorry, Mandy. You have to know . . . I love you and I . . . I'm sorry."

That did it. She went to the sink and began to pump water into a bucket then carried it over to the stove and started to heat it. Kendrick never moved. He just sat at the table, looking into space which surprised her because he'd never before just sat when she was lifting or moving something remotely heavy. Despite the fatigue that still lingered, she was determined to draw a bath for him. When the water was heated and poured it into the hip bath she began to heat another bucketful. Pulling Kendrick by the arm, she got him up and began to unbutton his shirt.

"What ya doin, Mandy?"

"Getting you into a bath. You smell positively vile and you look even worse."

"I just get worse all the time, don't I? I can't do anything right. Not ever. No wonder you don't want me." He tried to rise, lost what little balance he had and plopped back down in the chair.

She went to unbuckle his pants. Flushing, she stopped to ask him, "Can you take your pants off?"

"Rather you do it."

"Fine." It wasn't as if she hadn't seen him in his all togethers before.

She closed her eyes and pulled his pants down only to realize he was still wearing his boots. Fortunately, he was too drunk to realize that. She pushed him into a chair, pulled off the boots, finished pulling his pants off, applauding herself for not staring at his privates, despite a longing to see if her memory was as good as the reality.

Amanda got a buck-naked Kendrick into the tub and ordered him to start bathing. She started up the coffee and poured more hot water into the tub. It occurred to her there were no towels so she ordered him to *be careful* and went to get the towels. When she returned the coffee was ready and she poured him a cup. In between swallows of the brew Amanda washed his hair and gave into the enjoyment of shaving him. His grin told her he knew what she was doing, and he was enjoying it.

"Would you agree, Mandy, that my biggest claim to fame lately is making a fool out of myself in front of you?"

"Do you feel foolish, Kendrick?" She sounded interested, not unkind.

"Yeah, I do. Better that than broken hearted."

"Br . . ." She wasn't going to travel that road.

"We need to talk, Mandy. You and I. We need to talk."

Never one to run from trouble or hide from herself, Amanda agreed. "Did you want to talk now, or when you've sobered up a bit more and put on some clothes?"

"I'm sober enough . . . but yeah, as long as you feel well enough."

"I'll be all right. I just need to sit a bit."

He nodded. "Clothes."

She stepped away when he was ready to climb out of the tub and found him a few minutes later, sound asleep on the couch in the parlor. Taking a blanket Amanda covered him and, exhausted, wandered upstairs back to bed. At least they had had a conversation without arguing and irritating each other. He'd probably forget in the morning, just like when he was sick. Maybe that was the only way she could get through to him . . . if he was sick or imbibing spirits.

CHAPTER THIRTY-THREE

The next morning Amanda woke for the first time in weeks feeling rested and more like herself. She joined the Parkers for breakfast, noting Kendrick looked no worse for wear from his intoxication the night before. Brett mentioned he'd heard from an express rider that the war talk in the east was getting worse. More federal troops were being sent to the south and there were significant causalities in the few battles that had already been fought.

Kendrick shook his head. "Only one ending will come from this and it's not a good one. I'm starting to think I need to head back home and sign up."

"You sure that's what you want?" Brett asked.

"Not what I want. I just wonder if it's the right thing to do."

They hadn't spoken and Amanda didn't want to sway him one way or the other, but she felt she needed to ask. "When it's all over, won't they need lawmen to step in?"

"They need the law now."

"Of course. But if things continue as they are, with brother fighting brother, won't they need men who haven't been involved in the war to administer the justice? Someone without bias?"

"She's got a point there," Brett told them. "I hate to see you get caught up in all that, but you got to do what you think is right."

"I do have some thinking to do. Amanda, if I do decide to go back east, I can take you . . . if that's what you want."

"I . . . I'll let you know. I . . . I . . . If you will all excuse me,

I need some air."

Amanda stood and rushed from the table. Despite the warm spring air she felt chilled. It seemed to portend a life without Kendrick. If he went back east, she'd go with him and hope on the way they'd find their way to each other. Maybe he'd forgive her for losing their baby.

A few minutes later he stepped out and, without asking joined her on the porch swing. "Last night I said we needed to talk. It seems I didn't honor that at the time. Would you care to have that talk now?"

Amanda swallowed. She wanted to be a coward and say no. She wanted him to decide what he was going to do, and she would somehow simply be there with him "Of course. If you're sure you are up for it."

"I am. It's a talk we should have had a long time ago."

"Well, then let's not wait longer. After all, if you want me to pack and leave, I need to be doing that today."

"I don't want you to leave, Mandy. I want . . . I need . . . Amanda . . . ah shit." He stood, paced and came back to sit with her again. "Do you know why I didn't bring you back to St. Louis when I started thinking you weren't Bette?"

"Pride?"

"That was part of it. The other part was that I was already falling in love with you. You were unlike any other woman I'd ever met and I was afraid if I brought you back to St. Louis I wouldn't have a chance. That in the time it took for me to bring the evidence I had against Jenna's uncle here and returned, you would have found someone else. I thought if you were with me, you'd get to know me and by the time we got here you'd have feelings for me. Instead, I think it drove you further away from me. Then I think about what happened at the Haynes'. That's where we conceived our baby, isn't it? There?"

Amanda nodded.

"Why didn't you tell me?"

She shrugged and shook her head no.

He went down on one knee and took her hands in his. "Amanda, tell me honestly. Please. Did I force you? Did I hurt you and make you lie with me?"

She pulled one hand out from his grasp and cupped his cheek. "No. You didn't hurt me, and you certainly didn't force me. I wanted to be with you. I wanted what we had that night."

"Can you forgive me for not remembering that night? I mean, I do remember parts, feelings, but I don't . . ."

She cupped his chin, "You were sick, Kendrick. So sick. Your fever was so high you and the bed shook from the chills. Your teeth chattered so hard I thought you'd break your jaw. You were delirious and I knew I had to do something to warm you up or you'd die. I did the only thing I could think of — you yourself had told me, two sleep warmer than one. So in a way, I took advantage of you. I could have stopped you at any time. I wanted to be with you so I didn't stop you. Can you forgive *me?*"

"Forgive you? Amanda, you did nothing wrong. You saved my life, not once but twice. I was already crazy in love with you before we got to the Haynes'. I just wish I remembered what it was like being skin to skin with you," he sheepishly told her.

"I'd say it was nice except I was so worried about you."

"Then we got here, and I saw how you and Rick are. Do you have feelings for him?"

"Rick's a nice man. I think a good man. He's not you. Kendrick, you are the man I want to spend my life with."

"Then why didn't you tell me about the baby?" He spoke so low she barely heard him.

"I couldn't."

"But why? Why would you keep that from me? Did you . . .

Mandy were you ever going to tell me?"

"I don't know. I both wanted to and didn't want to. You . . . you're the kind of man who would want to do the right thing. You would have insisted I marry you. I wouldn't want to marry someone who asked me only out of obligation. You may not believe this, because of the way I speak, but I have feelings."

"I know you have feelings, Amanda. Really I do. And, I think you use those uppity words just to annoy me. Why do you think I call you Mandy no matter you tell me your name is Amanda?" He tried to smile, but the pain of losing his child was clear. "The baby though, would you really have kept that from me?"

"That's a hard question to answer now that I've lost . . . her. Would you really have wanted to know?"

He stood and stepped away from her, running his fingers through his hair. "How could I not? Amanda, I grew up without my parents. My mother, she died before I was barely a year old. My pa, he tried to keep me, but my grandparents, they were hard. They blamed my pa for my mother's death. My pa and me. Growing up, my grandparents, well I knew they cared for me, about me. But they never told me they loved me. Not once that I remember. My grandpa he did tell me that it was my fault my mother died and that she'd be alive if my pa hadn't brought her west and if I hadn't been born."

She stood and walked over to him, putting her hand on his shoulder. She felt him tense and then relax, just a bit. "Oh, Kendrick. I'm so sorry. What an awful thing for anyone to do to a child. It wasn't your fault your mother died. Or your father's."

"I know. In my mind, I know that now. But Amanda, I had a right to know about our child. How could you have planned to raise my child and not tell me?"

"I'm sorry. I'm so sorry. The baby . . . I didn't know how. You were, are, so strong, so determined and, as Rick said, you are a good man."

"He said that?"

"Yes, he did. At the social. When you were across from the church talking to those other men, he told me you were a good man."

Kendrick shook his head. "I thought he was saying sweet things to you. Courting things."

"No, all he ever said to me, any of the times we were alone was that you're a good man and I could do much worse than be with you. But that's why I was afraid to tell you I was in the family way. You would have asked me to marry you because it would have been the right thing to do, not because you loved me."

"Mandy! I *do* love you! I told you that. You are the only woman I've ever wanted to be with and that's probably why I've been such an ass."

"You've been so stubborn because you love me?"

"Yeah." His sheepish look was endearing, like a little boy who'd been caught with his hand in the cookie jar.

In that instant, more than anything, Amanda wanted to sooth the little boy Kendrick had been. To give him the love he'd craved his whole life "Kendrick, like you, I've known this since, well I think I knew the first time you kissed me how I felt about you, that I wanted you. That kiss felt so good, so right. I . . . this is so wrong of me . . . so brazen and wanton, but I wanted that kiss to go on and on. That night in bed . . . our bed, more than anything I wanted you to take me in your arms and kiss me again. And I wanted more. I wanted what we had in Nebraska. No matter what you decide, if it's to go back east, I would go with you, if you wanted me to."

"What if I asked you to stay here with me?"

"I would. More than anything in the world, I want to be

with you. Kendrick, I love you more than I ever thought I could anyone."

"Well, then, I'd like to stay here. The east, well my memories aren't all good. Here," he gestured at the house and ranch area, "here is family, warmth . . . love. I never doubted my pa or Brett's or Wolf's love. This is where I feel I belong, but Amanda, I'll go wherever you want, whenever you want."

"Here. I want to stay here. The east has nothing for me. Kendrick, the only place that holds anything for me is where you are."

He bent his head and kissed her hands. When he looked up at her his eyes were a deep shade of blue. Not icy. Not haunted but filled with love. "Amanda Davis, I love you with all my heart, will you do me the honor of becoming my wife?"

"Kendrick Parker, I love you and I will marry you. I certainly will."

Chapter Thirty-four

"Oh, Mandy, I knew it! I just knew it," Jenna gushed when she and Brett returned home to hear Kendrick and Amanda's news.

As Kendrick and Amanda both blushed, Kendrick assured Jenna she was right. "I think in some ways we were the last to know. Now that we do though, I don't want to waste another minute together. How soon do you think we can be married?"

"With how experienced the reverend has become the past year, especially with right quick marriages, probably by the weekend," Brett told him.

"Unless you have family and friends from back east to invite," Jenna put in.

"No. I don't," Mandy answered.

"I don't either. Not really," Kendrick concurred. "I've always felt this was my family, here. I just need to let my boss know I'll be out this way longer than expected. At some point I'll have to have my Washington attorney handle things there."

"What about things back east?" Brett asked.

"Mandy and I talked about that. I've already told her I'll go wherever she wants." He smiled and gave her a quick kiss on the cheek. "We'd like to stay out this way. The Haynes' told us they were looking for a deputy in Lancaster and while it's not here with you, it's closer than Washington."

"Why go there? Why not stay here?" Brett asked.

"Seems like you, Rick and Tom have things pretty well in hand."

"Town's growing and, well as much as I don't want to bring up a painful subject to the two of you, when Jenna's time comes closer, I'm going to want to be spending more time here at home. Why don't you and I talk to Rick and see what he thinks?"

"I'm fine with it, really," Amanda assured them. "I think I was more concerned about how Kendrick was handling the news, especially when I lost the baby."

"*We* lost the baby. We're a couple now, Mandy, so it's 'we.'" Kendrick told her, a smile on his lips, the faint look of the little lost boy that lurked inside him clear in his eyes.

"*We*. I like the way that sounds." Impetuously she gave him a quick kiss on the lips. "And Brett, if you and Kendrick could talk to Rick, more than anything I'd like to live here, in Alder Creek."

"That would certainly make me happy," Jenna assured them. "I always wanted a sister and a big family. And Marta would love to have the two of you to fuss over."

"You thinking we should live here, with you and Brett?" Kendrick asked, surprise evident in his voice.

"Big brother, where else would you live?"

"I'd be pleased to li . . . talk to my bride and see where she'd like to live best."

Amanda smiled. "You know, I think that's the first time you actually stopped yourself from ordering me around and making proclamations about what would happen."

"Told you I'd do anything for you." He gave her another quick kiss that quickly led to a deeper one until Brett cleared his throat.

"I'm thinking maybe we should see if the reverend is up and about tonight."

"Brett! No! Amanda deserves a real wedding and we're going to plan a beautiful one."

The next day the foursome drove into town. Their first stop was at the church and had the reverend grinning ear to ear. "Even with the rumors I heard about Sheriff Hansen courting Miz Davis here I knew the moment I saw you two together a wedding wasn't long in the making. If you're sure you can make your other arrangements by Saturday, we'll have a wedding."

"I'm an old pro at putting weddings together on the spot," Jenna happily told him. "And with help from Bea and Belle it will be beautiful. In fact, I'm thinking the white eyelet I wore for my wedding would look beautiful on you, Amanda."

"You'd lend me your wedding gown, really?"

"Of course! We'll start a family tradition."

At the jail Rick looked up as the foursome walked in, "Just what I need today, the entire Parker clan."

"Not the whole clan," Brett told him. "Wolf's not in town."

"Thank goodness for small favors. Sorry ladies, but I wouldn't be doing my job if I didn't pick on these two."

"Not a problem, Rick," Jenna told him with a smile.

Rick stood and pulled over chairs for the women before asking, "So what brings you all to town? Brett, you're not due to work till tomorrow."

"Got a favor to ask." Kendrick spoke up. "I guess first I should tell you, Mandy and I are going to be married. I know you were looking to court her, but . . ."

Rick put his hand up to silence the older Parker brother. "No offense to you, Mandy, I'm not looking to marry. I've seen the ups and downs courtship brings and the way these two carry on, I'm thinking it's going to be a long time, if ever, I decide to marry. I knew from the git go you and Kendrick belonged together and was only doing what I could to move that along."

"Well thank you, Sheriff. And no offense to you, I don't

think any other man could have captured my heart quite the way Kendrick has."

"So congratulations. I'm truly happy for the two of you. Would you be looking for a best man or someone to walk you down the aisle? Jenna can tell you I have experience at that."

"Oh he definitely does. And make no mistake, he won't allow for second thoughts on that count," Jenna told them with a laugh.

"I've already asked Brett to be my best man." Kendrick said.

"I hadn't thought about who would walk me down the aisle," Amanda softly told them. "It would please me no end for you to do so, Rick. Will you?"

"I most certainly will. So! When's the wedding?"

All four answered, "Saturday."

"Great! I'll ask Tom to take my shift and we'll be set."

"One other thing, Rick." Kendrick spoke up.

"Yeah?"

"Brett said — well he mentioned — you see, Mandy wants to settle out this way. I was thinking of seeing if the deputy job in Lancaster was still open. Brett said, well he was thinking . . ."

"You want the job, I'm more'n happy to have you. Town's growing. It'd be really good to have another deputy. When can I swear you in?"

Returning home that night, Kendrick walked Amanda to her room. "Something I've wanted to do all day today."

"What's that?"

"This." He lowered his lips to hers, his hands sliding along her waist, drawing her up close to his body, leaving no doubt what more he wanted to do.

She sighed against his lips, parting her own to welcome

him in while ever so lightly rubbing her chest against his. Accepting her invitation he dipped his tongue in to dance with hers, tasting the essence that was Mandy and only Mandy. He couldn't hold back a groan when she tangled her fingers in his hair, holding him firmly to ensure the kiss didn't end before she was ready.

Long minutes later Kendrick raised his head just enough to whisper in her ear, "You know I want you."

"I . . . I want you too. Kendrick, I have to tell you, I've wanted more than your kisses ever since that first one out on the trail."

"That's good, because I want to give you a lot more and when I do, I want to know it. Can you ever forgive me for not knowing we, that I . . ."

"There's nothing to forgive. I'm just going to spend the rest of my life reminding you how good it was."

"Was it good? For you?"

She nodded, her lips grazing his. "More than good. I'm looking forward to showing you how good."

He glanced up at the door. "Propriety says we need to wait six more days."

"Five. But there comes a time in life when propriety is over-rated."

Kendrick went still as a statue.

Amanda tried to pull away, "I'm sorry. I . . ."

"You sure? Cause I have to agree and since I promised you I'd do whatever it took to make you happy . . ."

She felt behind her for the door handle, he pushed it open.

She pulled him into the room.

Her hands went to the buttons of his shirt; his went to those on her blouse.

She fumbled with his buttons; he couldn't seem to find the buttonholes.

He shifted to pry off his boots, she kicked off her shoes.

All the while their lips remained locked together in a kiss that was so searing Amanda thought she'd go up in flames.

"I'm thinking," Kendrick told her against her lips, "that maybe since you undressed me at the Haynes' maybe I should be returning the favor now."

"I'm thinking you may be right, especially since I don't seem to be able to get my fingers to work right and I can't wait to run my hands up and down your torso to make sure my memory is as good as I think it is."

"You liked touching me, did you?"

"I did. And, I liked it when you touched me back."

"Mandy, I promise I'll never forget one second of making love to you again." With that he finished unbuttoning her blouse, peeled down her skirt and rested his hands on her hips. "You sure you don't want to wait till we're married?"

"If you'll recall, we were married, in Washington, after I met you at a Chekov play and fell in love with you. Our honeymoon has been too long delayed."

He needed no further encouragement. Her bloomers were gone before she could draw in another breath, his shirt unbuttoned before her chemise finished floating to the floor. Her sharply indrawn breath when she saw his shirt shot right to his groin, bringing on the full hardness he seemed to always have when he was around her, especially when she'd turn and snuggle deeper in his arms to sleep. He caught the glow of appreciation in her eyes when he shucked his pants, his manhood standing tall and proud before her.

She slipped back on the bed, lying against the pillows, her thighs parted ever so slightly, maidenly but all woman, and a woman who wanted her man.

"You sure, Mandy?"

Her answer was to tip her pelvis up, wrap her legs around him and guide him to the home he would always have.

CHAPTER THIRTY-FIVE

A light spring breeze scented with desert flowers welcomed their wedding day.

Bea and Henry invited Jenna and Amanda to spend the night in town so that Amanda could be fresh and rested for her wedding. Bea was practically bursting with joy when she informed Amanda, "You'll want to be well rested for your wedding night, I'll tell you. You wouldn't know it to look at my Henry, but he was most ardent then and remains so to this day."

"And she says that to you without even the slightest blush." Jenna smiled at her friend.

"Now don't tell me you don't enjoy your intimacies with Deputy Parker, Jenna," Bea retorted with a giggle.

Amanda debated telling them she'd already had firsthand experience on just how "ardent" Kendrick Parker could be. She also debated asking Jenna if making love three or four times a night was normal and something she could happily anticipate in the years to come.

She decided to wait until after the wedding to disclose those aspects of her life with Kendrick. Even though Jenna knew she and Kendrick had made and lost a child, it was better to let everyone think she and Kendrick did the proper thing by waiting till they were duly married to engage in relations with each other. Not that Jenna didn't know that once she agreed to marry Kendrick, he hadn't been sleeping in his own room but sharing hers.

That was probably why he groused so much when Jenna

and Amanda decided to spend the night in town. Not that he took Amanda for a light skirted woman, he just wanted to be as close as possible to his woman as much as he could. Amanda supposed that had to do with how he'd grown up and in her own way she looked forward to reassuring him over and over she wasn't going to leave him.

While Jenna bustled in and out of Amanda's room with breakfast, bath preparations, her gown and finally to do Amanda's hair, Bea chattered on and on about the wedding, the reception and the night to come. It seemed she'd appointed herself to act as the mother of the bride which Amanda found endearing.

"You don't settle down you're gonna scare her right out of the church," Brett told Kendrick. "That's the twentieth time you've paced to that window in the last fifteen minutes."

"Is not."

Rick's "Is to" was barely heard on the other side of the room where he sat, feet propped up on a chair, his arms crossed over his chest. "If the woman wasn't smart enough to hightail it out of town before this, she's not gonna figure it out now."

"Maybe you walking her down the aisle isn't such a good idea," Kendrick snapped.

"She's a nice woman. Real smart except when it comes to you, but believe me, I'm not interested." Rick sat up, putting his feet down on the worn wooden floor. "I've seen enough marriages in the past year to get me through a lifetime without my own."

"My marriage will be just fine." Kendrick told him.

"That's not what he means," Brett put in. "The past year we've had maybe thirty weddings, my own included. So far, all the marriages seem to be holding just fine. Even mine with the problems we had early on which weren't our fault. I think he's just saying he's ready for things to settle down."

"That'd be part of it. I just can't see tying myself down with one woman. Not when there's so many out there to choose from."

"Believe me, in Washington I had more than enough to choose from. You have no idea how relieved I am not to have to face another simpering miss again as long as I live." Kendrick held his hand up as if holding a china teacup, his pinky out while sticking his hip out the way he'd seen some women do. In falsetto voce he continued, "Why thank you Marshal, or can I call you Keeennnnndrick?"

The other men laughed.

"That'd drive me nuts," Rick told him between chuckles. "One thing's certain though, with Kendrick staying here, we won't have a lack of stupidity to laugh about."

"That's for sure." Brett agreed.

"I meant," Rick continued, "with the two of you together. If the scrapes you got into as kids is any indication, we're in for some roaring times."

"Don't forget Wolf," Brett put in. "Remember when he'd go on about . . ."

A knock at the door interrupted them. Kendrick stepped to the door to open it. "Reverend? Is everything all right? Nothing's happened to Mandy, has it?" He peered out past the minister, looking down the hallway.

"Nothing's amiss, but it will be if Sheriff Hansen doesn't get himself to the front of the church to escort your bride down the aisle and you don't come take your place at the alter in a few minutes. Your bride is waiting for you."

"Damn, I mean dang, I mean . . ."

"I'm sure you do." The reverend chuckled as he stepped aside to let Kendrick out of the room and took him to the front of the church.

A moment after he took his place Kendrick looked down the aisle to see Mandy standing beside Rick. She was, in a word, breathtaking. Amanda Davis was everything he ever wanted and in just a short bit she'd be his wife. Not the pretend wife he called her on the trail. His wife in fact and he'd spend the rest of his life making her happy she'd married him. He couldn't help but watch Rick's expression as he walked Amanda down the aisle. The man didn't so much as look at her, looking more like a big brother than anything else. When the minister asked "Who giveth this woman?" Rick answered, "I do" without reservation. But it wasn't until Amanda said, "I do" and kissed him, long and deep, he truly believed she was his forever.

EPILOGUE

A week later, after taking supper with the Parker boys and their wives, Rick patted his stomach. "That was a mighty good meal. You know, I was thinking, with you two having wives, maybe Marta would like to come cook for me."

"No how, Mista Sheriff. I'm not gonna give up the chance to take care of the babies Mrs. Jenna and Mrs. Mandy gonna be makin'. You can come here to eat any time you like."

"Thank you, Marta. There's no one makes a roast beef like you do." Rick stood and stretched.

"Aren't you going to stay for dessert?" Jenna softly asked.

"I'd like to but I gotta head back to town and relieve Tom. We're mighty glad to have you on board, Kendrick. See you in a couple of days."

As Rick tightened the cinch on his horse's saddle, he mentally shook his head. He couldn't explain it, but he felt antsy. He didn't really need to get back to town so early. Something was just edging him on to return right then. Maybe it was watching Brett and Kendrick with their wives. For all his talk about not wanting to get married, maybe deep down he did, and he just didn't see it. Not that he'd choose a bride the way those two did—a mail order who wasn't really a mail order and one accused of a crime she didn't commit. He was just glad Wolf hadn't found someone to marry throwing that aspect into the mix.

He headed out at a canter and had just about cleared the Parker land when in the distance he saw a shard of lightning split the sky, a puff of smoke in its wake. With the sky otherwise clear and bright he figured it was just a fluke until about half a mile from him another bolt hit. This time he saw the bluish haze left in its wake wasn't exactly smoke, rather it was like a cloud that seemed to encase a woman. At least he thought it was a woman, with the long-sleeved black shirt and tight fitting blue pants, a thick belt around the waist and what appeared to be a gun on the hip, he couldn't be sure. The dark brown hair in an intricate looking braid and the curves that filled out that shirt and pants were clearly female. He urged his horse into a canter. Before he was full out suddenly only wisps of the smoky image remained, the woman disappeared, only to appear before him as another jagged shard of lightning struck the ground just feet from where he pulled the horse to a stop.

The woman turned, hand going to the gun on her hip, her eyes wide. Just as the gun cleared the leather of her holster, her lids fluttered closed, and she collapsed on the ground.

Running to her, Rick reached her in seconds and felt for a pulse. With his hand resting lightly on her neck, she opened her eyes, "Who . . . who are you?"

"I believe," he said, "the man you're about to marry."

ABOUT THE AUTHOR

From earliest childhood Regan was an avid reader and upon discovering Alexander Dumas and Charles Dickens she was hooked on books that carried the reader away to a different time and place. Preferring the quiet of her room and a good book to spending time with people she traveled far beyond those four walls.

It was while working as a police dispatcher, first for the California Highway Patrol and then her local police department, she began to write fiction, primarily time travels and romantic suspense. In the spring of 2009 she returned to the day job she always liked best, working as a legal secretary. Although, curled up in her bunny slippers with her furfaced children, Missy and Lulu, while writing is one of her most favorite things to do.

www.ingramcontent.com/pod-product-compliance
Lightning Source LLC
Chambersburg PA
CBHW071259170626
46809CB00001B/283